TWO MASQUERADES AND JAMES

Chapter 1

The Seduction of Livie

February 28, 1816

The Sheffield Ball

Miss Olive Tyron's and Miss Daisy Wharton's first ball,

in their first Season

"I saw you dancing with the Earl of Winchester," Miss Olive

Tyron said to her cousin as they entered the ladies' retiring chamber

to repair Daisy's unraveling coiffure. "I can imagine you as a

countess!"

"The title wouldn't be worth it," Daisy replied, digging a

hairpin out of her reticule. "His lordship's hair is as thick as mine

and brushed straight up over his forehead. It waved back and forth

like a grove of trees in a high breeze while we danced."

"The 'Brutus' is supposed to look romantic," Livie observed. "Do you have any more hairpins?" When Daisy shook her head, Livie pulled a few hairpins from her own topknot and started anchoring her cousin's unruly curls in place.

"The earl's valet must have spent hours pasting his hair into place," Daisy told her. "He absolutely reeked of Pomade de Nerole." She wrinkled her nose. "I would never want to marry a man who wears more hair product than I do."

"There!" Livie turned her cousin to the large mirror hanging on the wall. "Just look how pretty you are, Daisy, without even a touch of pomade."

"You are far prettier," Daisy said loyally. "*You* should be a countess."

Livie shook her head. "That's not true. And as for being a countess, I think the earl looks more like a scallion than a tree, don't you think? Slim as a green onion with fluff on top."

Daisy choked with laughter. "A scallion in red heels?"

"Unusual for a vegetable," Livie agreed.

Daisy flipped open her fan and minced a few steps. "Here I am, a scallion in the field, waving in the breeze."

"No, you silly thing," Livie said. "A scallion's roots are—"

Her voice broke off. Out from behind the dressing screen that presumably concealed a chamber pot strolled a very beautiful lady with a *very* sour expression. She had golden hair, sky blue eyes, and a perfect nose (Livie was very observant of noses, wishing her own was more regal). She wore diamond bracelets on both of her upper arms and a diamond circlet on her forehead.

She was clearly a person of consequence, though Livie thought that wearing quite so many diamonds was rather vulgar. To be fair, her criticism likely stemmed from jealousy; as debutantes, Livie and Daisy were allowed to wear only pearl necklaces and muslin dresses.

"Good evening," Livie and Daisy chorused, dropping into deep curtsies.

The lady surveyed them head to foot, then inclined her chin in an approximation of a nod. Daisy gave Livie a delighted pinch. She enjoyed nothing so much as imitating the haughtiest of haughty aristocrats.

"Miss Olive Tyron and Miss Daisy Wharton," the woman drawled, in the bored tones assumed by elegant ladies. "Your first Season, I believe. Your first ball?"

"Yes, it is," Livie said, nodding.

The lady turned to the mirror and repositioned the diamond ring she wore on her left hand, over her long glove. "I am Lady Regina Charlotte Haywood."

Livie swallowed. Daisy's mother had warned them to stay clear of Lady Regina, labeling the Duke of Lennox's sister powerful and unpleasant.

"It is a pleasure to meet you," Livie said, elbowing Daisy.

"A pleasure," Daisy blurted out, bobbing a curtsy that caused several locks of hair to tumble to her shoulders.

"I can't say the same," Lady Regina said, turning away from the mirror, "since I gather that you—two young ladies of no particular distinction or beauty—think my fiancé resembles a vegetable."

There was a horrible silence.

Livie gulped. "I truly apologize for that unkind description."

Lady Regina focused on Livie with round eyes as hard as cobblestones. "Your insult was particularly noteworthy, given that you yourself are named after a vegetable."

"Actually, olives are fruit," Livie said, before she could stop herself.

"And you," Lady Regina said, looking at Daisy, "are presumably named after a favorite parlor maid."

"I was named after my grandmother," Daisy whispered.

"The earl shan't dance with either of you again. The real question is whether *any* eligible gentleman should dance with you." The menace in Lady Regina's voice was undisguised.

Livie could feel herself turning pale.

"I doubt anyone will be overcome by rapturous wonder glimpsing either of you across the ballroom. Oh wait, I forgot." The lady's lips curled in distaste. "You, Miss Tyron, find your cousin 'pretty,' do you not? Perhaps short and fat will be in style someday. Though it might be more accurate to say short, fat, and unkempt."

Daisy visibly wilted as a wave of anger ripped through Livie. Daisy may not be as polished as Lady Regina, but then, who was? The lady was as flawless as a China statue, but Daisy had her own kind of beauty. Now Livie's most darling friend in the world looked stricken, stripped of her joyful sparkle.

"My cousin *is* beautiful," Livie declared.

Lady Regina smirked. "Taste is so telling, is it not? I have always found that those of inferior rank are disposed to upstart claims of beauty."

"Yet everyone finds unkindness ugly," Livie retorted. She found Daisy's hand and turned to go. "Goodbye, Lady Regina."

She had just pushed Daisy through the door when she heard a hiss.

"You dare."

Reluctantly, Livie turned around.

Chapter 2

Mean Girls…or Toads?

Livie made sure the door swung shut behind Daisy before she replied. "Did you speak, Lady Regina?"

The lady shifted her diamond ring again. "I was considering how wearisome it is to see young women fluffing their feathers and shaking their tails at men who would *never* consider them for marriage. Your father, I believe, makes a living on a boat?"

"My father, Captain Sir Franklin Tyron, is the commander of His Majesty's *Royal Oak*," Livie said proudly.

"As I said, he makes his living on a boat." Lady Regina walked past Livie, pushing open the door and leaving without another word.

Livie pressed her hands to her burning cheeks. Society dictated that everyone must display fawning obsequiousness to that horrid woman. Her aunt, Lady Wharton, would be mortified by the fact that Livie had made an enemy of Lady Regina—but she would understand once Livie described the exchange.

Made his living on a boat?

Her father was not only a member of the aristocracy—albeit a third son—but he had also received a commendation for service. Under her father's command, the *Royal Oak* had become one of His Majesty's most prized vessels, instrumental in fighting off the French.

Lady Regina was a toad.

Livie absolutely refused to respect such an insolent person. She shook off her embarrassment, straightened her backbone, and returned to the ballroom where she found her aunt waiting.

"Livie, you must stay within my view," Lady Wharton hissed, as she drew forward a gentleman. "Lord Devin, I am happy to introduce you to my niece, Miss Olive Tyron."

Livie curtsied, then accepted the gentleman's hand. He had an open, cheerful face, as dissimilar to Lady Regina's as could be imagined.

"Are you enjoying the Season so far?" he inquired, as they waited their turn to process through the steps of a quadrille.

"Most of it," Livie confided.

"I have four sisters," Lord Devin said. "Did some fellow give you a pinch? I'll have him thrown out, since your father isn't here to do it for you. Commander of the *Royal Oak*, isn't he? You must be terrifically proud."

Livie beamed at him. Suddenly the evening didn't seem so dire. "I am!"

"So, tell me which rakehell made an improper advance," Lord Devin said. He had the kindest expression in the world, but suddenly Livie glimpsed a steely interior.

"Oh, it wasn't that," she said. "It's just that not everyone is welcoming."

Lord Devin grinned. "Jealous, are they? Well, you are frightfully pretty, if you don't mind my saying so."

Livie felt herself turning pink again.

"They say that yellow hair is the fashion, but I prefer a darker hue."

"You are very handsome as well," she said, twinkling at him. "So are your four sisters my age or closer to yours?"

He winced. "That's put me in my place, hasn't it?"

"I didn't mean it that way!" Livie cried. "You…of course, you are most handsome, and age doesn't matter to a man, does it? Ladies love a cleft chin!"

Lord Devin broke out laughing. "Do you always say just what you're thinking?"

"Far too often," she confessed. "My aunt is most displeased by my rashness. I'm afraid that earlier I was snubbed and I…well, I responded with unkindness." She felt a flash of shame. "I ought not to have been so forthright."

"So, you were insulted not by a rakehell, but by a lady," Lord Devin said thoughtfully. He raised one eyebrow. "May I have the details?"

He looked like the older brother that Livie had always longed for, so she told him the truth. "I compared her fiancé to a scallion, so of course she had the right to be angry with me. But she wasn't meant to overhear, and she was so nasty about it!"

Lord Devin burst into laughter again. "A scallion? As in a green onion?" he said, glancing around them. "Who is wearing green today?"

"It was really the Brutus hairstyle," Livie confessed.

"Presumably slender," Lord Devin said. "I must say, surveying the ballroom, I feel that beets are more in evidence. Red coats must be in fashion."

"The lady was justly angry. Unfortunately, she announced that she will ensure no eligible gentlemen will dance with me."

"We'll see about that," Lord Devin said.

Chapter 3

Success is the Greatest Revenge

The quadrille was ending, and by all rights, Livie's dance partner, Lord Devin, ought to return her to Lady Wharton. Her aunt would be waiting to introduce her to another possible suitor.

Instead, he nodded at a tall, thin gentleman. "Is that the scallion?"

"No," Livie whispered.

"A beansprout, but the nicest fellow," Lord Devin said. "Since you won't consider the older set—in short, *me*—I don't mind introducing you. He's a future baron, by the way."

Before Livie could apologize again, or tell him that she didn't care about titles, Lord Devin introduced her to Mr. Robert de Lacy Evans. After swirling around the ballroom with Mr. de Lacy Evans, Livie was introduced to Lord Argyle, who had sweet blue eyes and an obsession with timepieces.

Lord Argyle took her to supper, where they were joined by Daisy, escorted by Lord Fencibles. The four had just seated themselves when Lord Devin approached their table and introduced his sister Clementine, escorted by Mr. Peter Caron. Mr. Caron turned out to be a friend of Mr. de Lacy Evans, who used that as an excuse to join them. The seven of them sat around the table talking and laughing; when the music began again, they paid it no attention until Lady Wharton came and whisked away the three girls, taking them back to the ballroom.

By the time the event drew to a close, Livie had had so much fun that she didn't think twice about Lady Regina. When Daisy told her mother on the carriage ride home that the lady had been quite rude, Lady Wharton brushed it off; she was positively giddy after being assured by the other dowagers that Livie and Daisy were certain to make excellent matches.

"Lord Devin laughed repeatedly while dancing with you, Livie," Lady Wharton crowed. "Everyone noticed. He is the richest man in London."

"I wouldn't want to marry him," Livie objected. "I don't care how rich he is, Aunt Wharton. I'd rather marry someone without a title. A title seems to give people the excuse to act in an extremely ill-bred fashion."

Daisy nodded. "I agree. Lady Regina has appalling manners. True, we *did* compare her fiancé to a scallion, but how were we to know she was lurking behind a screen?"

"A scallion?" Lady Wharton sighed. "Never, *ever* say disparaging things about another person without considering first whether you would wish them to learn of your comment. Pretend they are in the room. They, and those who love them."

"I don't believe that Lady Regina loves the Earl of Winchester," Livie observed. "She didn't defend his looks."

"It's her second betrothal, so love doesn't come into it," Lady Wharton said, stripping off her gloves. "I dislike gossip, but the consensus is that her former fiancé fled on closer acquaintance. Lady Regina is unfortunately getting somewhat long in the tooth, given that she debuted later than most. She's lucky to have secured an earl."

"Who was her previous fiancé?" Daisy asked.

" Lady Regina was betrothed to Mr. Peregrine. Her brother, by the way, is the Duke of Lennox, a great admirer of Livie's father. The Duchess of Lennox is in a delicate condition and has retired to the country, or I would have introduced you."

"Lady Regina was engaged to a mere *mister*," Daisy commented, raising an eyebrow.

"The man is rich as Croesus," Lady Wharton stated.

"Who is that?" Livie asked.

"A king," Lady Wharton said vaguely. "Or perhaps someone in the Bible. It's just something one says, Livie. You mustn't always be asking for clarification."

"But darling Liv is like that," Daisy pointed out, winding an arm around Livie's waist. "She is our encyclopedia."

"What is an encyclopedia?" Lady Wharton asked, and then waved her hands before they could answer. "Don't tell me! My head is crammed with information about eligible gentlemen. Oh girls, I am *so* happy. I shall write to your mama this very night, Livie. Perhaps the news will give her the strength to rise from her bed."

Livie doubted that. Her mother was at the mercy of a weak set of nerves. She spent her days cycling between a bed and a daybed, a handkerchief soaked in violet perfume clutched in her hand. It was due to her mother's poor health that Livie had joined Daisy in the Wharton nursery over a decade ago.

"Invitations will pour in through the door tomorrow morning," her aunt rejoiced. "Now that hostesses realize the most eligible young men enjoy supping with you two, they shan't dare put on a party unless you're there, for fear your suitors will try to find you elsewhere."

Daisy squeezed Livie's hand.

"The best of it is that you didn't put on any airs or dampen your petticoats," her mother continued. "You were yourselves: natural and unspoiled—more than a few chaperones mentioned that to me. Lady Castlereigh confirmed your Almack's vouchers will arrive tomorrow."

Lady Wharton sat back against her seat, smiling into empty space.

"Lady Regina can stuff herself," Daisy whispered in Livie's ear.

"She can keep the green onion," Livie whispered back. "Is that too mean? I don't want to turn into someone like her."

"I shan't let you," Daisy said. "If you marry a titled man, and begin thinking too much of yourself, I shall spank you. Clementine overheard Lady Regina tell Abigail Dwyer that she was to be grievously pitied for her shape."

Livie frowned, trying to remember the lady.

"Miss Dwyer is delightfully curved," Daisy explained.

"That wasn't nice," Livie agreed. "We should avoid Lady Regina because she brings out all my worst instincts. I oughtn't to have said she was unkind, given that I was being the same."

"Oh, well," Daisy said. "You know how scallions are sold in a bunch, all the fluffy roots together?"

Livie started laughing.

"Lady Regina, the earl, an heir, and a spare," Daisy said triumphantly. "Her hair rose higher than his!"

Chapter 4

The Recipe for Disaster

Livie had never worried much about the world's opinion of her—until the world despised her.

After all, she was the darling daughter of a high-ranking officer in the Royal Navy, Captain Sir Tyron, commander of the HMS *Royal Oak*. Both of her parents came from noble stock, and she had a fair-to-middling dowry. Moreover, her hair curled naturally, and her lips had been described as "sultry" by her first beau, the local squire's son.

The news arrived while Livie was circling the dance floor at Almack's Assembly Hall. One moment, the world was smiling at her—to be precise, Robert de Lacy Evans was eagerly telling her about his plans to alter his country estate once he inherited the barony, which she interpreted as something close to a proposal.

But after he deposited her back at her aunt's side?

The world changed. Lady Wharton's normally cheerful face had turned faintly green. She caught Livie's arm. "We're leaving."

"Why?" Livie asked. Past her aunt's shoulder, the Countess of Silverton whispered something in Lady Regina's ear. As the countess drew back, Lady Regina's lips curled, her eyes glinting with disdain. She looked Livie up and down with a terrible look of enjoyment on her face, like a cat that has cornered a mouse.

What on earth had happened?

Livie gazed back, keeping her face calm. She hadn't done anything wrong. She certainly hadn't enticed Lady Regina's fiancé into the bushes, behavior that according to rumor had led to the demise of the lady's first betrothal.

Daisy popped up at Livie's shoulder. "Mama, the most peculiar thing just happened. I was to dance with Lord Marcellus, but he said that under the circumstances—"

"Follow me," Lady Wharton snapped. She didn't walk around the ballroom; she cut straight through all the clusters of people waiting for the next dance to be called. Livie had always known that her father's older sister was a formidable person...

But now?

When the same people who normally bowed and scraped before her drew back, whispering behind their fans, looking away?

Lady Wharton swept forward like a ship in full sail without regard for anyone in the room.

Lady Castlereigh was standing in the hallway with Mr. Paine, the Master of Ceremonies at Almack's. "Lady Wharton, I shall have to withdraw your vouchers," she said in a pained voice.

"This is a travesty, Amelia, and you know it." Livie's aunt snapped.

"In the event there has been a miscarriage of justice, all will be forgotten, as you know," Lady Castlereigh stated. Her face was placid and expressionless, like a pond without a breath of wind.

Normally, Lady Wharton would curtsy before the Almack's patroness; instead, she snatched her pelisse from a waiting footman and flew through the door, Livie and Daisy hurrying after her.

"Mama!" Daisy cried, the moment she entered the carriage. "What—"

"Be quiet," her mother commanded. "I feel distraught. I am *never* distraught." She sat upright, staring into space.

When Daisy opened her mouth anyway, Livie squeezed her hand and whispered, "Hush." Her cousin habitually sent her mother into a fury, as when Daisy ran out to visit a bookseller without a maid in attendance. But this felt different. *This*, whatever *this* was, was of a different magnitude altogether.

For one thing, their vouchers had been withdrawn.

Livie had never heard of such a thing. Of course, young ladies, even those from good families, didn't always receive a voucher. One of the patronesses had to personally vouch for you, your family, and, it was rumored, your dowry.

Her mother would be devastated.

With Livie's eventual debut and need for vouchers in mind, Lady Tyron had carefully tended her childhood friendship with Lady Castlereigh with years of monthly letters, even though she confessed to finding the exchanges dull.

And now those vouchers had been *withdrawn*?

Livie's heart sank to her toes. Beside her, Daisy managed to hold her tongue, though she was clearly simmering like a pot on the boil.

Finally, Lady Wharton drew in a breath. "I can't see any way to soften the truth."

"What?" Daisy burst out. "Mama, I didn't do—"

"Livie, your father has been arrested for crimes of high treason."

Chapter 5

Social Ruin is Certain

The news of her father's arrest struck Livie like a blow to the head. One minute she was confused, and the next she was seized by rage and horror. "Father is not a traitor!" she cried.

"A crime of high treason? Uncle would never do such a thing!" Daisy chimed in, her hand tightening around Livie's. "As you said, Mama, it's a travesty. What do they say he supposedly did?"

"No one at Almack's knew the details," Lady Wharton said grimly. "When the *HMS Royal Oak* docked this afternoon, the Secretary of the Navy was waiting for my brother, and they took him into custody. The news only leaked this evening."

"Do you… Do you mean my father is in *prison*?" Livie gasped.

"I'm afraid so." Her aunt was twisting a handkerchief in her hands. "They must have evidence, or they wouldn't have taken such a drastic step."

"Nonsense," Livie said sharply. "There can be no evidence, as my father is innocent. Isn't treason an attempt on the life of the King or his heir? Father is a loyal Englishman."

"Other crimes fall under the same definition," Lady Wharton said. "Aiding and abetting the enemy, for example."

"What enemy? Napoleon? He's immured on Saint Helena, and Father *despises* him!" Livie pressed the hand Daisy wasn't clutching against her stomach. "I feel ill."

"I don't," Daisy said. "I feel like killing someone. Do you think they put Uncle in a prison cell with criminals?"

Lady Wharton shook her head. "You needn't worry about that. My brother will be housed in relative comfort. He's been taken to Beauchamp Tower."

"The Tower of London!" Livie gasped. Her mind boggled, thinking of the fates of famous noblemen who had lived—and died—within the Tower's walls. "This is a nightmare."

"Beauchamp has housed royal prisoners, Livie. Your father will have his own room; I'll send fresh bedding and clothing over tomorrow morning. Surely, they will allow his valet to attend him.

I'll dispatch a groom to my husband. Unfortunately, Lord Wharton is in Scotland so the message will take weeks to reach him."

"Mother couldn't arrive for at least three weeks," Livie said, thinking of the long trip to Lancashire. "If she comes." The truth was, the news would give her mother spasms, and Livie couldn't imagine her rising from the couch under those circumstances.

"Your father's aid and comfort rest on our shoulders," her aunt stated, tacitly agreeing that his wife likely wouldn't travel to London. "I'll write to our family solicitor. Hopefully he will be allowed to visit the captain. Certainly, he should be able to receive a copy of the charges against him."

"May I visit Father?" Livie asked, her voice breaking.

Her aunt shook her head. "I'm afraid not, dear. I doubt they admit family in cases of treason."

"Surely he can write to me. He writes me every day!" Tears started sliding down Livie's face. "He hasn't missed a day since I learned to read."

"Of course, he will write to you," her aunt said, leaning forward to hand Livie a handkerchief.

"This has to be a mistake!" Daisy protested. "They must have him mixed up with someone else."

"Father received a commendation for the Battle of the Dardanelles," Livie said miserably. "How can this be happening?"

"We will fight it, Livie, with everything we have." Lady Wharton took a deep breath and looked at her daughter. "We must, because the aftermath of my brother's arraignment will not fall on Livie alone."

"I don't want a voucher to Almack's if they don't welcome my cousin," Daisy said immediately, winding her arm around Livie's waist. "I'll happily never enter that door again!"

"The consequences are far graver than a voucher," her mother stated. "We must prove your uncle's innocence, Daisy, or your chance of a good marriage will be very slim indeed." Lady Wharton turned to Livie. "As will be yours, Livie." The grimness of her tone left no room for doubt.

"Marriage into the family of a traitor," Lady Wharton continued, "is unheard of. A convicted man's personal possessions are forfeited to the Crown, which means Livie will be left without a dowry. While we will always care for you and your mother, Livie, we must face the fact that your personal circumstances would be much changed should your father be found guilty. Moreover, this won't be settled immediately. Months will pass before a date for the tribunal is set."

Daisy startled. "Our ball!"

"I shall cancel the ball in the morning," Lady Wharton said. "No one will show their face in our home while Captain Sir Tyron is in custody. I was just saying how tiresome morning calls had grown, was I not? Far too many young men traipsing through our drawing room on the slightest of pretexts, leaving our tables crowded with odious flowers."

Her aunt had indeed complained, but Livie knew Lady Wharton had been proud of Daisy's and Livie's herds of suitors.

"I should never have thought of the ball. What a despicable comment, when our every thought should be with Uncle," Daisy declared. "Please forgive me."

Her mother patted Daisy's knee. "There's the daughter I know and love. We shall face this as a family, and surmount it as a family, dears. Your father is not alone, Livie. I have powerful friends, and so does my husband."

"The Duke of Lennox!" Livie exclaimed. "You said that he had great respect for Father."

"Indeed," Lady Wharton agreed. "They know each other by way of His Grace's military service, though, of course, the duke did not serve in the Navy." She frowned. "It's unfortunate that the duchess is in a delicate condition once again, or they would be in London. Perhaps I shall travel to Cheshire and speak to him myself."

"I haven't met anyone I wanted to marry, anyway," Daisy declared. "Have you, Livie?"

Livie shook her head. "What happens to traitors who are convicted?"

Her aunt didn't answer.

Chapter 6

The Right Hat Brings Attitude With It

By the time they arrived home, Livie was wracked with sorrow and fear. She sobbed on and off through the night and woke in the morning with her face wet.

Lady Wharton greeted Livie and Daisy at luncheon with the news that Captain Sir Tyron had been accused of "adhering to the King's enemies"—a charge tantamount to plotting an armed insurrection against the government. She squawked with derisive laughter. "My brother is a decorated naval commander! This is nonsense, utter nonsense. It *will* be resolved."

"What does the charge mean?" Livie asked.

"I don't have the details yet," her aunt said. "Take a slice of beef, if you please. We must keep up our strength. I intend to go out directly after breakfast and begin marshaling the troops."

Livie thought, not for the first time, that Lady Wharton would have made an excellent commander in the Navy. All the same, she couldn't eat a bite. Thankfully, a somber, yet cheering letter from her father arrived an hour or so later—along with a large packet of all the daily letters he'd written since the last time the *Royal Oak* docked.

"Father's solicitor visited last night," Livie exclaimed. "He writes that it will take some time to clear up these erroneous allegations, but the outcome is assured. Men are being sent to France to bring back witnesses."

She frowned. "Apparently, his arrest stems from an event *two years ago*! Back when Father received a fraudulent message saying that an Englishman needed rescue from France. Do you remember that, Aunt?"

"Only vaguely," Lady Wharton answered. "Your father will supervise the investigation from his confinement. I shall undertake the equally important task of rousing the most important people in the land to rally to his aid."

"If anyone can do it, you can, Mama," Daisy declared.

"I shall demand an apology from Lady Castlereigh," Lady Wharton said broodingly. "We will simply wait this out, my dears. Luckily, you are both young. Hopefully your mother will feel well enough to join us during the next Season, Livie."

Livie's aunt might be a bit dictatorial at times, but she was always kind. The fiction that Lady Tyron would someday feel well enough to spend time with her daughter had been endlessly repeated since Livie first joined the Wharton household at the age of five.

"Mother and I am so grateful for your help," Livie said. "I know that Father will feel safer with you supporting him."

Lady Wharton squared her shoulders. "I fancy there are few women with as much power as I have in society. I have never enjoyed my consequence, but now it will be of use."

"I do wish we could ride in the park," Daisy said, bouncing a little in her chair. "We cannot remain indoors for a whole year, Mama."

"I suppose you're going to be as obstinate as a mule about it," Lady Wharton said, eyeing her daughter.

"My cousin is not suited to being cooped up," Livie said, trying to soften the truth.

"You and Livie will be given the cut direct by people who have professed themselves your friends," Lady Wharton pointed out. "It will be most unpleasant."

"I don't care," Daisy said. "We were prepared to be wallflowers, weren't we, Livie?"

Livie nodded. Back in the nursery, Daisy had spun marvelous tales of what would happen when they debuted. Often they were wallflowers and then spinsters, left to find their way in a world full of rapacious squires.

"I suppose you may leave the house, though we certainly shall not attend any society events," her aunt decreed. "Be it on your shoulders if you or your cousin are treated unkindly, Daisy. I told you that Mrs. Hedborough attempted to give me the cut direct this morning, did I not? I cooked her goose; I inquired about her son, and everyone knows he is a degenerate. She hurried away."

"Yes, you did tell us, Mama," Daisy said. "We shall ignore people like Mrs. Hedborough. I simply cannot stay in the house for eight months until my uncle has his trial. I shall wither and *die*."

Lady Wharton rolled her eyes.

"If anyone is unkind to me because of my father's circumstances, I shall not care about them, for they are quite unlikable," Livie declared.

"And we shall have no hesitation in informing them just that!" Daisy added.

"Your generation is remarkably different from mine," Lady Wharton commented. "At your age, my sister and I were crushed by the slightest insult."

Daisy said what Livie wouldn't have dared to. "I don't believe you, Mama. Not for an instant. Most of the ladies in the ton are terrified of you. Even Lady Regina is polite to you, and she is horrid to everyone!"

As the month wore on, the household adjusted to its new circumstances. A letter arrived from the country announcing that on receipt of the terrible news, Livie's mother had suffered a serious relapse, which surprised no one. Lord Wharton was presumably making his way from Scotland. Lady Wharton left the house nearly every day, often staying out into the evening, rousing support for her brother.

Livie's father wrote her every day, as he had for as long as she could remember, which made the whole thing fantastically…mundane.

He had been assigned a spacious room in the Tower. His valet came and went, delivering excellent meals prepared by Lady Wharton's cook. His first mate was in constant attendance. A tailor had been dispatched to the prison, ordered to create a magnificent uniform for the tribunal, with the best brass buttons down the front, gleaming epaulets on the shoulders, and Venetian lace at the throat.

When he wasn't consulting with solicitors, her father had begun designing a better ship's boat, combining a whaleboat and a jolly boat—whatever the latter was. He informed Livie that he found life tolerable, almost enjoyable.

Livie and Daisy rode daily in Hyde Park in the wee hours of the morning when paths were empty. Little by little, as the weeks passed, they started going farther afield, visiting bookstores and *modistes*.

Lady Wharton had been right: members of polite society acted extremely discourteously. Lord Devin was one of the few exceptions, always stopping to greet them and asking after their welfare.

One morning in early April, they ventured to a haberdashery after Lady Wharton declared their bonnets shamefully out of fashion.

"It is our duty to look our best," she had announced. "Any untidiness will be taken as an admission of guilt. Both of you *must* keep your curls under control."

Once in the shop, Daisy tried on a small straw bonnet that tied under the chin with plaid ribbons, trimmed with three curled feathers. "Do you think this brim is too daring?" she asked. "I fear that Mama will say that it's designed for the *demimonde*, not for an unmarried girl."

Livie was trying to decide whether to try on an adorable bonnet with a rose over one ear. She hadn't spent any of her pin money…but what if her father needed every penny to pay for solicitors? Yet Lady Wharton seemed to be so assured of her father's release… Livie was admiring the silk rose when a sharp voice interrupted them.

"I can scarcely believe my eyes," Lady Regina said. "Scarcely *believe my eyes*."

Chapter 7

A Young Termagant with Irritated Nerves

Livie was so startled by Lady Regina's entrance into the shop that she just stared at her. Out of the corner of her eye, she saw Daisy raise an eyebrow.

"Are you shocked by this bonnet?" her cousin asked the lady. "The plumes *are* daring, but also darling, don't you think?"

"Good morning, Lady Regina," Livie said, curtsying. And turning to Regina's friend, "Miss Massinger."

"Actually, Miss Massinger is my older sister, Prudence. I am Miss Petunia," the companion said, offering a vacuous smile. "We're twins, but she arrived before me."

"Do *not* curtsy to either of these women, for obvious reasons," Regina snapped.

Petunia had already dropped into a curtsy, but she jerked upright like a puppet on a string.

"You've stopped curtsying, Lady Regina?" Daisy's voice had a dangerous edge. "You *are* a maverick in society, aren't you?"

Lady Regina picked up a straw bonnet and turned it over disdainfully, eyeing the hat Daisy wore. "Plaid ribbons are not in style. Moreover, *La Belle Assemblée*'s most recent issue depicted only pleated silk headpieces."

"What a pity that flaxen hair goes so poorly with straw," Livie said, her eyes drifting over Regina's head. "A different bonnet that might suit you better—something black, perhaps."

Next to her, Daisy made a sound, like a choked-off laugh.

Lady Regina swelled up like a turkey-cock and turned an alarming red. "I am not interested in bonnets from *this* establishment. Not now that I realize who their customers are. I do not parlay with the criminal classes."

"Oh, so you mistook your way. Where were you meaning to shop?" Daisy inquired. "I hear one often gets lost as one grows older."

Miss Petunia coughed, which might have disguised a chuckle.

"You!" Lady Regina called to the store clerk. "Fetch the owner of this establishment, if you please."

The girl dashed into the rear.

Daisy reached over and picked up a petty bonnet. "You must try this on, Miss Petunia. The rose is just right for a girl in the bloom of youth. Your dark hair will suit it so."

"Yes, I think I will try that bonnet," Petunia replied, pulling out the hatpins that anchored her headpiece.

Daisy smilingly handed the bonnet to her.

A stout woman swathed in a white apron bustled out of the back of the store. "My name is Mrs. Mogbetty, and I am the milliner. What can I help you with?" she asked. "Ah, I see you're trying on my newest Parisian bonnet," she said to Daisy.

"I should have known it was French. Pleated silk is already out of style, isn't it? I believe I shall have it. My friend is considering the one with the rose," Daisy said, beaming at the shopkeeper.

Petunia had put her own bonnet to the side; now she plopped Mrs. Mogbetty's creation on her head.

"Actually, we shall take our custom elsewhere," Regina announced in a threatening voice. Her narrow nose rose in the air.

"I do like this bonnet," Petunia said, ignoring her friend as she tied it firmly under her chin.

"The rose over your ear looks like a cauliflower," Regina snapped.

"I disagree," the milliner said with frigid emphasis.

"Do you know who I am?"

"I have no idea," Mrs. Mogbetty said, "but I can tell that you're suffering from irritated nerves, and if there's one thing I can't abide, it's a young termagant with irritated nerves."

"Regina is often agitated," Petunia remarked.

She didn't seem to notice the threatening glare she received from her friend. Instead, she adjusted the bonnet. "Do you think that perhaps I ought to have *two* pink roses, one over each ear? Or two over the same ear?"

"Two would overweigh the straw," Mrs. Mogbetty said, coming over to adjust the headpiece.

"In all good conscience, I could not give my custom to a store that offers nurture and comfort to traitors to the Crown," Regina proclaimed. "And neither should you, Petunia. Your mother would be horrified."

Mrs. Mogbetty's eyebrows flew up.

"My father has been wrongfully accused of treason," Livie explained. "He's supposed to have done something nefarious in France, but he's innocent. He wasn't even in the same place as the plotters."

Regina sniffed. "The mastermind of a fiendish plot would never remain in its vicinity."

"My father is no criminal mastermind!" Livie cried. "He is a war hero!"

"*My* father was a member of the aristocracy, very close to the royal family," Regina retorted. "Your father is accused of plotting to overthrow the king." She shuddered. "I feel this very store is tainted."

"Coppers are prone to errors," the milliner said. "I can tell you stories from my own family."

Petunia was still paying no attention; she was twisting to the left and right, looking at herself in the glass. "This bonnet is very flattering."

"I cannot believe that you would consider purchasing something from this horrendously vulgar person," Regina said with acid emphasis.

Livie recognized the signs of a woman losing her composure; Daisy had better control these days, but when they were girls, her temper often led to objects flying around the room. She elbowed her cousin. "Good thing there's no teacup within her reach," she whispered.

"I only did that once," Daisy protested, *sotto voce*. "I don't look *that* unattractive when I'm in a temper, do I?"

Their gibes were far from subtle, and Regina's mouth clenched into an even less attractive look.

"No, darling Daisy, you don't look at all unattractive in a temper, but I'm afraid not everyone is as lucky as you are," Livie said. She deliberately glanced at Regina's mouth and then away.

Which was mean.

But somehow she didn't feel an ounce of regret.

Her father was *innocent*.

Chapter 8

Mrs. Mogbetty's Rules for Hats & Birdhouses

Petunia untied the hat and drifted to the store counter, taking

out her reticule. "I wish you could be calmer, Regina," she said over

her shoulder. "You are likely to come down with a sick headache

after expressing so much emotion."

"I am nearing the end of my patience," Regina spat.

Petunia put down some coins and gave the shopgirl one of

her vacuous smiles. "I shall wear this out of the shop, if you'd please

have my old bonnet delivered to #38, Grosvenor Square."

"Certainly, ma'am," the shopgirl murmured.

"I shall never return!" Regina announced.

"No loss," Mrs. Mogbetty retorted.

Petunia turned around. "I must say, Regina, there's

something fantastically commonplace about your mind when you're

in a temper."

The shopkeeper pointedly opened the door. Petunia drifted

through it, putting her head back just long enough to say, "Well, do

come along, Regina."

"I am the daughter of a duke," Regina informed the shopkeeper. "My monthly allowance is more than the rent on this despicable little hovel that you call a shop."

"*I* am the daughter of a decent man," Mrs. Mogbetty retorted. "I can't imagine what your father was like, but unless you replace that bonnet you're holding, I'll call him a thief and you his true daughter."

Regina looked down at the straw bonnet she still held. She made for the exit, throwing the hat disdainfully back into the shop as she left.

Livie snatched it out of the air—not for nothing had she shared a nursery with her excitable cousin for so many years. "What a lovely bonnet," she said, plunking it on her head and turning to the glass. "I look quite pretty in it, don't you think, Daisy?"

"I doubt that you could look any prettier than you are," Mrs. Mogbetty said frankly. "You have those eyes they talk about, Miss."

Livie was adjusting the bonnet's ribbon, so the bow was under one ear. "My eyes are not blue, my hair isn't yellow, and my chin isn't pointed, Mrs. Mogbetty. But that said, I much appreciate your kindness!"

"You have dancing eyes," Mrs. Mogbetty stated.

Daisy wound an arm around Livie's waist and kissed her on the cheek. "She's right. I don't care how beautiful Lady Regina is."

"Oh, is that her name?" Mrs. Mogbetty said broodily. "I have customers in high places."

"She's not worth the trouble," Livie said. "We intend to ignore her, don't we, Daisy? It's just that at the moment we're excluded from society, so we haven't had the chance."

"Next Season, after Livie's father is cleared of these unfair charges, we shall go to *all* the balls and ignore Lady Regina at every one!" Daisy agreed. "It will be an enormous pleasure. Almost as much fun as finding a beau."

"*More* fun," Livie said. "You can't imagine how everyone bows and scrapes before her, Mrs. Mogbetty. It's turned her into a monster."

The milliner grinned. "I can see the two of you straightening out high society in no time. That is not the bonnet for you, Miss Livie, if you don't mind my calling you that. You've too much hair for it."

"But it's so adorable."

"If your hair is atop your head, the hat will perch up there like a birdhouse. And if you wear it down, as you have it now, a horse's tail seems to spring from the back of your neck. I shall find something better."

Livie peered over her shoulder and sure enough, mahogany curls rioted down her back.

Mrs. Mogbetty returned holding a delicious scrap of coral silk: a circle topped with small roses. "This is designed to be worn by a lady with a wealth of hair. Just look at this." She tweaked something in the brim, and a veil unfurled.

Daisy took the hat and held on top of Livie's head. "The little veil hides your horse tail, Livie."

Livie swatted her. "You have just as much hair as I have."

"You're holding it backwards," Mrs. Mogbetty said. She flipped the circlet about and set it on Livie's head as if it were a coronet, anchoring it with a hatpin.

"I can see through the veil," Livie exclaimed. She lifted the silk and smiled at Mrs. Mogbetty. "It's translucent."

"This is a masquerade hat," Mrs. Mogbetty explained. "Masques and masquerades are all the rage these days. The hats are worn by ladies who go to Vauxhall and such, where they do not wish to be recognized by their husbands." She blinked. "Not that you should know anything about that, and I regret bringing up such a disgraceful topic."

"How interesting," Livie said. She walked over to the window. "It's as if the street is blushing. Everything is pink."

"I want one," Daisy cried.

"Young ladies—" Mrs. Mobeetie began.

"We were invited to masquerades," Daisy interrupted. "We were invited to *everything*, Mrs. Mogbetty. Now we must stay in the house, barring small excursions to the bookstore and the like. But next Season we shall go to masquerades, and we might as well be prepared."

Livie was experimenting with tucking the silk veil behind one ear and then letting it flutter free again. "I love this hat."

"I can't be responsible for young ones such as yourselves sneaking off to Vauxhall," Mrs. Mogbetty said. She frowned at Daisy. "I've seen your ilk before, and you are not one to stay quietly in the house."

"That is true," Daisy conceded.

"I don't want to go to Vauxhall, whatever that is," Livie said. "I shall wear this hat in the park. When fine ladies see me, they turn away so sharply that I feel as if their heads will twist off their necks. But wearing this hat, I could ride in the park, and no one would know who I am! Please sell me this hat, Mrs. Mogbetty."

"Sell me one as well," Daisy pleaded. "I couldn't allow Livie to go for a ride alone in Hyde Park. I'll buy the bonnet I'm wearing as well, of course."

Mrs. Mogbetty sighed; she knew when she was beaten. "I have misgivings," she grumbled, but she opened a cabinet, pulled out a circlet topped with silk violets, and handed it to Daisy.

"This is exquisite," Daisy breathed. "I promise, word of honor, that we won't go to Vauxhall."

"My cousin always keeps her promises," Livie chimed in. "She can be astonishingly naughty—you know that's the truth, Daisy—but my aunt is always frustrated when it turns out that she hadn't explicitly forbidden whatever Daisy had done."

"No Vauxhall," Daisy promised. "Well, not this year. Not until we're older."

"What is Vauxhall?" Livie asked.

"I don't know," Daisy said laughing. "But I'm certain I shall enjoy it…someday."

Mrs. Mogbetty groaned.

Chapter 9

Rebellion is Reaction to an Unfair World

By March, they were used to their new reality. Livie and Daisy spent their time exploring London, trailing a groom behind them as they visited the British Museum in Montagu House, the exhibits at the British Library, the Old Bailey sessions house, the Adelphi terrace, and St. Paul's.

"I never wanted to be so educated," Daisy groaned one evening, throwing herself into a chair in Livie's bedchamber. They were alone; her mother had left for Cheshire to visit the Duke of Lennox that morning and wasn't expected to return for at least three weeks. "*You* like learning things, Livie, but I don't! That whale, for example, was a waste of two ha'pennies."

Livie looked up from the account she was giving her father of the great sea beast's skeleton. "Not true! Just imagine such a giant animal floating about the ocean. I expect Father has seen them in the deep."

She finished her sentence, added her love, and sanded the letter.

Daisy was pawing through a basket she'd brought in from the drawing room.

Livie glanced over as she placed her father's morning letter into the trunk beside her desk, where it joined all the daily missives he'd sent since she learned to read at the age of five. "What do you have?" she asked.

"The invitations we received for this Season," Daisy said. "They used to be piled in the hallway, but Mother moved them to a basket." She scanned each missive before tossing it to the rug.

Livie thought of pointing out that she was making a mess, but she held her tongue. Her cousin found near-confinement far harder than she did. Daisy worried about her uncle, but not with the same nagging fear that Livie felt every waking hour.

No matter how often her father assured her that someone had borrowed his identity and met with scoundrels in France, Livie couldn't help fearing that the truth wouldn't come out or couldn't be adequately proved.

"I found it!" Daisy triumphantly held up an invitation. "It's an invitation to a masquerade ball, given by Lord and Lady

Rothingale." She flashed Livie a grin. "This invitation admits two, and you don't have to identify yourself, because it's a *masquerade*!"

"Rothingale is a degenerate," Livie objected. "He *eloped* with his wife last Season, Daisy. Your mother wouldn't have allowed us to go, even without this business about my father hanging over our heads. In fact, I'm surprised she received an invitation."

"We could go for one hour," her cousin cried. "Just an hour, Livie, that's all. If I don't have a chance to see people and hear music and dance one measure, I will *die*."

Livie rolled her eyes.

"Lord Rothingale lives at an excellent address, not far from here, so we needn't call up the carriage. We'd take a footman, of course."

"What if anyone discovered who we are?" Livie argued. "We would be disgraced as well as exiled! Aunt would be so disappointed. No, she'd be furious."

"We shan't be discovered! We'll wear the red domino cloaks that Mother had made for last Twelfth Night ball. We could even wear masks beneath the masquerade hats we bought. Besides, no one really knows us, do they? We scarcely debuted, and now it's two months later."

"Lady Regina knows us."

"Lady Regina would never go to a masquerade ball thrown by Rothingale," Daisy pointed out. "Plus, how could she possibly recognize us if we each wear a domino cloak, a mask, *and* a masquerade hat with the veil down? We'll be as good as nuns, Livie. *Please?*"

Livie groaned.

And gave in.

A few nights later, two young ladies, swathed from head to foot in voluminous cloaks, their curls tied up and their veils down, strolled up to the door of #45 Wimpole Street, with invitation cards in hand.

"Proper prime ones, they are," the butler muttered to his new footman after the two guests disappeared into the ballroom.

James gaped. "They were lightskirts?"

"Lightskirts?" Mr. Bridges snorted. "You sound like my grandfather."

"Jezebels?" the footman hazarded. "Courtesans?"

"High up in the *demimonde*," the butler said. "Did you smell them when they passed?"

James shook his head.

"Them women in the *demimonde* smell as good as ladies themselves," the butler pronounced.

"Maybe they *are* ladies," James said.

"Too young and pretty," the butler opined. "No chaperone."

"They had a footman," James pointed out. They had sent the man down to the servants' quarters to join the others of his ilk.

The butler snorted again. "Man-hunting, they is. No question about it. Not that I think any less of them for that," he added. "This house ain't what it used to be, under the old master. All sorts are welcome now."

James's eyes rounded. His mother had warned him of the dangers of the great city, and here they were. He felt shaken to the tips of his toes.

"Scarlet cloaks," the butler concluded. "That says it all, doesn't it?"

One of the ladies—the *demi*…whatever Mr. Bridges called her… Her curls had glistened in the light of torches outside the door as if they were made from spun silk. The little veil she wore ended just above her mouth, and…

Her lips?

James swallowed hard.

Chapter 10

Introducing Major Joshua Charles FitzRoy of the 5th Dragoon

When Major Joshua Charles FitzRoy of the 5th Dragoon Guards walked into Lord Rothingale's house, he instantly realized that he'd made a mistake.

Not having known it was a masquerade, he had no mask or domino cloak. A footman handed him a strip of black silk with holes cut in it, but he stuffed it in his pocket. Everywhere he looked, lush women bursting out of their scanty costumes were dancing with men in cloaks and masks.

This was no normal costume ball—nothing like Twelfth Night balls he'd attended before he took a commission in the 5th Dragoon Guards. These men may be gentlemen, but the women were certainly not ladies.

It wasn't a marriage market, and Joshua wasn't interested in other pursuits.

Or, as of late, anything else at all.

Perhaps it was the effect of going to war. After serving in the Peninsula in 1811, followed by the Battle of Salamanca, and a lengthy recovery from a gunshot that nearly took his life…

Ever since his earlier dinner with three friends from Oxford, Joshua had been wrestling with the realization that he'd outgrown them. Back in university, they'd called themselves the Arch Rogues, which was such a stupid label that he shuddered to think of it.

He had matured, and they hadn't. Or so it seemed over dinner.

He found himself repulsed by his oldest friend, Clay Trywhitt—*Clod* Trywhitt, they called him now, or so Clod had cheerfully told him. Clod had become a gambler and told Joshua that he was looking to marry a lady with a substantial dowry in the same breath that he boasted of healing from a bout of syphilis. What Joshua knew of syphilis suggested that Clod would infect his would-be wife, not to mention whatever brazen-faced (albeit masked) woman he bought for the evening.

Joshua had just decided to cut Clod Trywhitt from his life and return home when he heard a crash and a recognizable bellow.

Shouldering his way through the crowd, he discovered his friend flat on the floor, staring up at a young vixen who had apparently landed him a blow that had taken him off his feet. Not only that, but her delicate slipper was positioned on his chest.

She was pulling on his neck cloth, shouting. "Oh, you would, would you?" Every time she yanked on the fabric, Clod's head rose from the floor and then thumped back down again.

Clod wasn't resisting because he was in the bind of a gentleman who has apparently misbehaved—and is confronted not by a high-flier, but by a young lady. Her voice was crystal clear, and her inflection enraged. Joshua guessed her family was high-born, not mere gentry.

What on earth was she doing here?

Clod stirred, and she stamped her small foot, pressing her slipper into his sternum. "Don't you dare move, you repellent blackguard!"

Joshua found a genuine smile on his face for the first time since he returned to England. "How can I help?" he asked her, and then, looking down, "What an ass you are, Clod."

"Clod? As in a clod of earth?" the lady demanded. She yanked on his neckcloth again and let his head thump back down. "He is a disgusting, repugnant Beelzebub!"

"That's a bit strong," Clod whined. "Damme, my head is starting to hurt. Would you please take your foot off my chest?"

"Why should I?" she demanded. "So that you may behave in that brazen manner with another lady?"

"Lady? You're the only lady here!" Clod protested. "For God's sake, it's hardly *my* fault that you—whoever you are—walked into a house full of canary-birds."

"Canary-birds?" she repeated, frowning.

She turned her head to Joshua and whispered, "Do you think he suffered a head injury?"

Joshua coughed. "Canary-bird is a name for...for a ladybird. A bird of paradise."

Even through her veil, he saw puzzlement in her eyes. "No one in the room is capable of laying an egg."

She was aristocratic, very young—and naïve as well.

"My grandmother would have termed most guests trollops," he explained, hoping he wouldn't need explicate further.

The lady's lips formed a perfect circle. Her mouth was cherry red and delightful, and for the very first time since the Battle of Vitoria, Joshua felt a stirring of interest.

"If you're done with the vocabulary lesson, I'd like to get up," Clod grumbled.

"If I may be of assistance," Joshua said, placing his foot firmly on Clod's chest next to hers, "I can hold this position as long as you wish."

He could just see long eyelashes blinking at him through the translucent silk of her veil. She removed her foot, shook out her skirts, and said, "I have to find the friend I came with. We must leave immediately."

"What in the bloody hell are you doing, putting your foot on me, FitzRoy?" Claude said loudly.

"Don't use that language in front of a young lady," Joshua retorted, the edge in his voice telling Clod that he would have no hesitation grinding down with his heel.

"Oh, for—" Clod broke off. "Let me up."

A small hand caught Joshua's sleeve. "You should release him," the lady whispered. "We are attracting a great deal of attention."

Joshua lifted his boot, and Clod ponderously got himself to his feet.

"Who are you?" Clod asked the lady peevishly.

"I shan't tell you," she replied, tossing her head. "You're not a nice man at all, In fact, I suspect that you are a *libertine*."

Which was apparently worse than being Beelzebub.

"I shall escort you home," Joshua stated.

The lady came up on her toes, looking around as best she could. "I must find my friend first. We were separated in the crush."

"*Two* young ladies here?" Clod groaned. "What's the world coming to?" His cravat hung open, and his white shirt bore the distinct impression of a small shoe across the chest. He shook himself like a hunting dog emerging from a stream and shuffled off without another word.

Joshua concluded that he had no need to break off the acquaintance with Trywhitt. They had come to a natural parting of ways.

"There she is," the lady cried. She was still clutching Joshua's sleeve, which he rather liked. There was no ring on her finger, which he also liked.

"Do you know whether she is dancing with a bad man, like your friend?" Her hand tightened. "If so, we'll need to rescue her."

"Trywhitt is not my friend." Joshua turned and surveyed the ballroom. "What is she wearing?"

"A scarlet domino cloak just like this one, and a masquerade hat, but hers is ringed with violets."

He saw the lady instantly. Thankfully, she was circling the dancefloor in the arms of a man he recognized; moreover, he appeared to be in the middle of delivering a stern lecture.

"She's dancing with Lord Devin," Joshua said. "Can't be anyone else, not with his height and shoulders."

"Oh, thank goodness," the lady cried. "I like him. He's quite decent, isn't he?"

Further evidence that this lady moved in the highest of circles. "Absolutely," Joshua confirmed.

"Too old and too gentlemanly to be as horrid as that fellow."

"Age is not a predictor of behavior," Joshua noted.

"You're not very old, are you?" She stared up at him. "Have we met? Actually, I can't tell you who I am, so ignore that question."

"We have not met. May I introduce myself? I am Major Joshua Charles FitzRoy."

She dropped a graceful curtsy but added, "I'm sorry not to share my name, but we made an error coming here."

"I agree," Joshua said, taking her arm to lead her to the side of the room, hopefully before she caught sight of the couple leaning against the wall to their right.

His head was swirling with questions: Who was she? How did she come to be here? Was she spoken for?

Surely not. Hopefully not.

"*You* came here," she remarked.

"I didn't know the quality of the event. I ran into Trywhitt at our club, and he brought me with him, which is why I don't have a domino cloak or mask."

She scrunched up her little nose, just visible through the light veil. "You, sir, should make better friends."

"I plan to."

Chapter 11

Conquering the Clodpole

Despite her circumstances, Livie felt a wave of happiness. Major FitzRoy was absurdly handsome, that is if one liked sandy hair cut very short (she did), and stubborn, clean-shaven chins (she did). He had lines around his mouth, the kind that suggested he'd suffered pain in the past.

She didn't want to like those lines, or even think about why they were there…but she couldn't help but find them frightfully attractive.

Just now he was frowning at her, while she smiled back like a loon.

"How on earth did you push Clod to the ground?" the major asked. "He's a large, study man, and you are small."

"He's the size of a barrel of beer," she agreed. "But I assure you, sir, that I am not small. I am accounted very tall, if not overly so, for my sex. My father is taller than almost anyone on—in—" She broke off, remembering that she couldn't give him any clues about her identity.

"In the House of Lords?" the major hazarded. "I am fairly good at sorting accents."

They had reached a settee. Livid plumped down on the seat. She had just been accosted by a degenerate for the first time in her life; she had foolishly entered a den of iniquity; and yet she couldn't stop smiling.

She had not needed saving, but she was certainly safe now. The major wouldn't allow a man to wrap a hand around her buttock the way his disgusting friend had done.

She didn't even think about what to say next. It just tumbled out of her mouth. "I can't tell you how I tripped the clodpole, because what if I need to topple you at some point?"

The major blinked down at her. For a dreadful moment, Livie thought she had misjudged their interaction so far. She had been certain that she had seen warmth in his eyes—yet what did she know of flirtation, after all?

He seated himself beside her. "You shock me." Thankfully, his voice was teasing, not critical. "If you won't share your name, what am I to call you?"

"Lady Macbeth. I was *ferocious*, didn't you think?"

"Not precisely at the level of wielding bloody daggers, but yes. Unlike the murderous queen, I would guess you are a young lady under that veil. Perhaps in your first Season."

"How many ladies in their first Season could *trample* a rakehell after such an insult?" Livie demanded proudly.

"What exactly did Trywhitt do?"

The steel in his voice was unmistakable. He looked ready to whip out a dagger of his own and carve out the clodpole's heart.

"He made me an improper proposal and touched me in a way that I considered indecorous. So I bamboozled him, before knocking him to the floor. I conquered Clod!"

Major FitzRoy picked up her hand and threaded his fingers through hers. Livie blinked down at their hands, wondering how it was possible to feel a shock that affects one's whole body, especially through a glove. "This is also indecorous," she observed. "My aunt would be horrified, sir."

"Surely you need reassurance after such a disturbing experience." His eyes told her that wasn't the reason. He wanted to hold her hand.

Livie found her lips tipping into an uncertain smile. "I suppose I might feel a trifle unsure." He had dark brown eyes, beautifully shaped. And his lower lip was…

"I can't kiss you until we're betrothed," he said nonchalantly.

That shocked Livie back into sanity, and she pulled her hand away. "We are *not* betrothed! I mean, we will not be betrothed, either."

"Are you promised to someone else?"

"No."

His big body relaxed. "May I lift your veil?"

Livie couldn't bring herself to say no. Her breath caught as he slowly reached out and pulled aside the small scrap of fabric, tucking it behind one ear.

"You may not remove my mask," she told him.

"I knew you were exquisite," he said conversationally.

"I'm not," she protested. Who would have thought flirtation was so easy? Livie simply had to catch the eye of a handsome man, and here they were, laughing and talking as if they'd been friends for years.

"Your mouth is perfectly shaped," the major observed.

"That's what the local squire's son said," Livie told him. "A sultry mouth."

His body went still.

She rolled her eyes. "No, I didn't kiss him. His name is Silas, and I've never liked that name."

"What do you think of 'Joshua?'"

It must have been an attack of madness in the aftermath of Conquering Clod. Livie wanted nothing more than to lean forward and brush his lips with hers—to kiss Joshua, the way that couple against the wall had been kissing.

Joshua was a trifle somber, but otherwise…perfect. She wanted to run her fingers along his jaw and ruffle that short hair. She wanted to make him laugh. If holding hands was improper, tilting her face up for a kiss was positively dissolute. Nevertheless, a sweet tide of joy was racing through her veins, making her feel reckless.

It was just one secret evening, after all. He didn't know who she was. He would *never* know.

She raised her chin and looked at him through her lashes.

Joshua had experienced this feeling before.

Once, before the Battle of the Pyrenees, while morning mist still drifted among the mountain trees through which he would soon send his brigade charging. Another day, after a flash of light seen from the corner of his eye, which turned out to be a musket ball taking him to his death.

Almost to his death, as it turned out.

The time when his colonel appeared at his bedside and told him that once he had convalesced, he would return to the military at the rank of major.

Moments when his life changed.

The lady was looking at him with an unmistakable invitation. Her eyes were wide, fringed with dark lashes, but the interest in them was clear. When he froze, the rules of gentlemanly behavior speeding through his mind, she bit her lush bottom lip.

No soldier survives without learning how to make split-second decisions. Joshua's hands closed around her shoulders, and he captured her mouth.

Chapter 12

Kissing Lady Macbeth

If this was his mystery lady's first kiss, she had a natural gift. Sensation burned down Joshua's body. The months of painful convalescence were forgotten; passion roared in his blood the way it used to before his injury.

She pressed closer with a purr. A tide of desire broke free inside Joshua, and he pulled her to him, plundering her mouth.

A long moment later, he remembered where he was. In public.

Kissing a *lady*, in public. If this were a normal gathering, all inconsequential conversation would have halted, and they would be kissing in a pool of disapproving silence. At this particular masquerade, likely no one even noticed. Still…

"Hell," he gasped, drawing away.

She swayed and murmured something. Somehow her mask was still in place, but under it, her eyes looked intoxicated.

"Have you been drinking champagne?" he barked with a sudden bolt of guilt.

She shook her head. Her gloved hand went to her lips, as if they were tingling as much as his. "My goodness," she whispered.

Relieved, Joshua took a deep breath. Luckily, if he was bewitched, so was she. Behind her hand, his lady's mouth was smiling.

Her domino had eased open when they kissed, revealing a modest neckline. Candlelight from the chandeliers overhead cast patterns on her creamy skin, deepening the cleft between her breasts. A light fragrance of apple blossoms in spring combatted the sultry perfumes worn by ladies bouncing around the dancefloor.

Joshua swallowed hard; he was a *gentleman*. His mother would be horrified by his behavior this evening. He reached out and pulled tight the strings that held her cloak closed, tying them in a bow.

She raised a delicate eyebrow.

"The men around us are not behaving like gentlemen, and I don't wish anyone to ogle you." He hesitated and added, "I apologize for that kiss. I lost my head."

"If I had minded, I would have told you as much," she informed him. Then she added thoughtfully, "Perhaps I would have bitten your lip. Or your tongue." She had dimples; the sight of them made his heart skip a beat.

Crucial questions ranged in his mind: Who was she? Where could he find her father to ask for her hand? What in hell's name was she doing, sneaking out to a masquerade of this nature?

That wasn't what came out of his mouth.

"Please tell me how you toppled Clod?" he asked again.

"I'll tell you if you make me a promise."

From what he could see, she had a piquant little face, with the kind of charm that could make a man drop to his knees before her.

"Anything."

She tapped him on the hand with a finger. "You oughtn't to be so trusting, Major. Here's the promise: whenever I ask you to jump, you must do so."

He blinked. "What?"

"If I ask, you jump. You needn't jump very high." Her voice was merry.

His body offered a clear interpretation of that request: he wanted to jump forward and cover those smiling lips with his or, even better, to jump on top of her. He cleared his throat. "I promise to jump whenever you ask."

"In that case, unless I truly need to, I promise not to sweep your feet out from under you," she said, laughing.

"I think you already did," he said frankly.

Around them, the ballroom was filled with women determined to dazzle and bewitch the fashionable men who bowed before them. This was a market for the *demimonde* of London: the underbelly of polite society. Not as obvious as a brothel, but a market, nonetheless.

Each woman was fishing for a gentleman who would give them a home and an allowance in exchange for intimacies.

His lady wasn't fishing, but she had caught him.

"That was a good kiss, wasn't it?" Her smile widened. "It was my first."

Joshua nodded. "I thought as much."

"Was it all right? *Not* that I should be kissing strange men, but this is a unique evening, don't you think? Out of time, as if it didn't happen at all."

"It is happening," Joshua said, knitting his brows. He wasn't sure how to tell this joyous sprite that he would be taking her home—and perhaps even having a word with her father, given that she'd put herself in danger.

Yet she was brave and independent; he certainly didn't want her to change. Before he enlisted, he had attended local assemblies, of course. He had met many marriageable maidens, from languid to giggly. None of them could have swept Clod's feet out from under him. They paled in comparison to her.

Only rarely did ladies follow their husbands to the site of a battle, but there were those few who embraced adventure. Lady Florentia Sale, for example, famously accompanied the British forces led by her husband, Major Sir Robert Sale. He'd known Robert for years and envied him the "Grenadier in Petticoats," as Robert's officers called her.

Maybe…just maybe…

"I'd like to see you again," he said, choosing his words carefully.

"That's impossible," she replied. He could tell from the regretful tone in her voice that she truly meant it. She thought he would kiss her and walk away. Or that she could kiss him and expect never to see him again.

What had been lust in his veins became a pounding instinct to make her his—the only excuse he had for the thoroughly ungentlemanly action of picking her up, putting her on his lap, and gathering her curvaceous body close.

"Major FitzRoy," she scolded. But her eyes were sparkling with mischief. The cluster of standing candelabra behind the settee cast golden light over her scarlet cloak and made strands of her hair gleam like polished mahogany.

"I am breaking every rule my mother taught me," he told her.

She leaned back, fitting into the curve of his arm as if she were designed for him. "I am certain your mother would not approve of your attendance at this event, let alone the way you are holding me, Major. I can assure you that my father would be furious."

"I promise to bow before you in Almack's," he told her, his voice a hoarse throb. "I will court you."

"You will?" She gave him an impish smile. "You had best not behave like this, Major, or my aunt will have you thrown out of the Assembly Hall! But the truth is that I won't be at the Almack's ball next Wednesday."

"The week after, then," Joshua said.

She shook her head. "I'm afraid not. My cousin and I shall not attend any festivities this Season. You must woo some other lady, sir."

"A death in the family?" he hazarded.

"No! Just…no. For family reasons we withdrew from festivities for this year. My excuse for being here is that my cousin is frightfully tired of being in the house, so we snuck out to this masquerade. Obviously, we mistook the nature of the party. I cannot believe that my aunt was invited! She would be horrified."

"Horrified by your attendance or by the invitation?"

"By the nature of this…this event." She glanced about them. The room was lined with mirrors with gaudy, gilded frames that caught light from chandeliers overhead and standing candelabra tucked in the corners of the room. In the reflections, women curtsied so deeply that their breasts almost fell from low bodices, and drunken couples grappled on the dance floor and leaned against the walls.

"You do not appear to be horrified," he observed.

"Since I kissed you, it would be hypocritical to cavil about that couple kissing to the side of the room. Pink satin seems to be in fashion."

Joshua looked around with disinterest. "I prefer white muslin."

She twinkled at that compliment. "I cannot wait to be allowed to wear more interesting fabrics. Perhaps next year my aunt won't insist on such innocuous clothing. She is very strict about fashion. For example, my aunt thinks patches are quite out of style, but people at this party, both men and women, are wearing far more patches than I've seen at balls."

Joshua's mind boggled at the idea of explaining that patches often covered syphilitic sores. "If you won't tell me your name, may I know the nature of the scandal that exiled you from Almack's?"

Her body went still.

"Or not," he added quickly. "You needn't tell me anything."

"It's not my story to tell," she told him, her brows drawing together. "By the time we meet again next Season, you will know the whole of it, but the pleasure of this evening is that you know nothing of me or my…my family." Her profile was delicate, but her chin was firm, even stubborn.

A scandal in the family might have ended the lady's Season, but Joshua saw no reason why that should hamper his courtship.

He was confident that he could discover her identity. The exquisite lace at her neckline probably cost as much as many women's entire gowns, at least those worn in this room. Now that she was nestled in his lap, the flounces of her white muslin fell short; her slippers were pale blue, each adorned with a small sapphire.

Her family had wealth and standing, and thankfully, so did he. As a second son, he was always meant to join the army, but his godmother's bequest meant that he could support his wife in the manner to which she was accustomed—with sapphires on her shoes *and* her fingers, if she wished.

She peeped at him from under long lashes. "We have agreed that our relatives would be horrified by our rash behavior, Major. I should find my cousin and return home before we engage in any other improprieties."

The twinkle in her eyes? He hoped to see it every day of his life.

Likely, she was the daughter of a country nobleman, sent to London to debut under the chaperonage of a neglectful aunt. His own aunt was a marchioness who boasted of knowing everything about everyone. He would know his lady's name by tomorrow morning, and he could pay her a call.

A proper call, presenting a bouquet of flowers and remaining only the requisite few minutes. Certainly no kissing.

Thinking of that, he claimed her lips again. She melted against him, throwing an arm around his neck as if they'd been kissing for years. As if this wasn't the second kiss in her life, and the second in his that meant something.

Desire raced through him again, along with a new, unfamiliar feeling. One made him catalog the little sound she made in the back of her throat, the way her hand tightened on her hair, the way her tongue tangled with his.

Their kiss tasted like his future.

He was so absorbed that he almost didn't register the barking voice that accosted his ears: "Major FitzRoy!"

Chapter 13

How to Compromise a Lady

Wrapped in the major's hard, warm embrace, Livie paid no attention to their surroundings. Simmering desire made her squirm on his lap, her pulse beating frantically in her throat.

One of her hands was buried in his thick, cropped hair. The other lay flat against his waistcoat, fingers spread against his chest. Those fingers trembled, ready to slide upwards and caress his neck.

"Major FitzRoy!"

She heard...and didn't hear. She didn't want to hear.

Behind heavy lids, Joshua's eyes gleamed fever-bright. "Kiss number two," he whispered, his voice a silky murmur.

Then he glanced up. "Lord Devin," he acknowledged.

Livie squeaked, and would have jumped from Joshua's lap, except he had an arm wrapped around her waist. She risked a look up at Lord Devin. Sure enough, the kindly face she remembered from her very first ball had transformed into that of a stern dragon.

His lordship looked every inch the scandalized nobleman, albeit a slightly disheveled one. He was dressed in an exquisite coat, gray silk with cream embroidery, but his cravat was not in its usual precise folds. He wasn't wearing a mask or domino, and his black hair was tousled, as if he'd run an irritated hand through it.

Daisy stood beside him, still wearing her veiled hat. When Livie glimpsed the two of them dancing, Daisy had been in a state, her mouth set in a rebellious line. Her cousin had probably quarreled with Lord Devin throughout the dance.

But now she was staring with wide eyes, unquestionably because she had seen Livie *kissing a strange man.*

Livie started up again, but Joshua pulled her back against his chest.

"Not yet," he murmured.

With long experience, Livie read Daisy's surprise: of the two of them, Daisy was the one who fell into mischief, while Livie tried to persuade her to be respectable. Daisy was rash and impetuous; Livie always attempted to follow her father's precepts.

Not this time.

"Take your hands off her," Lord Devin snarled. "Do you realize that you have accosted a lady?"

"I do," Joshua said, not moving. In fact, his arm tightened around Livie.

"Perhaps you should allow me to stand," Livie suggested. "We need to leave."

"The ballroom is twice as crowded as when I entered, and these idiots are four times as drunk," Joshua said. "Lord Devin, be careful!"

An inebriated dancer bowled into Daisy, who gave a scream and returned a hard shove that sent the man careening away and her flying toward Lord Devin. He caught her against his chest.

The drunkard crashed to the floor, his arms thrashing in the air.

Livie looked up at Joshua with a giggle. "He looks like an agitated turkey with that odd, pointed nose on his mask."

"That's a Venetian mask," he told her. "Will your cousin jump on top of his chest, as you did to Clod?"

"Oh no," Livie assured him. "That would be most unladylike."

"But *you*—"

"Yes, but as you can see, Lord Devin has taken care of the matter."

Sure enough, his lordship leaned over the turkey and said a few words. Livie couldn't make out exactly what was said, but Lord Devin's icy tone spoke for itself, and the curl of his lip was frankly terrifying. The man rolled to his side, clambered to his feet, and scurried away.

"You must let me go," Livie told Joshua. "This has been lovely, but the evening is over. As you can see, Lord Devin is cross—"

"I'm taking these two nitwits home," Lord Devin barked.

"You mayn't call us names," Daisy cried, poking his lordship in the side. "Just because you are a stodgy man who never does anything out of line doesn't mean that everyone is like you!"

Livie was still nestled against Joshua's chest, so she felt his quiet chuckle as much as heard it. "What?" she asked, looking up at him. Daisy and Lord Devin had started quarreling with each other again, which meant that she could remain where she was for just a moment or two longer.

The expression in his eyes made her shiver: where they had been grave, now they held a spark of laughter. She might even have said tenderness, though Livie knew that was foolish. They were strangers, after all, and that's all they'd ever be.

"Lord Devin is stodgy?" Joshua murmured. "Let's just say that his lordship's wild oats were notorious."

Livie felt a stab of uncertainty. "Were yours? Not that it matters, because we likely shan't meet again, but I wouldn't care to think of you like that."

One side of his mouth curled up. "No."

"These are my wild oats," Livie exclaimed. "You don't know my name. I could have been one of those birds, a canary bird."

"You have no relation to a canary bird," Joshua stated. "Other than the fact that you inadvertently flew into this particular room. I am very glad that I found you, and that Lord Devin found your cousin."

"I'd rather be a parrot," Livie said. "At least parrots can talk, whereas canary birds and birds of paradise can only sing."

"Wagtails and hummingbirds sing as well."

"Do those words indicate the same…the same profession?"

He nodded. "Not that we should discuss such a disreputable subject."

"What does that smile mean?" Livie asked suspiciously. "Are you laughing at me?"

He shook his head, and then whispered in her ear, "I could coax you to sing, if given a chance."

She wasn't entirely sure what he meant, but she suspected it was naughty. "You, sir, are most impertinent," Livie informed him, but since she was still seated on his lap, and not struggling to escape, the reprimand had no force. "I am a terrible singer," she added, in case he didn't mean it as a provocation.

"I would prefer that you sow no more wild oats," Joshua observed.

Livie eyed him. He was somewhat older than she, but not much. He had obviously seen more of the world and knew more about it than she did, yet his tone didn't have the hectoring quality that her father inevitably employed in his letters. "I do realize that this could have turned out to be a dangerous excursion," she offered.

Joshua said in her ear, "I would be happy to instruct you in sowing grain at some future date."

That was definitely a provocation. "Are you being vulgar?" Livie demanded.

"Somewhat," he admitted.

"Vulgarity is a crime," she informed him, taking that directive straight from her father's most recent letter.

"I apologize." His eyes were grave again, but his mouth had a secret smile.

"If I am not to sow wild oats in the future, what about you? We arrived here mistakenly, but you?"

"The same. As I told you, I had no idea it was a masquerade. Neither did I know the invitation list. I have been convalescing in the country and only came to London a few days ago."

"Were you wounded in battle?" Livie asked, worry tightening in her stomach. She always feared that her father would be injured, so it was a familiar sensation.

"A mere trifle," Joshua told her. She didn't believe him, not given the lines around his mouth. Still, he seemed to move easily. She almost said something about her father and the dangers of war, before she remembered that she was in disguise.

"Have you noticed how much the room smells?" she asked, changing the subject. "When we first arrived, there was a reek of perfume, but now…"

"Sweat and garlic," Joshua said, wrinkling his nose. "Do you dislike strong smells, Lady Macbeth?"

There was an odd light in his eyes, as if the question really mattered. "I don't care for strong perfume," Livie told him. "Daisy cannot bear the odor in the stables, but I quite like it." She saw approval in his gaze.

"Now let me go," she commanded. "My cousin has an excitable nature, and a terrible propensity to lose her temper. If I don't intervene, she may toss a glass of champagne at Lord Devin's head."

Joshua lifted Livie to her feet, keeping her tucked against his body. The crush of dancers was spilling to the corners of the room. Their settee was instantly occupied by three women with rouged cheeks and avid smiles, leaning forward to allow a clear vision of their bosoms.

Livie's aunt would say that it showed lack of breeding. She had the distinct impression that "breeding" was not a quality these particular ladies cared to cultivate.

"Lord Devin knows who you are," Joshua said, gently touching her nose with a finger. His other arm was still wrapped around her waist. "Shouldn't I know your name?"

His lordship broke off a heated sentence and turned his head, narrowing his eyes at Joshua. "No, you should not. Unhand the lady."

"*The lady* being the woman I intend to marry?"

Chapter 14

Quixotic Madness

The words dropped between them like a stone tossed into a pool of water. Lord Devin blinked, and there was an audible gasp from the woman at Joshua's side.

"What?" his chosen bride cried, jerking away. "Don't be absurd." Her cheeks turned pink, and her dimples disappeared.

"That was more than flirting," Joshua said, the ruthless instinct of a hunter prickling the back of his neck. "You are mine."

"More than a ballroom flirtation, I'll grant you that," Lord Devon remarked.

Her eyes widened with shock. She rounded on Joshua. "But no one knows who I am!"

"You kissed him," her cousin put in. When most ladies would be censorious, she sounded envious. "We all saw it. Actually, I think you do have to marry him. You know your father would agree."

"This proposal—if one could call it that—is no more than quixotic madness. The kiss...the kiss meant nothing."

"It meant something to me," Joshua stated. "I compromised you."

"You can't compromise me if you don't know who I am!" she retorted. "Compromise implies that my reputation is impaired. If no one knows who I am, I cannot be considered tarnished."

"That's true!" her cousin confirmed, changing sides.

Joshua gave the cousin a swift glance, just long enough so that he would recognize her snub nose and the wash of white blonde hair that had fallen from her topknot when he saw her again. The lace on her bodice had to have cost fifteen guineas, not to mention the foaming layers of white muslin that made up her gown. Both ladies had the natural command that comes from being daughters of the nobility.

"Lord Devin, don't you agree that the lady was compromised by that public kiss?" he asked.

"No, I do not."

Joshua leveled a surprised glare at his lordship. Devin and he didn't know each other terribly well, but they were both gentlemen. Why wouldn't the man acknowledge that by kissing a lady, Joshua had put himself in a position wherein he was obliged to declare himself?

Every arbiter of polite society would insist that a proposal of marriage must follow a kiss.

Lord Devin responded with his own question: "Major, you recognized no one at this damnable excuse for a masquerade, did you?"

Joshua narrowed his eyes. Devin looked as if he was about to whip out a swordstick and cut out Joshua's liver. He had thought the man mild-mannered, but at the moment he looked fierce enough to lead a brigade.

"I did not recognize anyone but you," Joshua answered, truthfully enough. "If anyone asks me, which they will not, I will say that I was surprised and disappointed to find that Rothingale has fallen to such a low that he hosted this event full of disrespectable strangers."

"Including your friend Clod," his lady reminded him.

"He is a stranger to me from this night," Joshua stated. The truth was that the next time he encountered Clod, he intended to knock him down.

"Clod?" Lord Devin repeated, frowning.

"Trywhitt," Joshua supplied. "An old friend who now calls himself 'Clod.'"

"A hell-raker at best," Lord Devin snapped.

"Mr. Trywhitt was saucy with me, but I tipped him to the ground," his lady said demurely.

Her cousin clapped. "It worked just as the stableboy promised, Li—" She broke off.

So, her name began with 'L.' "Liza?" Joshua asked.

His lady flicked him a glance. "Certainly not."

"Lily? Lillith?"

"Do I look like Lillith? If I remember correctly, the biblical stories connected to her are not very nice."

"Lady Macbeth isn't a nice lady either," Joshua pointed out.

Lord Devin broke in. "I shall escort these young ladies to their house—not that you know where that is, Major FitzRoy, because you have no idea *who they are*."

Never mind the fact that Joshua would always be able to pick out this lady's lips, her chin, her eyes.

"I have no idea who they are," he agreed. He reached out and tweaked his future wife's veil so that it swung free, covering everything but that enchanting mouth of hers. Damn it, one glance at her lips, and scorching desire raced through his limbs again.

She was smiling. "Goodbye."

There was a knowing laughter in his lady's eyes; whether or not she acknowledged it, she knew that he was hers, as much as she was his.

He wanted nothing more than to catch her up and acquaint her with the ravaging hunger roused by her kisses. By the sultry hum in the back of her throat. By her laughter, the intelligence in her gaze, her arguments, her bravado, and her willfulness, too.

By everything about her.

"I have no idea who these ladies are—yet," he clarified. "But I mean to amend my ignorance at my earliest opportunity."

"No," Lord Devin stated, his tone adamant. "I insist that you do not attempt to discover their names. Next Season I shall introduce you. Until then, this evening never happened."

"I should prefer to be introduced before next Season," Joshua said stubbornly. "I must obey orders, and I may not be in England next spring."

His lady gasped, then pulled her veil back so she could see him clearly, tucking it behind her ear. Swift color came up in her cheeks. "Back to war?"

"I go where they send me."

"You already know—" her cousin exclaimed, before she cut herself off again.

Joshua shot her a query, but she had buttoned up her mouth.

A small hand crept into his and curled around it. "We are not well acquainted, Major FitzRoy, but I would be most displeased if you were once again injured in battle. Or worse."

Joshua saw worry in her eyes, and he smiled. "Have no fear. I have much to live for."

Her hand slipped from his. "I shall pray for your wellbeing, Major."

"Enough," Lord Devin announced. "It is time to leave. Major FitzRoy, I look forward to introducing you to these ladies in the new year." His hand shot out and caught Joshua's wrist.

They were both big men, of a similar height, though Joshua was more muscular. He had the impulse to shift his weight and throw Lord Devin into the crowd of dancers. Instead, he glanced down at his wrist and then up at his lordship. "I must ask you to unhand me."

"Do not attempt to discover this lady's identity," Lord Devin said, his eyes looking steadily into Joshua's. "I ask you as a gentleman, on your honor." He dropped his hand.

Joshua shook out his cuff. He was livid, but his blood was icy cool. Being the youngest major of his rank had led to jealousy; he had learned to overlook insolent behavior.

There was only one response to be made, so he made it. "I shall obey your injunction, Lord Devin. In return, I depend upon you to introduce me at your earliest convenience."

"You mustn't quarrel with each other," his future wife cried. "Major FitzRoy, I promise, there are the best of reasons for our secrecy."

He met his sprite's eyes. "I do not wish to wait until next Season to court you, my lady. 'Tis a year away. I leave for the battlefield in a month or so."

He saw her slender throat bobble as she swallowed, anxiety deepening in her gaze. "You shall return, safe and well, after which I will greet you in a ballroom, Major FitzRoy."

Lord Devin folded his arms over his chest and nodded. "Next year."

Everything in Joshua refused this notion. He loathed the idea of leaving England without speaking to her father and making his intentions clear. Once they were betrothed, they could correspond. What if her father decided to give her to a lesser man, not knowing of Joshua's interest?

He caught her elbow and spun so that his back was to the other two. Then he ran a finger down her cheek. "We haven't known each other long, my lady. Will you wait for me until next Season?"

"I have no suitors," she said, turning pink. "That is, I had suitors before, but they…they left. Because of the scandal."

Thank God for the idiocy of his peers. And for that scandal, whatever it was.

"I would like to speak to your father—to ask him for your hand in marriage—even if you and I cannot meet again until next Season."

"That's impossible." She shook her head. "My cousin and I did not have permission to attend this masquerade. My father would be appalled by knowledge of this evening and must never know of it."

He took one of his cards from inside his coat and gave it to her. "If you ever have need of me, just send a message. I shall delay my departure from England for another month. Thereafter, my household will forward your missive. Your letter might take some weeks to reach me abroad, but I will always answer you."

He had been pressing to return to the front, though his doctors were reluctant. Now he planned to exaggerate his injury rather than trivialize it.

She tucked his card inside her domino cloak, dimpling at him. "It would be most inappropriate of me to send you a letter. My father would be outraged. He would *die*."

"In that case, your parent would be in the grave several times over if he learned of this evening," Joshua remarked. "Please write me at least one letter?"

She shook her head.

"So that I can take it with me to battle, folded in my breast pocket," he added, catching her hands in his and bringing them to his lips.

"Oh goodness," she murmured, her plump lips curling into a smile. "I shall write to you once, Major, and only if you promise not to question my footman." She glanced over her shoulder and sighed. "They are quarreling again. My cousin has a dreadfully excitable disposition."

"And you?" he asked. "Are you excitable?"

"Oh no. Compared to her, I am practically a nun."

He burst out laughing.

"I mean it! My aunt swears that she has aged ten years in the last year alone because of my cousin's misadventures."

"I might age ten years if I thought the two of you would continue racketing about London in masquerade masks," Joshua said honestly.

"I shan't do that any longer." A curious little smile played around her mouth. "I believe my wild oats are sown. We already made a promise not to visit Vauxhall, so our masquerade hats will not come into service again."

The look in her eyes and her rosy lips… Joshua succumbed to his basest instinct. He reached out to bring his lady's hand to his mouth again, changed his mind, leaned in, and stole another kiss. A hard, audacious kiss.

Her lips softened under his, and their tongues met. Then:

"Shoo!" she cried, giving him a little shove. "Go sow your wild oats somewhere else, Major FitzRoy!"

As he turned, laughing, he met Lord Devin's amused eyes. The truth didn't need to be articulated; they both understood it.

There hadn't been many wild oats, but there would be no more, whether or not Joshua had to wait a full year to court his future bride.

Chapter 15

A Maiden of Questionable Modesty

Livie hopped down from Lord Devin's coach—he had insisted on driving them the four blocks from the Rothingale residence—and dashed to the side door of the Wharton townhouse with Daisy and their footman Peter close behind her.

The house was as still and quiet as it had been when they snuck out a few hours ago. Once inside, Daisy pushed both dominos into Peter's arms and hissed, "Please store these away without anyone seeing you."

Their favorite footman scowled. "If it wouldn't have created a scene, I'd have come upstairs and hauled you off the dance floor. That party was not for young ladies. The conversation in the kitchen was about how far the household standards have fallen."

"It was terrible," Livie agreed, trying to look somber despite her giddiness. "Lord Rothingale is thoroughly debauched, judging by his acquaintances."

"I found it very interesting!" Daisy cried. She rolled her eyes at Peter's frown. "We shan't go back there again or have anything further to do with Rothingale. Word of honor."

"Daisy always keeps her promises," Livie told the footman. "But Peter, who would have imagined that such a gathering could take place only a few blocks from here?"

"Lady Wharton would be furious if she learned of this night," Peter said glumly. "I'd be turned off without a reference."

"Aside from Lord Devin, no one discovered us," Livie assured him. "Daisy and I have sworn him to secrecy, so you needn't fret."

With that, she pulled her cousin up the back steps, down the corridor, and into her bedchamber.

Daisy closed the door and leaned back against it. "Tell me everything!"

Livie scarcely knew where to begin. She went to her bed and sat down. "It was so…" Her voice trailed away. How could she explain her outrageous behavior?

Daisy threw herself onto her side on the bed, repeating, "Everything. Tell me *everything*!"

Livie cleared her throat. "First, a man named Clod Trywhitt made a most improper suggestion and squeezed my buttock, just as if he were purchasing a day-old loaf of bread."

Daisy gasped. "How revolting!"

"I pretended not to be insulted, begged him to jump, and then swept his feet out from under him," Livie said, feeling more cheerful. "He hit the ground with a whopping thump. It was so satisfying, Daisy."

"Good! Next time we're in the country, we must remember to thank Fred for teaching us that technique. Who would have thought a stableboy's trick would work on a lecher? I have to say, Trywhitt was an idiot for agreeing to jump."

"I believe he may have been inebriated. I was scolding the clodpole when Major FitzRoy arrived." Livie stopped, finding it difficult to put into words what happened next.

"How did your scolding translate to a public kiss? I've been told my entire life that I'm the more impulsive of the two of us, but you have a claim to the title now."

Livie took a deep breath. Even thinking about Joshua made molten honey sink into her veins. "The major had arrived at the party with Clod Trywhitt."

Daisy's eyes flickered.

Livie was used to reading her cousin's thoughts. "I informed the major that he needed better friends, and he agreed. Thereafter, a couple began kissing against the wall. He pulled me away, to protect my sensibilities, I believe."

"You were too innocent for such a sight, so he kissed you himself?" Daisy's tone was skeptical. "I can't believe you sat on the major's lap, Livie. In public, no less!" She shook her head wonderingly. "I've always thought of *myself* as the rebel, and *you* as the good girl."

Livie felt a little dizzy at the memory. "I lost my head," she admitted. "I can't explain it. First we were sitting together, and he kissed me—which was scandalous enough in itself—and somehow I ended up on his lap, and we kept kissing."

"Thank goodness you kept your mask on. Just imagine what your father would say. Or Lady Regina!"

Livie felt the blood draining from her cheeks. "She would say horrible things about me. I would deserve every cruel thing she said."

Not to mention her father's reaction. One of his favorite directives was that she should be acquainted only *with those whose names are never branded, and whose modesty is never taxed.* Not only had she been in a room with unladylike women, she had become one of them!

"Betrothed couples are always having their wedding date moved forward, for evident reasons. After that, the scandal is forgotten," Daisy pointed out.

"Daisy! That will never happen to me. Oh, my father would be *so* angry if he knew!"

"You always try to be proper," her cousin observed. She leaned forward and dropped a kiss on Livie's cheek. "I'm glad that your father's lectures haven't taken hold. If you obeyed everything he said, you wouldn't be *you.*"

"But I don't want to marry Joshua because of a kiss. He was forced to propose once you and Lord Devin appeared."

"Lord Devin was truly horrid!" Daisy said, scowling. "Particularly to me, while we were dancing. I loathe the man."

"Really? He was so kind when he introduced us to all those gentlemen at the Sheffields' ball."

"Our erstwhile suitors?" Daisy swept her free hand through the air. "Where are they now? You'd think they would at least leave a card if they're too afraid to be seen entering the house." Her face was a blend of perplexed and enraged. "I could have sworn that Lord Argyle was on the point of proposing to me."

Livie nodded. "Would you have accepted?"

"Certainly not." Daisy gave her a wry smile. "His proposal would have sprung solely from the fact that my dowry includes the French clock downstairs that supposedly belonged to Marie Antoinette. That timepiece is as desirable to Lord Argyle as you are to Major FitzRoy."

"Don't be silly!"

"I'm not. Argyle is obsessed with clocks, which leaves no room in his heart for a woman. Major FitzRoy obviously fell in love at first sight, just like in an Eliza Haywood novel. I always knew you would marry a military man. It's in your blood."

"I have no plans to marry him." Livie silently repeated that statement to herself, because her heart thought it was an excellent idea.

"Why not? The major is *so* handsome, Livie," Daisy said, rolling to her back and staring dreamily at the ceiling. "Much better than Lord Argyle."

"He does have a perfect nose," Livie agreed.

"I don't understand your obsession with noses. I didn't even notice that. What I *did* notice was that he fit his breeches very well."

"Daisy!"

Her cousin snorted. "Too late to be missish now, Livie. Tell me you didn't notice?"

Livie had noticed. What's more, the major had seen her glance at his thighs. Recalling the desiring flare in his eyes made her feel warm. She groaned and fell back next to Daisy. Her skin prickled at the memory of how his lips had caressed hers until she opened her mouth and welcomed a deeper kiss.

"Given his impeccable appearance, I would never have imagined that the major would be so abandoned as to kiss a strange woman at a ball," Daisy went on, "which just goes to show that I don't understand men."

Livie agreed. Even after they'd kissed, Joshua's appearance remained faultless, whereas her curls and muslin flounces were left rumpled by his embrace.

Neatness was one of her father's strongest directives, and yet Livie rarely finished a day without smudges on her gloves and often her skirts as well. Likely, the major's cravat would still be snowy white when he removed it in the evening.

Just like her father's.

"What are you thinking about?" Daisy rolled back onto her side, propping her head on one hand.

"The major's valet."

"Why on earth?"

"I suspect that Major FitzRoy is always tidy," Livie said. "His valet has an easy task. As opposed to our maid, poor Margery."

"You do tend to get disheveled," Daisy agreed.

"Within an hour."

Daisy poked her. "A major's wife must be neat and tidy. You'll have to make a special effort next Season."

An uneasy silence fell in the bedchamber.

"Perhaps he won't disappear like our other suitors," Daisy offered.

Her father's teachings were crowding Livie's mind. "The major's career would be ruined if he was known to have kissed the daughter of an accused traitor, let alone that he'd proposed to one."

"Phooey," Daisy said. "That's absurd."

Livie understood the military better than her cousin. "Like our other suitors, he has to disappear—for his own good."

Chapter 16

The Case of the Disappearing Suitors

Livie's stomach had turned to a ball of ice. "What if Joshua goes to Lord Devin tomorrow morning and demands to know who I am, perhaps at sword's point?"

"Joshua?" Daisy repeated, giggling madly. "Of course, *Joshua* will pursue you in every way possible."

"Stop it, Daisy!" Livie snapped. "The major is a member of the military. He will be horrified when he discovers that my father has been accused of treason, and I'll be mortified if he learns who I am before the charges are lifted."

"He's very young to have the rank of major, isn't he? Think of how happy your father will be, although admittedly, Captain Sir Tyron wouldn't want his daughter to be kissing a strange man in public. Or privately, for that matter."

"Can you imagine?" Livie found herself whispering. "Father is always directing me to avoid occasions where people display light behavior. And he's thinking about Drury Lane theater, not a dissolute masquerade!"

"Captain Sir Tyron would not approve of Rothingale," Daisy agreed. "But how could we have known of the sheer depth of his depravity?"

Livie shook off that worry. "More importantly, Major FitzRoy's reputation would be damaged if anyone knew that he'd kissed the daughter of a traitor."

Daisy frowned. "You really think so?"

"Military careers—like naval careers—are vulnerable to scandal. Joshua's career would be finished."

Daisy bit her bottom lip. "There's always next Season, after the captain has been cleared of his charges."

"Yes, but what if people never accept that my father is innocent? Or, God forbid, if he's convicted?" Livie asked, her deepest fears spilling from her mouth.

Daisy shook her head. "That won't happen."

"Even once my father is released, some people will always consider his reputation besmirched."

"Are you worried that we won't have vouchers next Season?"

"I don't care about Almack's!"

"The charge is that Uncle met with a group of traitors in France. Once they find the Englishman who impersonated your father, no one can possibly believe the allegations."

"But what if they never find the imposter?" Livie asked, clearing her throat. "I'm so afraid, Daisy. I feel sick every time I think about it."

"You must have faith," Daisy said, leaning over to give her another kiss on the cheek. "Lord Devin is working on behalf of your father. He may be frightfully condescending, but I trust he will find the truth."

"What if Joshua—Major FitzRoy—decides that he has to marry me because of our kiss? What if he ruins his career over a point of honor?"

"I shall eviscerate Lord Devin if he says a word about our identity," Daisy declared cheerfully. "I'll write him immediately and let him know."

"I don't think you can bend him to your will. And you shouldn't correspond with a man, Daisy!"

"Pooh," Daisy said. "No more moralizing from *you*. You've lost all claim to being the more prudish of us. I'm not afraid of Lord Devin."

"He is old and powerful."

"He's not *old*," Daisy protested. "Just stodgy. He can't be thirty, because he was at school with Lord Argyle."

"That's ten years older than we are."

"He seems old because he's so censorious. We should go to sleep, unless…" Daisy leaned over and poked Livie. "You'd care to tell me more about kissing?"

Livie gave her a crooked smile. "Obviously, it was my first kiss, but I have to admit that it was rather wonderful."

"Like in *Romeo and Juliet*?"

"I have nothing in common with those two idiots," Livie said, sitting up. "If you think I'd stab myself over a man, you're vastly mistaken."

"Romeo's cousin took him to a masquerade just the way I did," Daisy pointed out. "You're not in an Eliza Hayworth novel, but a Shakespeare play!"

Livie shrugged. "Remember that production we saw in February, when Romeo kissed Juliet behind a convenient pillar? If we'd found a pillar, Joshua wouldn't feel compelled to propose to me."

"Romeo's cousin takes him to the ball so he can fall in love with someone better than Rosaline." Daisy waggled her eyebrows madly. "There's another masquerade next week, hosted by the Duchess of Trent—'The American Duchess,' they call her."

"I don't wish to forget Joshua," Livie protested.

"You just said that marrying you would ruin his career, even if your father is released from the Tower! We'll go to the duchess's masquerade, Livie, so you can find another gentleman whose nose is equally delectable. You might as well kiss the new one too, since you've gotten the hang of it."

Livie scoffed. "Don't be absurd. We'd be recognized."

Daisy shook her head. "When you and I first entered the ballroom and were separated by the press of people, I saw Lord Devin and smiled at him. Livie, he had no idea who I was! He was very nice until I told him my name. After that, he was decidedly unpleasant."

"He thought you were a ladybird!" Livie exclaimed.

"A what?"

"A lady of the evening, just like in *City of Eros.* A strumpet. Except Joshua referred to them as birds: ladybirds, birds of paradise, wagtails. I think parrots as well."

Since being evicted from polite society, Livie and Daisy had spent hours browsing bookstalls. A few weeks ago they had purchased—and Daisy had read aloud—*City of Eros,* a book of advice for young ladies supposedly written by a Madam running a brothel. It had been eye-opening, if occasionally mystifying.

"Did Major FitzRoy mistake you for a ladybird?" Daisy asked.

Livie shook her head. "I don't believe so."

"Well, Lord Devin smiled at me," Daisy said with satisfaction. "Before he went all holier-than-thou, he thought that I was for sale! I shan't let him forget that."

"In that case, he isn't very observant," Livie pointed out. "Most of the ladies were far less clothed than we. And their breasts are so large."

"As are mine," Daisy said, patting her chest. "It's my finest feature."

"You are nowhere near as endowed as those ladies," Livie said flatly. "Besides which, you have so many fine features that one can hardly count them, Daisy."

"We really must go to the Duchess of Trent's masquerade. If I'd had more time before I ran into Lord Devin, I could have found a major as well. I love a man in a uniform."

"Wait a minute—How did you discover that Lord Devin was helping with my father's case?" Livie asked, ignoring Daisy's implausible idea that masquerades were littered with unmarried military men.

"He was scolding me for attending Rothingale's debauched party, and when I said that I had to find you before I could make my escape, he grew even more angry," Daisy admitted. "He's part of the group in the House of Lords that is investigating the supposed treason. He called us idiots, and said that the last thing your father needs is for you to create another scandal."

Livie groaned. "He's right."

"We shan't go to the Duchess of Trent's masquerade," Daisy promised, reversing herself. "Even if you turn into Romeo and start withering away from unrequited love, and I never find a major of my own. We'll have to wait until next Season to find husbands, Livie."

"I don't think that Lady Regina will ever forget the fact of my father's arrest," Livie said, the certainty growing in her mind. "She didn't like me before that scene in the milliner's shop, Daisy, and now she loathes me. Even had she been inclined to generosity— and I doubt the woman ever feels the impulse—she would make a point of excluding me from society as revenge."

Daisy sat up and wound an arm around Livie's shoulders. "I shan't allow it."

Livie let out a weak chuckle. "You looked so much like your mother just then. I'm fairly sure that Lady Regina is spiteful enough to ban you as well."

Daisy tossed her head. "She can try!"

"She *will* try. Remember that your mother told us that Regina has an eagle eye for the smallest fault."

"How can I forget?" Daisy said wryly. "I'm 'short and fat,' remember?"

116

"She's a dreadful woman," Livie said. "I'm sorry she was so unkind to you."

"She's met her match in me," Daisy said, her expression not the least perturbed. "I felt shaken after our first meeting, but that was mostly because I was ashamed to be overheard comparing her fiancé to an onion."

"Lady Regina has power," Livie insisted. "By next Season, she'll presumably be a marchioness."

"She consistently demonstrates lack of breeding," Daisy retorted. "I look forward to making that clear to everyone. And as for her marriage…I'll believe that when I see the scallion waiting at the altar. Her first fiancé escaped, and likely the earl will make an attempt as well."

"If she does become a marchioness, you'll have to marry very highly in order to combat her."

"Lord Argyle will not do," Daisy agreed. "Next Season I must scoop up a duke."

Livie started laughing. "It's not so easy, Daisy."

"Actually, I think it *is* so easy. Just think of those young ladies who debuted with us this Season, Livie. I don't know how to explain it, but their conversation was rather flat."

"None of them were allowed to speak freely because their mothers were watching them like hawks," Livie pointed out.

"Yes, well," Daisy said, shooting her a mischievous twinkle. "It is my distinct impression that young men do not care to marry *flattened* ladies, and I do intend that pun. I shall find a duke, after which I will squash Lady Regina beneath my slipper."

She jumped from the bed and arched her back. "Obviously, men can be brought to heel by a generous show of bosom. Just look at the women who flocked to Rothingale's house! Luckily for me— and my future duke—I have the best bosom on the market. The rest of you are too slim."

"You do look like the figurehead on the bow of Father's ship," Livie said, giggling. "The *Royal Oak* features a buxom lady, who supposedly represents Queen Elizabeth."

"Just wait," Daisy said. "This bosom will mow down polite society as easily as the *Royal Oak* plows through the waves!"

Chapter 17

Grounds for Judgment in Trivial & Treasonous Trials

Early in the morning, Hyde Park is not yet thronged by elegant carriages, ladies walking their recalcitrant dogs, and gentlemen swinging their ebony canes. Rather than camouflage for children playing hide-and-seek, the poplar trees serve as racetracks for excited gray squirrels. The horse-chestnut trees flaunt brilliant pink and yellow fluff, not yet competing with ladies in bright cottons and silks.

It was the only time that Livie and Daisy could ride without being snubbed.

Moreover, if they arrived early enough, they could even gallop down Rotten Row—something that no properly-bred young lady would do.

"Race you to the end?" Daisy asked, raising an eyebrow at Livie as she pinned back the veil of her masquerade hat.

Livie patted her mare, Jacqueline. The Row stretched ahead, the gravel still neatly raked. No one was in sight to chide them. "Jack and I will slay you!"

"One, Two, Go!" Daisy shrieked.

"What happened to 'three?'" Livie called, but she loosed the reins anyway.

Her mount snorted and surged forward on her powerful front legs. A groom had brushed Jack's mane to sleek elegance, draped on one side; now it flared up and tangled in the air. Wind whipped past Livie's face, and the poplars lining the path merged into a green blur. Instead of the chirps of London sparrows, she heard only the pounding of Jack's hooves and the spray of gravel; it was as if she rode the crest of a tidal wave roaring toward an unseen shore.

Livie laughed aloud, loving the wild freedom that came from ignoring ladylike behavior. Daisy was ahead by a length, but Jack was steadily catching up—until a huge black horse flashed past. The rider veered close to Daisy, reached across the gap between them, and snatched her reins.

Livie pulled up Jack abruptly, her mare snorting with displeasure and rising onto her back hooves in protest. Livie barked "No," pulling the reins down. In the country, she could cling to the saddle with her thighs while Jack bucked, but in London she was forced to use a side-saddle, which made it harder to control her mount.

As soon as Jack's hooves were back on the ground, Livie turned—and grimaced.

Lord Devin held Daisy's reins.

Her cousin's face was red with fury. "You risked tripping Iris and perhaps *injuring* her!" Daisy shouted. "Just what did you think you were doing? You bacon-brained buffoon!"

"You appeared to have lost control of your mount." Lord Devin's genial mouth was compressed into a grim line.

"I'm not one of your little sisters." Daisy yanked her reins from his hand. "I never lose control of Iris. Ever."

"Good morning, Lord Devin," Livie said, nodding to him. Temper tantrum forgotten, her mare pranced sideways, coquettishly introducing herself to his gelding.

"I suppose you think that Livie's mount had run away with her as well?" Daisy cried. "That we're both such wretched horsewomen that our horses were startled at the same moment?"

"I was of the belief that young ladies didn't ride helter-skelter down Rotten Row," his lordship said icily. "Though I see now that I was mistaken." He doffed his hat. "Good morning, Miss Tyron. How are you?"

"Very well," Livie said. "I am glad that our paths have crossed, Lord Devin, as I wished to thank you. Daisy tells me that you are helping with my father's case."

"I am."

"When his lordship is not busy interfering in races that have nothing to do with him." Daisy's hair had tumbled down past her shoulders. Pulling hairpins from her pocket, she began twisting up the heavy coil of hair again.

Livie ignored this sour comment. "I have to request, Lord Devin, that you please do not share my name with Major FitzRoy, should he ask you again. Until my father's charge is dismissed, I think it would be best to have no contact with the gentleman."

Lord Devin nodded. "I agree. Apropos of that matter, I learned today the case will be decided by the House of Lords rather than by a Navy tribunal, with the Lord High Steward, Lord Paget, presiding."

Daisy edged her horse over and caught Livie's free hand. "What does that mean?"

"A panel of Lord Triers, your father's peers, will consider the facts of the case," Lord Devin said to Livie, ignoring Daisy.

"But they haven't found the traitor yet," Livie responded. "How can they possibly hold a trial?"

"The trial isn't imminent," Lord Devin said. "We have men searching throughout France, and we will find the degenerate who assumed your father's identity. The prosecutor has the two witnesses he needs. We merely need to find one more on our side."

Livie brightened. "You do have one witness who maintains that it wasn't my father?"

"No one can clearly identify the scoundrel, as it was dark when the impersonation occurred. We have a witness who is certain that the man calling himself by your father's name was under six feet tall, whereas Captain Sir Tyron is well over. The revolutionaries had no reason to disbelieve his identity, as the traitor had been using the captain's seal to communicate with them."

"My father had lost it!" Livie cried. "He wrote me that it had been misplaced. After that point, all his letters were sealed without an impression."

"Presumably, the traitor filched the seal," Lord Devin said, "using it to convince rebels to join his cause. Believing a lord and captain of the British Navy was at their back, a group of French revolutionaries found the courage to imagine they might commit regicide."

"My father would never have anything to do with such a nefarious plot," Livie said passionately. "Never!"

"English lords are true to their country," Lord Devin said.

Daisy scoffed. "Except when they are not. Why are you wasting your time sending people around France? It was most likely an Englishman who stole the seal, and certainly one who presented himself as the captain. His rank, by the way, seems irrelevant to me."

"Not precisely irrelevant," Livie put in, seeing Lord Devin's eyes kindling with anger. "But Daisy does have a point, my lord."

"We are investigating every possible avenue," his lordship said stiffly. "Your father seems quite comfortable in the Tower, Miss Tyron. Have you visited him?"

"My aunt was under the impression that I would not be allowed to see him."

He blinked. "She may have wished to spare you a harrowing experience."

"I shall visit him this afternoon," Livie stated. She wished…well, she wished that her father had expressed a desire to see her. He wrote to her every day, but—barring a remark or two about the boat he was designing—he had reverted to the lists of admonishments and recommendations that had always filled his letters.

"I would like to return to the house," she said, before Lord Devin and Daisy could start sniping at each other again. "I shall visit my father after luncheon. It was a pleasure to see you, your lordship."

"I fear you won't be admitted without your aunt accompanying you," Lord Devin said. "My understanding is that she won't return from Shropshire for several weeks."

"I shall try," Livie replied, turning Jack and heading back down the Row. Anxiety was pinching her stomach. If she wrote her father and asked for permission to visit, he'd never grant it.

If her aunt was strict, her father was even stricter. He'd be happiest if she never left the house at all.

Her eyes narrowed, thinking of it. What if the worst happened, and Livie never saw her father again after the trial? All her worst fears leapt to mind. What if her final meeting with her father took place within the indifferent walls of a courtroom, perhaps without even being allowed to hug him before the bailiff took him away in chains?

No.

She could and would pay him a visit.

Chapter 18

The Art of Breaking in—and Breaking out—of the Tower of London

"Miss Jenny the Lion's cubs must be half grown by now," Livie observed as she, Daisy, and their maid Margery climbed down from the family barouche. Ahead of them was the Tower of London in all its gloomy glory.

Daisy and Livie had visited the Tower menagerie in the fall, when the lion cubs were only a month old. It was hard to imagine that golden time now, before she'd ever thought about charges of treason or imagined her father imprisoned.

"We're supposed to call her Missus Jenny, now that she has a family," Daisy reminded her with a giggle.

"The queen herself announced it," Margery put in.

"It's hard to imagine lions at the altar," Livie said wryly, as they made their way across the bridge, passing over the Tower's wide moat and approaching its imposing gate. "Daisy, why don't you and Margery pay the mama lion a call while I visit my father's chamber?"

"I prefer to greet Harry the Tiger," Daisy said. "I love the fact that he has a little dog friend. Maybe we should get your father a dog, Livie!"

"Do walk more slowly," Margery called from behind them. "My corns are paining me something awful."

"Father dislikes domesticated animals," Livie reminded Daisy. "You'll have to tell me how Harry is. Also Miss Peggy, the black leopardess."

"I don't think you should visit Uncle's chamber by yourself," Daisy said.

Livie shook her head. "By visiting him, I am disobeying your mother. I shall likely be scolded, and you shouldn't be part of it."

"She didn't expressly instruct us to stay away from the Tower."

"My father will likely be displeased as well." Captain Sir Tyron had little tolerance for what he called "Acts of Disobedience," even if they were as small as buying a "fattening, unnecessary" sweetmeat, or a "malicious" novel.

Consequently, Livie's reading had always been limited to her Bible or copy of *The Gentlewoman's Companion: A Guide to the*

Female Sex, which her father had given her at the age of ten. Needless to say, *The Gentlewoman's Companion* did not approve of frivolous expenditures of effort or thought, which meant that fiction was doubly forbidden.

Luckily, Daisy enjoyed reading aloud.

Daisy rolled her eyes. "If you'll forgive me, Livie, when is your father ever pleased?"

"He doesn't mean to be harsh. I just…I need to see him, but I don't want you to suffer consequences from my actions."

"Your father—" But Daisy caught herself.

"He would be disappointed to think that I led you into disobedience."

"Whereas it is always the opposite!" Daisy exclaimed. "Oh, very well, Livie." They were nearing the entrance to the West Tower. "I hope Captain Sir Tyron is not too cast down by his imprisonment. Just look at how the gateway hangs over the bridge like a harbinger of doom."

Livie glanced at the masonry, shining in the afternoon sunshine as if it had been polished, and shook her head. "All those novels have frizzled your brain."

Two warders in magnificent red uniforms guarded the entrance. As Livie, Daisy, and Margery approached, the yeomen raised their battle-axes, crossing them to bar the way forward. One man was old and stout, with a bulbous gourd for a nose. The other was taller and even older, his hair and beard yellowy-white like thick cream. The axes visibly trembled in the air.

"This is preposterous," Daisy remarked. "As if they could hold back a rebel horde!"

"Hush," Livie whispered.

"Halt! Who goes there?" the older man bellowed, looking over their heads.

"We're right in front of you," Daisy stated.

His chin tilted down, and he stared at them from under the wide brim of his hat.

"Good afternoon," Livie said, curtsying. "I am Miss Tyron, and I am here to visit my father, Captain Sir Tyron."

"I am Miss Wharton, the daughter of Lord and Lady Wharton, " Daisy said, flashing the yeoman the beaming smile that typically got her anything she wanted.

It had no visible effect.

"No one is allowed to visit the prisoners unless their name appears on the list approved by the prison warden," he barked. "You may not enter."

"Surely I could escort my dear cousin to her father's chambers and then visit the menagerie in the company of our maid?" Daisy asked, as if she didn't hear his statement. "I can't possibly allow Miss Tyron to enter the Tower without my escort."

"No visitors without prior approval," the stout yeoman bawled.

"But he's my father," Livie said, her eyes filling with tears. "I am not dangerous in the least. No one could consider *me* a threat to the security of the Tower."

The elder man peered at her over his spectacles. "What do you have in that basket?"

"Fruit, delivered from the country this morning," Livie said, whisking the cloth from the basket, revealing apples and peaches from Wharton greenhouses.

"There isn't a single file to be found!" Daisy put in.

The yeomen frowned at her.

"If we had an iron file, we could hide it amongst the fruit. Then my uncle could file the bars off the window, make a rope of his bedsheets, slide to the ground, and escape," she explained. "That's how Edmund Neville made his escape in the 1500s. He filed the bars from his window."

"Daisy!" Livie hissed.

The younger man's brow darkened. "We'll be searching that basket, and your pockets as well."

"We'll be having a look at that fruit," the other agreed, squinting at the basket.

In one practiced movement, the warders swept their battle-axes straight into the air, opening a path into the Tower. "Enter."

Behind them, Margery squeaked. "We should return home!"

"That is no longer an option," the elder yeoman said with magisterial emphasis.

"Oh, Daisy, what have you done?" Livie whispered.

"Gotten us into the Tower," Daisy retorted, taking her hand.

They walked under the ancient battlements, despite Margery's voluble protests, and were escorted into a small, damp office made of stone. The elder warder took the basket from Livie and slowly placed each piece of fruit on the wooden table before them.

"You should cut them in half," Daisy suggested.

The two yeomen looked at her.

"Daisy!" Livie cried. "The fruit is for my father!"

"I am merely assisting these gentlemen with their duty," Daisy said. "You can see how seriously they take their work. They may not have considered that had we pushed a file into one of these pieces of fruit, it wouldn't be immediately visible upon inspection."

Livie groaned.

Twenty minutes later, they had collectively discovered that the Tower's battle-axes were not kept as sharp as they ought to be. Most of the fruit had been destroyed as the yeomen systematically squashed and splattered each piece under the blunt edges of their axes. The small room had taken on a sweet, floral smell, like an autumn orchard littered with fallen apples.

Margery was cowering against the farthest stone wall, squealing every time an ax thumped against the wood. "Just like them murdering Frenchmen a-cutting off people's heads," she cried, more than once.

By the time most of the fruit had been "inspected," Livie was having to take deep breaths to control her irritation. A particularly juicy peach had splattered her pelisse and gloves; the ruffs at her wrists were spotted yellow.

Daisy, on the other hand, was having a marvelous time. "I truly admire how devoted His Majesty's servants are to the safety of the realm!" she exclaimed, placing the last peach in the center of the table. "Stand back, Livie. This one is quite ripe."

"What in God's name is going on here?" a stern voice barked from the entrance.

They all turned. Lord Devin stood in the entryway, looking the very picture of the aristocracy in navy velvet with silver stitching.

"That's all the zoo needs—a peacock!" Daisy muttered.

"The West Gate appears to be unguarded," his lordship observed.

"Not for much longer," Daisy told him. "We've checked almost the fruit for contraband, as you can see. These two excellent gentlemen have been most assiduous in pursuit of their duties."

"As I said, the West Gate is unguarded," Lord Devin repeated, his voice hard.

"We'll be with you in a moment, your lordship," the yeoman said. He slammed down his ax, smashing the last peach and spraying its gore around the room.

Lord Devin brushed a fleck of juice from his velvet sleeve and looked at Livie. "I suppose that this fruit was intended as a gift for your father." He nudged a bit of apple with the toe of his shoe. "They're not even good for pies now."

She nodded.

Lord Devin's gaze moved to her cousin. "Miss Wharton."

Daisy had been brushing stray bits of fruit from her pelisse. She looked up at him, eyebrow raised.

"Are you, by any chance, responsible for the destruction of Miss Tyron's gift to her father?"

"I suppose you could see it that way," Daisy said, a note of caution in her voice. Then she added, with a toss of her head: "I'm quite certain that *you* will see it that way!"

"Your marked delight in the outcome spoke for itself. Even given my low opinion of your intelligence and manners," Lord

Devin remarked, "I am surprised by your complete lack of consideration for your cousin's feelings."

Daisy gasped, red flushing her cheeks. "How dare you?"

"Lord Devin, will you please escort me to my father's chamber?" Livie begged.

His lordship nodded. "Certainly." He turned to the yeomen. "Clean up this mess and return to the gate. Your post may appear a sinecure, but you do have responsibility."

Daisy stopped scowling at Lord Devin and gave the yeomen a warm smile. "*I* want to commend you both on the thoroughness with which you carried out your duties! It has been a pleasure to see His Majesty's guards at work."

"I'll take you over to the Lions' Tower, miss," the elder yeoman said, hoisting his ax over his shoulder. "We can't have a young lady like yourself wandering around unaccompanied."

"Do take her away," Lord Devin said, his tone sour enough to curdle milk.

They all strolled through the gates, Daisy and her ancient escort following slowly.

"I must say goodbye to my cousin," Daisy caroled when they reached the courtyard. She caught up and gave Livie a hug, dropping something heavy into her pocket.

"A present for Uncle," she breathed, and then, more loudly: "Margery and I shall meet you in the barouche after your visit."

When Livie and Lord Devin reached the middle of the courtyard, he asked, "What did she give you?"

Livie stuck her hand in her pocket and brought out a curious object, like a folded knife.

"A file," Lord Devin said, his tone disgusted. "Didn't the yeomen search your pockets?"

Livie pried it open and stared down at the iron tool. "They were distracted by the fruit, which must have been what Daisy had in mind all along. I can't imagine where she found a file."

"I expect she sent a footman to buy one."

"Peter," Livie said, nodding. "He would do anything for her."

"So she imagines Captain Sir Tyron filing through the bars, rappelling down the walls, swimming the moat, and escaping?"

"She just wanted to help." Livie couldn't stop a shaky smile. It was so like Daisy to offer an audacious—if illegal—solution to her father's imprisonment.

"If he's discovered in possession of that file, he may be thrown into the darkest dungeon they have on the premises," Lord Devin said bitingly. "If you'll forgive me, your cousin is a bird-witted fool!"

"She is merely trying to help, just as you are, Lord Devin. Her methods may be unorthodox, but perhaps the gift would lift his spirits."

"Captain Sir Tyron is not a man to find humor in a dishonorable action."

Livie had to nod. "I suspect he won't be happy with my visit either, but I'm so worried about him. I can't *not* see him. I'm so grateful to have chanced on you once again, Lord Devin."

"Chanced? On the way home from the park, I realized that stubbornness likely breeds true in your family. The guard at his cell wouldn't allow you to visit without me, and even so I'm not certain I can manage to get you into his chamber."

"Then I am doubly grateful," Livie said, smiling at him.

"I'll take the file in payment."

Chapter 19

Beauchamp Tower

Livie followed Lord Devin into the Beauchamp Tower—a prison that housed only prisoners of high birth—trying to ignore her upset stomach. The fragrance that rose from her pelisse was making her so queasy that she might never eat a peach again.

Or perhaps her nausea stemmed from the smell of limestone spotted with mold and wet with river water.

"Why is the moat so smelly?" she asked Lord Devin as they climbed the stairway.

"The Tower's sewers empty into the water."

Livie's stomach lurched again.

At the top of the steps, a bored-looking guard snapped to attention. "Lord Devin!"

"Captain Sir Tyron's daughter for a visit."

Livie glanced at her escort and discovered Lord Devin at his most haughty.

The guard blinked rapidly. "Does she appear on the approved list, my lord?"

"I shall vouch for her. Move aside."

The guard turned a large iron key in the lock and stood back.

Lord Devin pushed open the door to a large chamber adorned with faded tapestries. In one corner a bed was hung with thick curtains, and directly in front of them, under a mullioned window, Captain Sir Tyron was seated at a table, presumably dictating a letter. His first mate, John Cassio, sat at the other end of the table, transcribing.

With a rush of relief, Livie realized that fear hadn't made her father gaunt. His thick, dark hair was brushed over his forehead with military precision; his shoulders were just as wide and proud as ever, his back just as straight.

"Put the tea tray on the table," he barked, without looking at the door.

"Father?" Livie breathed.

At that, his head whipped about, and he rose. Livie burst into tears and hurled herself across the room, wrapping her arms around his waist. "I've been so afraid for you!"

The captain cleared his throat, and the rigidity of his body registered in Livie's brain. She sprang back, dashed tears from her cheeks, and fell into a deep curtsy, head bowed. "Captain Sir Tyron."

When she rose, his arms were crossed, his eyes uncompromising. "You grieve me, Miss Tyron, at a time when I have other concerns. As I have instructed you in letter after letter, a gentlewoman should be ever reserved."

"I ap—apologize," Livie hiccupped, accepting the handkerchief that Lord Devin pushed into her hand.

"I have overlooked the signs of impetuousness you occasionally exhibit in your letters, as your years are green, but your presence here gives me doubt as to the strength of your character. It could be that your cousin is a poor influence. My sister describes her daughter as growing more impudent and feckless by the day."

Beside her, Lord Devin made a sudden movement.

Livie spoke quickly to cut off his lordship before he agreed with her father. "She isn't!" she cried, shaking her head. The captain's eyes narrowed at her defiance. "Daisy is everything good and kind, Father."

Lord Devin stepped forward and bowed. "Captain Sir Tyron."

Livie's father turned and bowed. "Your lordship."

"I deserve your censure for prompting this occasion," Lord Devin said. "I had hoped that the presence of your daughter would relieve the tedium of this unjust imprisonment."

The captain's rigidity eased, and he nodded to Livie. "I might have guessed that you would not be so immodest as to visit me unprompted. His lordship was much mistaken, but that reproach ought not to land on your shoulders. Those of your sex often fail to engage in complex forethought."

Livie drew in a shuddering breath. Her father was never precisely affectionate, but she'd never seen contempt on his face before a few moments ago.

"Lord Devin," he continued, "If you will forgive my admonishment, no gently-bred young lady should find herself in proximity to the male sex in a chamber containing a bed, as this cell does. I have always protected Miss Tyron from becoming a scandal or blemishing her family name."

Livie stole a glance at Lord Devin as he bowed once again, his face expressionless. "This experience shall better inform me hereafter. I apologize to Miss Tyron and to yourself."

After a tense moment, Livie's father nodded. "We will have tea." He pulled a cord to the side of the desk. "This establishment is not as well-run as the *Royal Oak*, is it, Mr. Cassio? You know my daughter, Miss Tyron. Lord Devin, may I introduce John Cassio, my first mate."

Mr. Cassio was a short man, with round, shiny eyes like a blackbird's. He stepped forward and bowed low before Lord Devin, then turned to Livie. She nodded, and he smirked, his eyes lingering on her bosom.

"Mr. Cassio, go to the kitchens, if you would, and remind them of their duties," the captain said, waving his hand.

Once his first mate had left the chamber, Captain Sir Tyron escorted Livie and Lord Devin to a group of comfortable chairs before the fireplace. "You'll forgive me for having the fire lit on such a lovely afternoon, but the walls are damp."

"Of course," Lord Devin said, seating himself.

"Where is your maid?" the captain demanded suddenly, turning to Livie.

"Outside," Lord Devin said. "I counseled that Miss Tyron leave her maid, as the woman would not be approved for entry to your chamber. If you are concerned about chaperonage, Captain Sir Tyron, I assure you that I consider myself an uncle to your daughter."

"I had forgotten the list," her father said, his face easing. "You may think me strict, Lord Devin, but in women I demand discretion, silence, and modesty above all."

He was still holding forth on that subject when Mr. Cassio reentered the room followed by a servant holding a tea tray. Mr. Cassio snuck another look at Livie and moved as if to seat himself in a chair beside her, but the captain abruptly sent him away before he could join them.

"I shan't have Mr. Cassio join us for tea, due to Miss Tyron's presence and the nature of this room," Captain Sir Tyron said, glancing at the bed before turning his attention back to Lord Devin. "You might wish to chat with him at some point. He was a member of the shore expedition on that fateful night."

Lord Devin put down his teacup with a sharp click. "I thought there were only five men in the boat, all of whom we have questioned."

"Mr. Cassio was there as well. I personally vouched for him, so he hasn't been investigated in our search for the true traitor," her father said. "I've known him since he was a lad, and he's been under my command throughout his naval career. I have nurtured him with the same attention to moral precepts as I have my daughter. I consider him to be the zenith of my labors: He is a dutiful soldier and a good man—loyal and upright."

He sipped his tea and then added, "Mr. Cassio is the son I was never fortunate enough to have. Of late, I have considered a match between Miss Tyron and Mr. Cassio."

Livie choked.

"Her status and dowry will improve his condition in life. My hope is that someday he will command the *Royal Oak*, as my son might have."

Livie winced at the tinge of bitterness in her father's voice. She'd known all her life that the captain would have preferred a son, but generally he wasn't so emphatic.

"I am certain Miss Tyron will have her choice of suitors," Lord Devin said. "Am I to understand that you separated from Mr. Cassio once ashore in France?"

"As I have said—I know not how many times—our landing on the beach was disorderly, since we were instantly set upon by enemy forces awaiting our arrival. I found myself alone in the dark, fighting adversaries whose faces were muffled in black scarves. The battle led away from the shore, and my men and I did not reunite until after the sun rose."

Livie's eyes widened, and she straightened. Surely no one had better access to a captain's seal than his first mate. Without thinking, she opened her mouth, but Lord Devin shot her a warning glance. She stilled, folding her hands in her lap.

"I have questioned Mr. Cassio about that night myself," her father continued. "My inquiry leads me to believe that he has no more information beyond that which I've already given you. Regardless, I would encourage you to conduct your own review of his account. Your questions might reveal some overlooked detail."

"I shall speak to him," Lord Devin said.

"He is my right hand," Captain Sir Tyron said, pride resonant in his voice. It was a tone Livie seldom heard from her father, and certainly one that had never been directed at her.

Lord Devin began explaining the trial that the Lord High Steward, Lord Paget, would conduct in the House. Livie listened quietly, watching her father. The captain was much the same as usual, not that she saw him often; he routinely spent a year or even longer at sea; the *Royal Oak* hadn't been in England for many months. Despite his circumstances—the looming trial, the imprisonment—he didn't appear worn down by care.

"I approve of Lord Paget," her father declared. "He fought like a true Englishman in the Battle of Waterloo last year."

As the conversation continued, Livie realized that Lord Devin was taking the trial more seriously than her father. Captain Sir Tyron seemed entirely convinced that there was no possible outcome in which his name would not be cleared and his command fully restored. Despite the burden of proof resting on the defense's shoulders, he expressed no concern about his fate.

Nor, she had to acknowledge, was he concerned about *her* fate, since he was considering marrying her to Mr. Cassio. She swallowed hard at that idea. His first mate combed his hair over to the top of his head to disguise a glaring patch of baldness.

His shiny black eyes had boldly scoured her body, quite likely because her father had made him aware of the possibility of marrying his daughter. Now that she thought about it, in the last two or three years, the captain had been interspersing references to Mr. Cassio amidst his usual admonishments. This proposed marriage had been in his mind for some time.

The thought made her feel as bitterly cold as the tea left in her cup.

Finally, Livie's father turned to her and said, "I commend you on holding your tongue, Miss Tyron. I know how hard it is for those of your sex to remain silent. Volubility in women reflects rudeness of breeding. I pride myself on your restraint."

Livie nodded.

"Your daughter's concern for you is a tribute to the soft-hearted nature of her sex," Lord Devin put in, his voice even.

The captain's brows drew together. "That is a good point." He reached out and patted Livie's hand. "I assure you that I am perfectly content. This folly shall pass. I look forward to presenting my boat design to the Admiralty. It will be of great value to ships that send their boats to shallow waters."

"I am happy to hear that," Livie said, forcing her lips into a smile.

"Given your ill-advised visit, I shall not write you a daily letter. Today's missive was to be a warning against levity and indiscretion."

"I see," Livie said, not daring to glance at Lord Devin. If her father ever discovered the previous night's misadventure, he might…he might disown her.

"Never expose yourself to the reproach of society, for no matter how high fortune has placed you, if you stoop to indelicacy, you will fall to the depths," her father advised. "Be on your guard throughout every occasion. Even a simple dance can create scandal due to a loose or light gesture."

"I don't… We are not presently participating in society, Father," Livie faltered.

He blinked. "Of course. I trust that you will make excellent use of this time before you re-enter the hollow world of high society. Give attention to the unpardonable faults that besiege your sex— immodesty and vanity. Tomorrow, I'll write with some advice as regards your looking glass."

"Thank you," Livie murmured.

"I choose that subject deliberately. As you know, I do not shillyshally with the truth, Miss Tyron."

Livie's heart sank.

"Your appearance is displeasing," he said flatly. "Perhaps your garb was becoming when you donned it this morning, but now you look a slattern, good for nothing more than scrubbing the washing."

Tears welled in Livie's eyes at his harsh tone. She bent her head and willed herself not to let them fall.

"A woman's garments ought to be clean and delightful," he continued. "Instead, yours are dirty, and an odor hangs about you. Were we aboard ship—and you a male—I would toss you overboard and have you swim after the stern or drown in your filth."

"I apologize, Father."

"As you know, Miss Tyron, I prefer my title," he said, rising. "Given the closeness of my quarters, I shall not expect to see you again until the conclusion of my trial. Farewell."

Livie stood, before sinking into a curtsy. "Farewell, Captain Sir Tyron."

"I am not unhappy to see your tears," the captain commented. "The eyes of women should be cisterns of sorrow, considering the gravity of their imperfections."

"Farewell," Lord Devin murmured, taking Livie's elbow and drawing her out of the chamber. The guard swung the door closed behind them.

Lord Devin didn't say a word as they walked down the stone stairs. Livie was also silent, her lips pressed tightly together to suppress the sobs rising in her chest. Despite herself, tears spilled down her cheeks as they walked into the sunlight.

"I don't usually carry on like this," she said, blotting her eyes with his handkerchief. "I'll have control in—in a moment."

"Were I you, I would be crying," Lord Devin remarked, rather oddly.

Daisy had not returned to the carriage. She was perched on a low stone wall on the other side of the courtyard, her white-blonde hair gleaming in the sunshine.

At the sight of them, she gave a wave and hopped off the wall. As her cousin began running across the grass toward them, Livie's vision blurred, and a sob tore out of her chest.

Lord Devin gave her a gentle push. "Go."

Daisy met Livie in the middle of the courtyard, wrapped her arms around her, and rocked her back and forth.

"Is your father much affected by his imprisonment?" Daisy whispered, when Livie had calmed.

"No," Livie said. "No, he isn't. He is just the same."

Chapter 20

An Epistolary Chapter (or at least, one that includes two epistles)

By the evening of the third day that had passed without a letter from Lady Macbeth, Joshua was seriously considering chasing down Lord Devin and demanding her name. His intentions were honorable, after all. What right had Devin to keep a man from the lady he intended to marry?

He and his older brother Frederick were seated in the library, which, despite the massive hearth at the front of the room, was as damp and chilly as the rest of the family townhouse. Joshua had his boots so close to the fire that his soles were liable to be singed.

Frederick was nursing his second glass of brandy, while Joshua sipped wine: his doctor was of the opinion that strong spirits were injurious to those recovering from blood infections. The thought of his wounds made him grimace. Perhaps a man should warn a woman before marriage if his right side is a mass of scars.

"You're as twitchy as a cat on a hot brick," Frederick commented.

Joshua put down his sherry. "I've found the woman I want to marry."

Frederick reached over and slapped him on the shoulder. "Bravo! Why aren't you out there courting her?" He blinked. "Wait…did you say 'woman' deliberately? Because our father isn't going to be happy if your wife isn't a lady."

"She is a lady."

"Who is she? Not that I've been going around to Almack's and the like. I didn't think you were, either. Where'd you meet her?"

"In Hyde Park," Joshua said, lying without a qualm. "I don't know her name yet, but I mean to."

"Humph." Frederick reached out a booted foot and kicked the bottom log. It cracked in half, sending a shower of sparks up the chimney. "Never fit me to play the older brother, but my advice, for what it's worth, is that there's something to be said for not judging a book by its cover. You remember that mistress I had before you left for war?"

"Lady Merivale?"

"No, the one who followed, Léonie. She was married to a Russian ambassador, who was eighty if he was a day. She was exquisite, from head to toe—and she wanted me to kiss those toes of hers." He kicked the log again. "Strip off all the powder and paint, and you'd discover a temper like the devil's. She hacked up my favorite vest—the salmon-pink one, with the gold embroidery. Cut it into pieces because she said I looked at another woman."

"Did you?"

Frederick shrugged. "I was so blind drunk the night before that I couldn't remember. My point is that your lady-in-the-park may be polished on the outside, but what of the inside? After you're wed? I was able to shed Léonie with a good-sized emerald, but you'd be stuck for life."

Joshua got up and put another log on the fire.

"For God's sake, we employ footmen to keep up the fires. So, are you trying to find her? Roaming the park with a posy in hand?"

"I haven't tried that yet."

"If she *is* a lady—and who's to say that she is, because these days ladybirds look as elegant as the rest—it'll be easy enough to find out her name."

"Due to some sort of scandal, the lady says she will be introduced next Season rather than this."

"Better check out the pedigree. You don't want to involve yourself with a dishonored family. Father won't have it."

"*Father* has nothing to do with whom I marry."

"True enough," Frederick said with a sigh. "Your fortune is your own. The same can't be said for mine."

"Is there someone you'd like to marry?" Joshua turned his head and surveyed his brother. Despite his future earldom, Frederick didn't bother with elegance: his coat was ill-fitting, his hair oft-disordered, his appetite for brandy excessive.

"Never," Frederick replied, unsurprisingly. He'd been adamant on that subject since the age of fourteen.

A rap on the door was followed by their butler, Mr. Oates-Plagitt. "A groom has delivered a letter for Major FitzRoy." He held up a thick silver plate with one letter squarely placed in the middle. "An *anonymous* letter."

Joshua bolted upright. "Did you allow the man to leave?"

The butler cleared his throat. "The groom informed me that he will remain in the kitchen long enough to drink a tankard of ale if you wish to reply, but that his mistress has ordered him to refuse all questions."

Joshua almost headed for the kitchen, but then he remembered he'd promised on his honor not to seek out his lady's name, nor question her footman.

"Well, let's have the letter," Frederick remarked. "Missive from the future Mrs. FitzRoy. We have, what, fifteen minutes to scribble a reply? We'd better get at it."

Joshua took the letter from the butler. "I don't suppose you recognize his livery?"

"Forest green with black trim," Oates-Plagitt replied. "No specific house comes to mind, but I can inquire after it at the next meeting of the butlers' club."

"When's that?"

"A fortnight."

"That will do," Frederick said with a wave of his hand. "Rip it open, Joshua."

Joshua waited until the butler left, closing the door behind him.

Dear Major FitzRoy,

I write to express my hope that you remain safe and well while serving in His Majesty's Armed Forces. 'Tis vastly improper of me to write to a gentleman, so this will be my first and last such missive.

I must also inform you that I can never be your bride, and I pray that you will put that idea far from your mind. My reputation was not impugned by our foolish behavior, so you need not think that honor demands our marriage. My father would never agree to such a union, and indeed, has informed me that he has already made plans for my betrothal.

I wish with all my heart that you find happiness.

With sincere best wishes.

"Damn it!"

"Ah, love," his brother said. "The riskiest endeavor of all. Let's see it." He held out his hand, leaning over and grabbing the sheet when Joshua didn't instantly comply. "Smells like a lady—just a touch of fragrance." Frederick looked over at Joshua. "I think I could give lessons in how to be a courtesan. I would emphasize how unpleasant it is to receive letters drenched in scent. A light spritz is all one needs."

"I promised on my honor not to search out her name," Joshua said. He was itching to go to the kitchens and bribe the groom with a gold coin. Or two.

"If you want her, you'll have to give up foolishness about honor and the like," Frederick said, with all the cheerful air of a man infamous for adulterous *affaires*. "This is a clear plea for help, so you need to find out her name. Her father is matching her to a degenerate, likely a man with one foot in the grave."

Joshua snatched the letter back. "It doesn't say that."

"You are not used to parsing elegant texts," Frederick said. He slid forward just enough that he could put his boot to the wall and drag down the velvet cord. A hollow bell sounded in the distance. "I suspect you don't know how to write a letter to a lady, either."

Joshua scowled at him. "Now there's a sooty streak on the wall from your boot. Can't you be bothered to stand up?"

"No," Frederick said simply, upending his snifter into his mouth.

The butler entered with an alacrity that suggested he had been hovering in the hallway.

"Writing desk, ink, fountain pen," Frederick ordered. "And writing paper. Give me a sheet of the impressive stuff. The crested parchment."

Oates-Plagitt walked to the far end of the room and returned with a lap desk fitted with a pot of ink. He handed it to Frederick along with several pieces of thick parchment. "Is there anything else you wish?"

"First, more brandy. Second, your help with a letter," Frederick told him.

Oates-Plagitt bowed. "My pleasure, your lordship." He returned with the decanter and refilled Frederick's glass.

"Our butler has the fanciest language of anyone in this house, to go with his double-barreled name," Frederick explained to Joshua. "He's helped me extract myself from a marital tangle now and then. Oates-Plagitt, we need to reply to a young lady who's begging my brother for assistance. I shall play scribe." Frederick dipped his quill in the ink bottle and tapped it on the rim.

"*Dear Lady Macbeth*," Joshua said obediently.

His brother scowled. "You can't go proposing to a married lady. It's not allowed. I assiduously pursue ladies wearing rings precisely because I need not fear the altar."

"Lady Macbeth is a character from a play. I surmise the title is a pseudonym," Oates-Plagitt put in.

"Pseudo-what?" Frederick asked. "No, don't tell me." He frowned at Joshua again. "You need to beguile the lady with elegant rhetoric and then demand to see her. She'll give in, be it from curiosity or desperation."

"Not a bad plan," Oates-Plagitt allowed.

Without waiting for Joshua's response, Frederick began scratching out a letter, speaking aloud as he went. *"Dear Lady, I am your humble servant.* What next?"

"Ask her if we can meet," Joshua said.

" I do heartily wish that you would honor me with a command to be your own, despite your father's wishes."

"We didn't speak to each other that way. Are you sure this is a good idea?"

"You know nothing of ladies, and I know everything," Frederick retorted. "If I ever need to lead a battle, I shall come to you." He cleared his throat, continuing. *"The passion which carrieth me to your service proves as unprofitable as extreme."*

"What does that mean?" Joshua asked.

His brother ignored him. *"Which forceth me to have recourse to entreaties, beseeching you to honor me with your commands.* What do you think, Oates-Plagitt?"

The butler stared thoughtfully into the distance. "Following *'your commands'—so that, other means failing, my obedience may oblige you to believe that I am your most affectionate servant.* Add brackets around *'other means failing.'* Close: *With a most earnest entreaty that we meet again.* No, wait!"

Frederick raised an eyebrow, quill in the air.

"With a most earnest entreaty that you grace me once more with the flower of your presence."

"She's going to think I'm a fool," Joshua said.

"She'll eat it up," Frederick promised. He sifted sand over the sheet. "Don't fold it until you're in the kitchen, Oates-Plagitt. I don't want our radiant prose smeared."

Joshua watched the butler leave, then reached out, snatched Frederick's glass, and took a deep swallow of brandy. "I hope you're right."

"I'm right," his brother said comfortably. "You command a battalion. I command a ballroom—or at least, a lady's chamber." He grinned at Joshua's scornful glance. "To each his own!"

Chapter 21

A Revelation that Changed Everything

"I wish Mother would return home," Daisy said idly.

Livie looked up from her half-hearted perusal of her father's latest letter. Why hadn't she ever noticed how critical they were? How much they assumed that she was licentious, if not worse?

"Are you missing her?" Livie asked.

"I am bored, and I am always enlivened by a good battle with my mother. I don't mean to be critical, darling, but you have been so melancholy since your visit to the Tower that the whole house is sunk in gloom."

"I am sorry," Livie said.

Daisy leaned forward and snatched the captain's letter, tossing it to the floor. "You must stop moping about your father. Lord Devin will make sure the trial goes well. He's frightfully powerful, you know. *The Times* wrote this morning that Devin is 'intrinsic to the nation,' whatever that means."

While her cousin chattered on, Livie reached down to pick up her father's letter. Guilt nagged at her heart.

Perhaps she *was* licentious. If not, she would never have kissed a stranger. The captain's new letter had dropped the question of her stained garments and moved to harping on her stupidity in entering the Tower of London, where ladies ought never to be seen: "You put yourself in danger of ravishing."

What would her father do if he knew of the Rothingale masquerade?

Wincing at the thought, she put Captain Sir Tyron's letter aside. For most of her life, she had always written him back the same day that a letter arrived, but now two letters lay unanswered on her desk. Normally, she skimmed his admonishments without much interest, but also without shame, judging them a sign of his affection for her.

Now?

She *felt* ashamed. She had kissed a man in public, knowing full well that she was flouting society's rules. She could hardly assure her father of her modesty when she had so easily discarded that attribute. Not only that, but she had written a letter to that same man.

And he had responded: the major's unopened letter was tucked away in her hatbox. She ought to toss it in the fire.

"So, what does your father say today?" Daisy inquired, noticing that Livie had rescued the captain's letter from the floor.

"He writes about vanity and indiscretion. Also, he says that there is no excuse for unladylike excursions, which makes me feel utterly guilt-ridden."

Daisy wrinkled her nose. "The captain wouldn't have appreciated our trip to the masquerade, but honestly, Livie, it's not as if you wandered off into the shrubbery with the major. That's what happened to Lady Regina's first fiancé, you know. Needless to say, said fiancé is now married to the shrubbery. No, that didn't come out right. Married to the woman he took into the hedge."

"I've been indecorous at best," Livie said, ignoring the discussion of shrubbery. "I am finding it difficult to write back to Father, since I feel as if I am lying by omission. Yet I cannot confess the truth. I think he might disown me, Daisy."

"Of course he wouldn't disown you. He would shout, but you are his cross to bear. Children exist to offend their parents," Daisy said comfortably. "I expect his father thought he was a terror as a boy."

"I do know he married my mother against my grandfather's wishes. Aunt let that slip one day."

"A love match?" Daisy asked. "It's hard to imagine. What a pity that your mother has always been so frail."

Livie just sighed. In her memory, her parents had never lived in the same house, let alone shown signs of being happily married. Her father was always aboard ship, in London, or at her aunt's estate. Her mother never joined them; Livie had seen her only twice in the last five years.

"I think you'll be more comfortable if you take it as a given that Uncle will be deeply offended by anything you do."

"Daisy!"

"It's true," her cousin insisted. "He once informed me that my laugh was neither demure nor humble, embodying the original sin of my sex. Poppycock, Livie! With all respect to Captain Sir Tyron, a world in which women were never allowed to laugh would be a dismal place indeed. More than this world already is, I mean. Likely he's told you the same?"

"I don't laugh around him."

Daisy jumped to her feet. "Where's that letter from the major, Livie?"

Livie's eyes instinctively flew to her hatbox.

Her cousin dashed over and snatched the box from the top of the wardrobe, running to the far side of the bed. "You don't mind my looking at your new hat, do you?"

"It isn't a new hat," Livie protested. "I merely returned to Mrs. Mogbetty and asked her to resew the veil. You know that!"

Daisy pulled the top off the hatbox. "I see an exquisite masquerade hat." She held up Livie's hat, now featuring a spangled veil. "Oh! I love the new veil!"

"Mrs. Mogbetty told me that her masquerade hats are all the rage," Livie said, hoping to distract her cousin. "Apparently, everyone invited to the Duchess of Trent's costume ball will be wearing one in lieu of a mask."

Daisy put down the hat. "I'm very pleased for her." She tipped the box, grabbed Joshua's letter, and held it up in the air. "And I'm even more pleased for you. How glorious—evidence of love's young dream!" She was giggling so hard that she wheezed.

"Daisy, you mustn't," Livie cried, springing up and coming to the other side of the bed. "It would be frightfully improper of me to engage in correspondence with an unmarried man. I've thought about it, and as long as I don't read the letter, we haven't corresponded."

"Then I'll read it aloud, just as I do the novels we both love," Daisy said, catching her breath. "Do you give me permission to open this letter, darling cousin?"

Livie bit her lip.

"Your father's precepts mean nothing to me," Daisy said bluntly. "He makes everyone around him uncomfortable with his complaining and carrying on. If *I* open this letter, and *I* write back to the young man who sent it, the sin is not yours. You may reply to his daily lecture with a clear conscience."

Livie still hesitated.

Daisy stuck her finger under the seal and wiggled it. "You can't ignore the major. He even used a seal on the letter, a proper one, with a coronet. What if he goes to battle and doesn't return, Livie? Think of that!"

"I suppose," Livie whispered, her heart squeezed by the thought of Joshua coming to harm. "You may read it aloud, but we definitely shouldn't answer."

Daisy ripped it open. *"Dear Lady, I am your humble servant. I do heartily wish that you would honor me with a command to be your own, despite your father's wishes."* Daisy looked up, eyes round. "Livie, he is asking you to run away with him!"

"Surely not," Livie said. "That's just fancy language."

"It is fancy," Daisy agreed. "Listen to this." She read a few more sentences, then wrinkled her nose. "I don't like his letters nearly as well as I liked him."

"I don't think he wrote it," Livie said slowly. "He didn't speak like this at the masquerade."

"I wish we had another example of his hand." Daisy squinted at the letter. "This isn't even signed."

"Well, we haven't." Livie flopped down on her back. "Oh, Daisy, what if I have to marry Mr. Cassio? I think I'd rather die."

"Which would be worse? To marry a man who wants you and possibly damage his career, or marry a man who wants you only so that he can have a career in the first place? To me, there's no question," Daisy said. She turned the letter over. "The major doesn't have to remain in the army. His family is clearly substantial. There's a crest on the letter."

"We suppose we could look him up in Debrett's Peerage," Livie said. "Though Father more or less announced that I was going to marry Cassio."

"You shouldn't listen to such twaddle," Daisy counseled. "I would never allow you to marry the first mate of a boat. Your father has obviously lost his head due to the stress of imprisonment."

"His letters have been talking about Cassio for several years," Livie said hollowly, pointing to the trunk at the bottom of her bed. "I didn't pay them any mind, because it never occurred to me that Cassio had anything to do with me."

Daisy was peering at Joshua's letter. "The crest has unicorns to the sides and a lion on top. There are always unicorns, aren't there? You'd think they could be more original. If I was making a crest, I'd place my mare in the middle…with a rooster on her head! That would stand out."

Livie shrugged.

"No one can force you to marry," Daisy consoled. "If need be, I shall ask Mother to give you the mantel clock downstairs. Lord Argyle will be at your feet in no time, given how he prattled on about that timepiece."

For foolishly sentimental reasons, Livie had been keeping Joshua's card in her pocket ever since she'd told Peter the major's address. She held it in the air. "His address might offer a clue to his family."

"Oh, of course," Daisy said, running over to take it from her. "We can ask—"

Her voice broke off.

"What?" Livie asked.

"He's—he's—"

"He's *what*?"

"He's related to Lord Paget. He must be if his address is Paget House," Daisy said.

"Lord *who*?" Just then, the name registered. Before Daisy could answer, Livie sat up and gasped. "Lord Paget! From the Battle of Waterloo?"

"Waterloo-Shmatterloo," Daisy cried. "The same Lord Paget who will preside over your father's trial as Lord High Steward!"

Chapter 22

The Second Masquerade

The Duchess of Trent's Annual Masquerade Ball

Livie pulled her crimson domino cloak tightly around her shoulders as she stepped down from a hackney cab in front of the Duke of Trent's mansion. Light spilled from a large window at the front of the manor, and she could see costumed people milling about inside. Thankfully, a fair number sported colored dominos, so she and Daisy wouldn't stand out.

"Fiddle-faddle!" Daisy exclaimed, hopping down to stand beside her. "I was certain that the duke and duchess would have opened the ball by this hour so we could sneak in without encountering the reception line. They aren't dancing yet, are they?"

As Livie shook her head, the door to the ducal mansion swung open and a butler appeared on the threshold, waiting for them to make their way up the walk.

"Ugh," Daisy murmured. "I'm so nervous that my knees are wobbling."

"You surprise me! You're usually the first to be up for a lark." Livie pulled a coin from her reticule to pay the driver, wishing him an excellent evening.

"This is more than a lark," Daisy said morosely. "My mother will *eviscerate* me if the Duchess of Trent recognizes us."

"It was your idea! Besides, Her Grace would think it funny."

"If the Duchess of Trent—who has known us for *years*—identifies either of us, it won't matter if she bursts out laughing. My mother will not be amused."

"The ball is crowded with masked guests," Livie pointed out, nodding at the window. "We can remain on the far side of the room."

Had Livie been attending this masquerade under normal circumstances, she might have been unnerved by the sheer magnificence of the costumes she glimpsed. Instead, all she could think about was Joshua.

She had told herself that the only reason she had once again breached societal rules by writing to a man—and this time begging him to meet her—was for the sake of her father.

But now? When she would see Joshua again any moment?

She found it impossible to stop smiling.

She meant to reveal her name and beg him for help, but in truth, her father's trial wasn't foremost in her mind.

She couldn't stop thinking of Joshua's kisses. The low groan in his throat that had made her blood race so quickly that she could hardly breathe. The way he had feasted on her, their mouths fused together. The way he'd wrapped his arms around her and deepened their kiss, stealing her breath along with her propriety.

He'd made her feel *alive*.

Her father's admonishments drifted into her head, but she dismissed them. Ever since arranging this meeting, Livie couldn't stop thinking about how perfect—how *wanted*—Joshua made her feel. In her father's eyes, she was a disobedient wretch. Joshua wanted her to be disobedient, celebrated it, even.

She longed for the moment when he lost control—when he made *her* lose control. She wanted more of him, more of that burr of pleasure that made nonsense of society's rules.

If she wasn't careful, her giddy smile would turn into a laugh, the kind of laugh Captain Sir Tyron deplored. She couldn't bring herself to care. Her father planned to marry her to his lecherous first mate, a man whom she scarcely knew, and who may well have even betrayed his country. The captain didn't deserve her loyalty, though he still had her love.

"Is your veil in place?" she asked Daisy. "Let's go!"

"We should have met the major in the park," her cousin moaned, as they approached the butler, who stood at the top of the steps, looking like a particularly well-fed pigeon.

"These days Lord Devin waits for us in Hyde Park every morning," Livie noted.

"That irritating curmudgeon is certain I'll topple off my mount," Daisy brooded. "Still, we should have offered to meet the major elsewhere." She came to a halt. "I don't have a good feeling about this. Please reconsider, Livie."

"Where else could we meet Joshua? In case you've forgotten, I'm still a pariah, and I can't just walk around London in a masquerade veil, Daisy! It's odd enough in Hyde Park. People invariably stare and whisper when I'm in a bookshop, and I daren't even enter a café."

"We could have found a place that no one in the fashionable world would dream of visiting. I have a great uncle buried in the

Ironmongers Graveyard. I can see the note now: *Meet me on the family tomb.* Even better: *Kiss me on the family tomb.* The major would be there in a shot!"

"To quote you, 'fiddle-faddle!'" Livie exclaimed, catching her cousin's arm and drawing her up the steps. "Good evening!" she said to the butler, imitating her aunt's imperious diction as she handed over the entrance ticket that had been tucked inside Lady Wharton's invitation.

The butler frowned, likely wondering why two young ladies had arrived without a chaperone.

Fortunately, a large coach rattled to a stop on the street before he could ask for their names. Livie glanced over her shoulder as four liveried grooms leapt down and took their positions on either side of a door emblazoned with an impressive escutcheon.

A lady emerged, dressed in a gown fashionable two decades ago in the French court. Her voluminous skirts were trimmed with braided gold thread, incongruously topped by a masquerade hat, trimmed with its own golden braid and adorned with a gold-tinted veil. And on top of that?

A coronet, glittering with diamonds, just like Marie Antoinette might have worn.

"Lady Dolphinton is particularly resplendent tonight!" Livie exclaimed, turning back to the butler. "Perhaps one of the royal dukes accompanies her."

The butler squinted toward the street and then handed back the entrance ticket. "Their Graces, the Duke and Duchess of Trent, have chosen to welcome guests inside the ballroom." He bowed with perfunctory haste and trotted down the steps.

"Lady Dolphinton looks as if someone vomited gold braid all over her masquerade hat. I haven't met her. How did you know whose coach it was?" Daisy whispered, as they entered the house.

"I have no idea who she is, or who owns that coach," Livie replied.

Daisy shook her head, grinning. "After two decades in which my naughtiness was the talk of the nursery, you are stealing my title, Livie!"

A footman stepped forward and bowed. "Good evening. May I announce your arrival?"

Livie cleared her throat. "Just a moment, if you would." She drew her cousin over to the side of the wide entrance hall.

"We mustn't greet our hosts," Daisy hissed. "Let's hide in the ladies' retiring room until the duchess opens the dance, then slip into the ballroom from a side door."

"No, I must find Joshua!" Livie protested. "What if he gives up and leaves? Now that I've made up my mind to tell him who I am, I have to get it over with. I can't lay awake another night!"

Daisy groaned. "The man won't leave before meeting you, Livie. I'm sure he was up at night too, thinking of you." She leaned in and said in a naughty whisper, "Not just thinking."

Livie rolled her eyes. Ever since Daisy read *City of Eros*, she believed that men took solitary pleasure everywhere—even behind curtains at a ball.

"You are mistaken," Livie told her. "That act is so undignified...and Daisy, this isn't the time or place to debate it."

"Obviously, Lord Devin doesn't pleasure himself," Daisy said, pursuing her own train of thought. "He's far too haughty. I suspect he considers himself above bedplay."

"He attended Lord Rothingale's masquerade," Livie pointed out. "Unlike Joshua, Devin knew perfectly well who was invited to that house, which suggests he was looking for an amorous encounter." She could hear the party from the large coach coming up the path, chattering at the top of their lungs.

"Consorting with loose women is not a point in his favor," Daisy said loftily.

"Lord Devin isn't coming tonight, is he?" Livie asked, alarmed. That particular gentleman would not only recognize them, but promptly drag them out of the ball.

"No. I inquired yesterday morning—in a casual way, so he didn't suspect," Daisy said, glancing to her side at the open door leading outside. "We must go, or we'll be herded into the ballroom and discovered."

"No, wait," Livie said, but Daisy whirled to face the footman.

"Oh, no!" she cried in a high voice. "My flounce ripped when I climbed from the carriage! I assume the ladies' retiring room is still next to the library?"

The footman bowed and began to reply, but she rushed past him and down the long corridor leading to the back of the house.

Livie had no intention of waiting until the Duchess of Trent signaled the first dance to see Joshua. Marie Antoinette and five or six other costumed revelers were about to enter, and another carriage had drawn to a halt on the street. Their Graces might be caught in the receiving line for an hour or more.

She needed more than Joshua's help. She needed that steady gaze of his that told her she was worthy, even though her father thought otherwise. She needed kisses that made her feel not just desirable but cherished. Livie drew in a shaky breath.

She could follow the next group of guests into the ballroom and disappear into the crowd while they greeted the duke and duchess. She pulled out her fan and waved it before her face.

"I shall cool my face while I wait for my cousin to return," she announced for the benefit of the hovering footman.

Before he could respond, Marie Antoinette traipsed through the door, followed by a throng of babbling guests. The gentlemen began relinquishing their hats and the ladies adjusting their millinery. Mrs. Mogbetty had certainly been right about the popularity of her masquerade hats.

To Livie's horror, one voice immediately rose over the clamor.

"Be attentive, if you please," Lady Regina said sharply to the footman, who had rushed to attend her. "Stand farther off. I shall be most displeased if my skirts are stained by greasy hands."

Lady Regina, dressed as Marie Antoinette, was ready to command the commoners to eat cake, since they had no bread.

Livie turned away, vigorously waving her fan and pretending she was fascinated by the wallpaper. Regina would undoubtedly lead the way into the ballroom. Livie could trail after the group and slip away.

"Who is that?" Regina asked the butler in piercing tones.

The butler murmured something.

"Nonsense," she said. "I recognize her. Miss Petunia Massinger was undoubtedly chaperoned by her sister." She raised her voice. "Petunia, were you waiting for me?"

Obviously, Livie should shake her head and retreat. She should turn and rush down the corridor.

But Daisy was right: Livie didn't feel like her father's docile daughter any longer. Just this moment?

She couldn't resist temptation.

"Good evening!" she chirped, turning toward Regina.

Chapter 23

Rebelling against Regina

"So kind of you to wait for me, dear, though you will have to strike out on your own sooner or later," Regina said, walking over to Livie.

Whom Regina thought was Petunia, her best friend.

"Once I am a marchioness, I shan't spend my time with old maids," she continued. "Not that you should despair. Even the most hag-ridden ladies occasionally achieve a respectable alliance. Not that I mean to imply that *you* are hag-ridden!"

Given her behavior in the millinery shop, Petunia didn't seem the type who would—or should—put up with abuse, so Livie protested. "That isn't fair, Regina, since you are at least a year older than me and also unmarried."

Regina bridled before collecting herself. "You seem to require both a lesson in civility and the peerage," she said acidly. "I am betrothed to an earl and only eleven months older than you!"

"I forgot the precise number," Livie retorted. She shrugged. "Eleven months, a year…"

"Are you coming down with a cold? Your voice is rather low," Regina said. "I cannot bear ill people about me. My constitution is not as strong as some."

"I am quite well," Livie replied.

"Come to the side, won't you? Hold this glass for me."

Livie obediently held up the small mirror that Regina had taken from her reticule, hoping that the militant sparkle in her eyes couldn't be seen through her veil.

She ought to rush away, but she could not bring herself to flee.

Not from Regina.

Regina powdered her chin, adjusted the veil on her masquerade hat, straightened her diamond tiara, and said, "Well, come along, Petunia! My brother and his wife are already in the ballroom. You have that manner of drifting along like a seedpod caught in a breeze, but it often makes us late, doesn't it?"

"Unfair," Livie commented.

Regina examined "Petunia" from head to foot. "I am gratified that you wore a red domino, as I requested. The color will set off the gold in my gown."

"You're not worried that you have overdone the gold trim?" Livie gave Regina the same head-to-toe examination. "Personally, I am concerned that the bustle attached to your rear will make a waltz challenging."

"You must be jesting." Regina twirled, which caused her bustle to wag from side to side, rather like the rear end of a happy, overweight dog. Facing Livie once again, she pointed her toe, holding out a high-heeled slipper adorned with a diamond cluster. "My skirts are daringly short, as you can see. My ankles have been called exquisite by more than one gentleman."

"How is your bustle constructed?" Livie asked. "I thought they were made of cork, but that looks far heavier."

"It's padded cotton. My maid fashioned it."

"I suspect she used a bolster," Livie observed, noticing that the bustle was still quivering of its own accord.

"Sophisticated apparel is not your forté, Petunia. Just look at the spangles on your masquerade hat. You resemble a porcelain

Turkish dancer," Regina declared, taking hold of Livie's arm and heading through the ballroom door.

"Your costume has all the sophistication of a donkey wearing an Easter bonnet," Livie retorted.

Regina gasped and dropped Livie's arm. "You forget yourself!"

"Perhaps I have simply found my voice," Livie suggested. Taking advantage of their position at the top of the steps leading into the ballroom, she began looking over the crowd for Joshua.

"Who are you looking for?" Regina asked suspiciously. "Oh, bloody hell, there's Winchester."

Livie almost blurted out "Who?" before she remembered that the Earl of Winchester, the scallion himself, was Regina's fiancé.

"At least he's not wearing green," Regina added. She caught Livie's upper arm again. "Do you see him, over to the right?"

Livie peered through her veil until she found the earl, as tall and slim as ever, his hair brushed upward into the Brutus.

"Is he wearing orange?" Regina asked, jutting her chin toward her fiancé.

"Apricot," Livie said, though it was hard to distinguish the precise color through her rosy veil.

Regina let go of Livie's arm and offered her elbow.

Livie frowned.

"Take my arm," Regina commanded. "As I said, your domino sets off my costume." After Livie complied, they took the last few steps to the ballroom floor and joined the outskirts of a large group surrounding their hosts.

"I also instructed Winchester to wear red to provide a foil for my gown," Regina said in a discontented undertone. "I suppose his coat might appear orange because of my yellow veil. Those scrubby little schoolgirls would probably refer to him as a carrot. What are you grinning about?"

"I am not *grinning*," Livie said with dignity. "I've merely glimpsed your brother, talking to our hosts."

"That oink," Regina snapped. "His wife was horrendously rude to me in the carriage, and he did not defend me."

"Oh?" Livie said innocently.

"She called my fiancé a turnip."

"A scallion, a carrot, and a turnip," Livia mused. "Given tonight's attire, one might want to add an orange or apricot to the mix. Which is preferable? Marriage to a vegetable, or to a piece of fruit?"

Regina's scowl was clearly visible through the gold net of her veil. "Have you been at the champagne, Petunia? Wine will mar your complexion, not to mention make you fat. I believe I see a spot on your chin."

"The Earl of Winchester does not resemble a turnip," Livie said, ignoring the question of spots, since she knew perfectly well that her skin was unblemished.

"The conversation addressed his intelligence rather than his girth," Regina said sulkily.

"Ah."

"I think of the earl's intellectual ineptitude as a strong point," Regina said with a trace of defiance. "It makes him biddable. There's also his title, of course."

"His docility is remarkable," Livie agreed. "As is his hair. So magnificently high. I can see it from here, waving like an ostrich feather."

"Where? I've lost sight of him," Regina said. She picked up her veil and peered about, then drew in a sharp breath. "Look at that handsome man, Petunia! Over there, making his way from the other room."

Livie's heart skipped a beat.

Regina had found Joshua.

Livie let her eyes greedily range over Major FitzRoy, happy to discover that she was just as taken by him now as she had been at Rothingale's masquerade. His letter had been so disappointing that she was slightly afraid that the man she kissed was a coxcomb, as affected as his writing.

But no. Joshua was not mincing his way through the ballroom but striding, without a trace of dandified affectation. His loose-limbed gait befitted a man of action, and the deeply-carved lines by his mouth made Livie long to coax him into smiling.

"I have always found a man in uniform very appealing," Regina declared. "I believe I know who he is. That chin…a remarkable chin, isn't it? Now where have I seen that chin?"

Joshua wore neither a domino nor a mask, so he must consider his dress uniform to be a costume in itself. He was wearing a double-breasted crimson coat with golden epaulets, and his collar and cuffs were striped green. His boots were worn high over his white breeches, nearly reaching the top of his calves.

"Not the chin of a biddable man," Livie commented.

"Who cares for that?" Regina said, letting her veil drop. "Marriage is not a consideration when admiring men like him. Military men are notoriously rusticated, not to mention impoverished. A woman of our stature could never marry such a man—no matter how desperate you may feel, Petunia. Your household would have scarcely more than a maid and a footman. You might as well become a fruit-and-vegetable seller."

"I'd sell a turnip before I'd marry one," Livie bit out.

"Winchester is a *noble* turnip. A slim figure is far more appealing than a brutish set of shoulders, such as that soldier's," Regina said. "What if one's children inherited that trait? More befitted to a farmer than a nobleman. Oh, wait…that reminds me. I do know who he is."

Livie felt a wash of anger. She would love her sons to inherit Joshua's shoulders. Winchester wasn't just a turnip; he was a young turnip, pulled before it was full-grown.

She took a breath, preparing to say as much, when Regina exclaimed: "Of course! That man is Lord Paget's son. Second son, of course. You could do worse, Petunia."

"Indeed?" Livie said dangerously.

"He has a fortune from his godmother. Equally importantly, everyone says his elder brother won't ever marry."

"Why not?"

Regina lowered her voice. "The heir refuses to bed anyone but married women! It's only a matter of time before an angry husband challenges him to a duel, and since he's an inebriate, he will surely lose. That means the second son will inherit the title and estate."

"That's terrible," Livie said, feeling a little sick.

Regina shrugged. "It's a new earldom, and not as desirable as Winchester's, but it's still an earldom." She went up on her toes. "Drat, where has he gone? I thought he was walking in our direction."

Livie had to slip away before she utterly lost her temper. "I see him to your right."

"Where?" Regina swung in that direction, her padded rump swinging so freely that it bumped into Livie's hip.

"Jump," Livie suggested.

"*Jump*? I do believe you've lost your head, Petunia. No lady jumps."

"True, not every lady is able to jump," Livie replied sympathetically. "Could you hop?"

"*Hop?*"

"Another word for a *chassé* step." Livie demonstrated. "Few people in society are capable of a proper *chassé*. Only those who are light on their feet can master it since both feet need to leave the ground. I'm not sure you can do it, given that bustle."

"Your *chassé* has no elegance, Petunia. You look like a ginger beer bottle going pop."

"Oh," Livie said, schooling her voice to sound crestfallen. "Won't you demonstrate?"

Regina sighed. "Put your feet together elegantly. Slide one leg forward, and keep your eyes up, facing your partner."

"Of course," Livie said.

Regina jumped.

Chapter 24

Joshua Opens the Ball

Earlier that evening

"Shall I announce you by title or character?" the Duke of Trent's butler inquired, as Joshua and Frederick paused before the entrance to the ballroom.

Frederick raised an eyebrow. "My character is frequently impugned by gossip columns, but I don't care to have that broadcast."

The butler ignored this frivolity. "Some guests have chosen to be announced in costume, as in the Sultan of Sultania."

Joshua intervened. "Lord Frederick FitzRoy-Paget and Major Joshua FitzRoy."

His brother elbowed him. "Lord Frederick FitzRoy-Paget and Major Joshua FitzRoy-*Paget*."

The Trent butler squared himself to the ballroom and bellowed, "The Right Honorable Lord Frederick FitzRoy-Paget, and Major Joshua FitzRoy-Paget."

The Duke and Duchess of Trent were waiting at the base of the steps to greet their guests. Joshua was itching to dash off and find Lady Macbeth, but he managed to school himself enough to accept their congratulations. His father had sent notice of his promotion to *The Morning Post* and hyphenated Joshua's name to allude to the new earldom, without heed for his younger son's dislike of public acclaim.

Joshua found his father's nomenclature—Lord FitzRoy-Paget, Earl Paget—absurd.

The duchess was chattering to Frederick in her charming American accent, so Joshua tried to engage the duke, but the man was busy glowering behind his mask.

The fact that Frederick was flirting madly with his wife might explain His Grace's foul mood.

Joshua kicked his brother in the ankle and bowed once again. "Your Graces."

"You pulled me away just when I'd come up with a compliment that was guaranteed to infuriate the duke," Frederick complained, after they'd moved a few steps away. "A charming reference to the duchess's bosom. It would have made her giggle, which does marvelous things to her cleavage, in case you didn't notice."

Joshua hadn't noticed and didn't give a damn. "I've told you before that I prefer to introduce myself without hyphenation. The title was conferred after I left my father's household. I see no reason why *I* should change my name, and I have not done so."

"You deserve to be hyphenated for pulling me away from our hostess," Frederick retorted. "Regrettably, after more than a decade of marriage, Her Grace still seems to be in love with her husband. It must be her American blood. The British don't dance with their spouses, let alone dangle after them."

"You would know," Joshua said wryly.

"I *do* know. The duchess flirts with me merely to annoy her duke, but I am happy to engage." He threw Joshua a smirk. "In lieu of bedfellows, she and I have become close friends."

"Both my lady and her cousin are wearing scarlet dominos," Joshua said, ignoring his brother's folly.

"I already know that," Frederick said, sighing. "I read the note, and you reminded me in the coach. Brandy is presumably to be found in the cardroom, so I'll let you know if a scarlet domino is hovering over the dice." He set off.

Joshua scanned the mass of revelers, noting the palpable difference between this event and Rothingale's masquerade. There, the ladies' apparel had hinted at a state of undress, and most men had been in black with brandified noses and lecherous smirks.

By contrast, only the very top of society had been invited by the Duchess of Trent and, if anything, the nobility were wearing more clothing rather than less. Joshua recognized the unmistakable girth of a royal duke, garbed in sky blue, skin-tight pantaloons, with a Roman toga incongruously pinned to the shoulders of his tailcoat.

No scarlet domino was to be seen. Joshua made his way through the crowd in the ballroom before striding across a room set out with trays of hors d'oeuvres, glancing into the game room where men were smoking cigars and watching a billiards game, and even walking into a room set aside for tattling dowagers.

Not a single guest wore a red cloak. Frustration pounded through Joshua's veins. He wanted to see her. He wanted to learn her name, pull her into his arms, and assure her that she needn't marry a repugnant man chosen by her father.

He couldn't stop imagining her eyes dark with worry instead of shining with desire. Her lips tight with anxiety rather than sweetly inviting. Her—Joshua became abruptly aware of a lady's lingering glance below his waist. With a muttered curse, he made for the edge of the room and leaned against a wall, staring into space as he willed his body to calm down.

Frederick had been right about his lady's distress: her follow-up missive had begged Joshua to meet with her, calling it "a matter of life and death."

Life and death, indeed. If her father married her to another man, Joshua would go off to the battlefield without giving a damn about his fate. Their brief meeting had changed something in his very essence.

He was literally starving for her touch.

His brother suddenly appeared at his shoulder. "Found her!"

Joshua jolted upright. "Where?"

Instead of telling him, Frederick started braying with laughter. Joshua reached out, caught him by the back of his collar, and gave him a hard shake.

"Watch that!" his brother barked, shoving him away. "I've poured the better part of a decanter of brandy into an empty stomach."

"Where is she?"

Frederick's mouth again curled into a wicked grin. He waved his hand at Joshua's waist. "I feel as if we're lads of fourteen again. You've put all the family jewels on display."

"Oh, for God's sake," Joshua snarled, adjusting his breeches. The conversation had already deflated him to half-mast.

"She just entered the ballroom," Frederick reported. "Wearing a scarlet domino and accompanied by Lady Regina rather than the cousin you described. I recognized her companion by the circlet of diamonds she dons at every opportunity."

Joshua wheeled about and headed for the ballroom.

"Regina, by the way, is the prettiest and most poisonous lady on the market," Frederick said, following him. "Can you believe that she informed my godmother that I was an inebriate whom she wouldn't consider marrying?"

"Yes," Joshua tossed over his shoulder.

"I was appalled. Not that she's wrong, but ladies aren't supposed to be so forthright."

"Why not?"

"No one but a termagant would say it aloud," Frederick grouched. "Wasn't your lady's presence here supposed to be a secret? If so, she should be careful. Regina is not only pugnacious, but a virulent gossip."

Joshua began making his way through the ballroom, heading toward the entrance on its far side. He didn't see a red domino, but the duke and duchess stood at the base of the steps, surrounded by a crowd.

Frederick trailed after him, still grumping about Lady Regina.

Just as they neared the throng of costumed guests, there was a commotion: a clamor of voices and the unmistakable sound of a body hitting the floor.

Damn it, some reprobate had touched her again.

He dove into the crowd, shoving past a Caesar and two Cinderellas before skidding to a halt just in time to avoid stepping on a woman lying on the floor.

The fallen woman wore one of those masquerade veils, along with a diamond coronet tipped over one eye. Lady Regina, presumably, though his lady was nowhere to be seen. Like a boat stuck on a sandbar, the lady seemed to be unable to regain her footing. The bolster under her gown held her thrashing legs in the air like an upturned turtle, stuck on its back in the sand. The group of party-goers who surrounded her stood stock still, watching her shriek at them with evident curiosity.

So much for *polite* society.

Stifling a sigh, Joshua leaned over and extended a hand. "Good evening. May I help you to your feet?"

Regina wrenched off her veil, and her diamond circlet skittered across the floor. She blinked up at him with huge blue eyes. "It's you," she breathed.

Which made no sense, but Joshua didn't give it a second thought. He needed to get her up so he could resume his search. He bent farther, slipped an arm around her slender back, and brought her to her feet.

"Oh, my goodness!" their hostess exclaimed, popping out of the crowd. "What on earth happened, Lady Regina?"

"Too much champagne," someone said audibly.

Her Grace frowned in the direction of that ill-mannered remark.

Joshua steadied the lady and stepped back.

"I tumbled to the ground while demonstrating a *chassé* to a bungling friend," Lady Regina explained, fluttering her eyelashes at him. "Our feet tangled." She glanced about. "Likely, mortification has sent her away in tears."

"I see," Joshua said, retreating another step.

"Lady Regina, may I introduce your rescuer, Major Joshua FitzRoy-Paget?" the Duchess of Trent asked.

The lady dropped into a deep curtsy; Joshua suppressed a sigh and bowed. "Good evening, Lady Regina."

"Good evening," she said, smiling at him. He noticed— disinterestedly—that she was exquisite, though her eyes were hard as blue marbles. Drunk or not, Frederick was invariably accurate in his assessments: Lady Regina was pretty *and* poisonous.

"Speaking of the *chassé* step," the duchess said, "we shall open the ball with a country dance. Major FitzRoy-Paget, if you would please accompany Lady Regina?"

She turned and waved at the orchestra, seated on a balcony.

Lady Regina beamed and stuck out a bony elbow; Joshua slipped a hand through it. The musicians fell silent, and guests drew back to the edges of the ballroom. The Duke of Trent joined his wife, and the four of them faced each other in a square in the center of the room.

When the music began again, he and the duke bowed to their partners. As he straightened, Joshua caught sight of Frederick, furiously waggling his eyebrows. He gave his brother a look, silently commanding him to find the lady in the red domino.

Frederick gave him a mad grin and turned away, so hopefully he understood.

For the next half-hour, Joshua and Lady Regina skipped and hopped their way through the country dance. All eyes were on them until another four dancers joined in, and then another. When the dance finally ended, the floor was filled with twirling, jumping aristocrats…and Joshua was irritated beyond belief.

He had a hard time mustering up a smile when Lady Regina curtsied at the music's close. Together with her avid eyes and oft-wiggling bottom—thanks to the pillow she had strapped under her dress—he was forcibly reminded of a bird engaging in a mating dance.

Surely he was wrong about her interest in him. After all, an ostentatious diamond glittered on her left hand.

"I owe you so much for rescuing me," Lady Regina cooed. "I shall award you the supper dance, Major FitzRoy-Paget, so that I can thank you at leisure."

Despite himself, he made a grouchy sound, but her smile only widened.

"I know masterful men such as you prefer to ask your partners, but I saw you looking at my betrothal ring." She leaned closer. "A daughter of a duke can change her mind even the day before the altar."

She slipped away before he could come up with an excuse.

That *was* a mating dance.

Damn it.

Chapter 25

A Ballroom can be a Battlefield

After watching Regina bounce on her bolstered bottom, Livie fled to the far side of the ballroom, grinning like a loon.

Regina was so *mean*. She deserved a tumble.

Once her back was to the wall, Livie began searching for Joshua's face amidst the crowd of veils, masks, and elaborate hats. She didn't think he'd be on the dancefloor; he seemed more like the Duke of Trent, a man who danced only when his wife commanded it. She was about to slip away to search other rooms when people began backing up, clearing the floor so that the duke and duchess could finally open the ball.

Strains of music began. The lady in front of her gasped and said loudly, "That is *not* her fiancé!" Whispers sprang up all around.

Livie rose on her toes to see what was happening—and then came down on her heels with a thud. Joshua was bowing before Regina! The two of them were opening the ball with the Duke and Duchess of Trent—an honor that was often the precursor to an announcement of betrothal.

Her mind reeled before she remembered the Earl of Winchester. Regina wouldn't marry Joshua rather than the turnippy earl. For one thing, the major was *not* biddable.

Livie rose back onto her toes. Joshua was going through the steps of the dance without a flaw, but with none of the flourishes that elegant gentlemen relished, most especially when being watched by all society. He showed no signs of being dazzled by Regina, either; his expression was pleasant, but unenthusiastic.

She was so fascinated by the spectacle that she didn't notice that someone was approaching her from behind until a deep, somewhat slurred voice spoke in her ear, "Not a fabulous dancer, is he?"

Livie came down on her heels again and turned around. A tall, rather disheveled man was leaning against the wall beside her, looking as if he needed the support to remain upright.

"What did you say?" she asked cautiously.

"I was commenting on the major's determined but graceless dancing."

"*I* think he's an excellent dancer," she said instantly.

"Oh, good, I was afraid you might be the wrong red domino," the man said. "I'm his brother, by the way."

Livie blinked at him. "Joshua's brother?"

"The same."

"You don't look alike!" she blurted out. He appeared to be far older than Joshua, his hair already streaked with white. Though when Livie looked closely, she made out Joshua's nose and chin albeit blurred, as if sculpted in soapstone rather than marble.

This had to be the heir to the earldom, the man whom Regina predicted would die unmarried.

"Likely because I've spent a good deal of the last decade pickling myself in brandy," he explained cheerfully.

"I see."

"And you're the lady whom Joshua commanded me to find," he continued.

Livie felt herself blushing. "I suppose I am."

"Going to tell me your name, or must you wait for a big revelation?"

His eyes twinkled at her in a kindly fashion, but she had to tell Joshua first, given her father's—and *his* father's—situation. She shook her head and whispered, "What is your name?"

"No need to keep your voice down. Everyone is so boggled at seeing my brother dance with that tigress that we could burst out singing and they wouldn't notice. Or would they?" His eyes lit, and he opened his mouth.

For a second, he looked exactly like Daisy.

"Don't you dare!" Livie gasped, poking him in the stomach. His middle was soft, even paunchy—not like his brother's.

He sighed theatrically. "I can see that you will be as dictatorial a family member as Joshua. He's my *younger* brother, in case you're wondering, and my name's Frederick FitzRoy-Paget. You don't seem to have memorized Debrett's, the way many eligible ladies here have done. He's a good catch. A future earl."

"You shouldn't say that," Livie said instinctively. "You might stop drinking brandy. Fall in love and get married. You don't *have* to only…only…married women," she faltered.

His smile widened. "I gather you've gathered your information not from Debrett's but from quite accurate gossip. I like you. Trust Joshua to have found a gem in this wasteland of glass stones. At any rate, darling, I have no intention of marrying, but you'll have to drag Joshua off the battlefield if you want to keep him safe."

Livie shook her head. "I would never do that. He's a soldier to the bone."

"He plans to return to war even though he's not fully recovered from the last injury—did he tell you about it?"

"He mentioned it," Livie said. She could feel herself blushing. "We haven't talked very much."

"You're well-bred, all right," Frederick muttered. "I'm guessing there's an army man in your family, and that your father is a baron or above."

She couldn't help smiling at him. "Neither."

"Then *his* father is or was a baron or above."

"True!"

"If not army, navy?"

She nodded.

"How on earth did Joshua find you?" Frederick mused, bracing his shoulder more firmly against the wall. "My brother told me about the Rothingale masquerade, and it sounded like a hurly-burly brothel, if you don't mind plain speaking."

Livie cleared her throat. The crowd around them had thinned as couples paired off and joined the dance. "The guest list was surprising."

"Ladybirds."

"Not just ladybirds," Livie said, grinning at him. "Birds of paradise, wagtails, and parrots. Your brother enriched my vocabulary in that respect."

"That's not his style, in case you're wondering," Frederick said. "Not that I've ever heard 'parrots' in that context. Not my style, either. I don't mind drinking myself to death, but I'll be damned if I'll die of the pox."

Livie nodded. "At least one is a choice rather than a malady."

"Oh, they're both maladies," Frederick said wryly. "Don't ever take up drinking—it's too hard to give up. You're rather unusual, aren't you? I'd think most young ladies would be prostrate with horror at this conversation."

Which reminded Livie of Regina squawking on the floor, so her smile widened. "Not me."

He cocked his head, and suddenly he really *did* resemble Joshua. "Were you responsible for that commotion up front? From what I heard, some woman fell on her arse."

"Why would you think I had anything to do with it?" Livie asked, knowing her eyes were dancing.

"I saw you enter with Lady Regina. I'd tumble her if given a chance," Frederick said feelingly. "And I'm definitely not referring to 'tumble' as a bedsport."

"She's unkind," Livie said. "As well as shamelessly ambitious with regard to marrying a nobleman."

"She won't get there by way of marriage to Joshua. He's as loyal as they come, and he has his sights fixed on you. Many a younger brother would have written me off as an intoxicated boozer, kicked me to the side—if not into the river—and started planning to take over the estate once our father is gone. Not Joshua."

"Of course not," Livie said indignantly. "That would be horrid. Murderous."

"Tries to get me to stop drinking, of course. But not in a loathsome way."

Livie bit her lip.

"You won't be able to talk me out of it, either," he continued, a note of apology in his voice. "I'm a four-bottle man, and there I shall stay. Before you inquire, brandy, not wine."

"Four bottles of brandy…*every* day?"

"It doesn't floor me."

"I suppose it's your choice," Livie said. "Is the world much better after a bottle or four?"

To her surprise, Frederick took that seriously. "Yes. It is."

"Well, then," Livie said. "I'm sorry, because your world must be dreadful when you're sober."

He gave her a crooked smile and moved away from the wall. "The dance will be ending soon, and I'd like to stow you away so that Lady Regina doesn't come after you with a pitchfork in hand."

Livie winced.

"She never forgets an insult. A few years ago, I was three sheets to the wind and told someone loudly that the only way Regina would be judged a 'diamond of the first water' was if she pasted one on the end of her nose."

"Very unkind," Livie said, trying to keep her face solemn.

"Naturally, she was informed." He swayed slightly and caught himself against the wall. "Since you're going to be my sister-in-law, I'll share the aftermath."

Livie's eyes rounded. "I haven't agreed—"

Frederick waved his hand, cutting her off. "Regina takes every opportunity to inform people that I'm a tippler, never mind the fact that *she* had once hunted me as if I was a stag who'd gobbled fermented berries. And here's the kicker."

"What?" Livie asked, when he fell silent.

"Forgot what I was saying," Frederick muttered. "Oh! You know how she decks herself out in diamonds?"

Livie nodded. "I have seen it."

"Unladylike," Frederick said. His eyes were full of wicked humor. "But pointed, wouldn't you say? I think she did her best to follow my guidance."

Livie snorted.

"How unladylike of *you*," Frederick chortled. "Now, let's stow you somewhere so I can swill a little more brandy, collect my brother, and bring the two of you together. It's rather Biblical, don't you think?"

"How so?" Livie asked.

"Obviously, I'm God, and you're Adam and Eve. No, Eve and Adam—well, you're just Eve—You get the idea, don't you? Of course, there's Mary and Joseph, but I beg you not to have any children out of wedlock. It gives people ideas, and before you know it, they're painting your portrait with a gold halo rather than a wedding ring."

"I won't," Livie promised.

"Come along. The duchess is a friend, so I know precisely where to put you," Frederick said.

"Where?" Livie asked, following him.

"Somewhere no one will find you except my brother. Are you afraid of the dark? I'd better give him your location before having more brandy, because what if I forgot? They'd find you years later, withered from lack of love, not to mention lack of food."

Livie sped up. "The dark does not bother me, but starvation does."

"I have a dramatic turn of phrase," Frederick told her. "Ignore me. My father and Joshua do. Well, Joshua doesn't, but he doesn't pay me any mind, either. I promise not to let you wither, how's that?"

"Excellent."

"Or marry that disgusting fellow your father has in mind. The prospective spouse *is* unlikable, isn't he?"

"My father's plans are not agreeable to me." Livie took Frederick's arm because he seemed incapable of turning his head to look at her while walking in a straight line.

"I expect he's betrothing you to a disgusting lout, a fate that befalls far too many women. Why do you think I have so many married lady friends? By the way, don't think the Duchess of Trent is one of them. She is tiresomely in love with her husband."

He stopped outside a door. "What is the prospective husband like? A white-haired, irresponsible, drunken, future earl?"

Livie couldn't help grinning at him. "That would be better."

"No, it wouldn't." Frederick pushed open the door. "'Come in,' said the spider to the fly."

Chapter 26

Wardrobes are not just for Narnia

After dancing with Regina, Joshua was dismayed to find that he was unable to continue searching for Lady Macbeth. The opening dance, together with the butler's announcement, had allowed most guests to not only identify him but also come to the conclusion that he would inherit his father's new title.

Young women kept popping up in front of him with glowing smiles, pretending they had met before. Only by muttering excuses about finding his next dance partner was he able to shake them off.

By the time he felt someone jerk his sleeve, his nerves were frayed from dodging debutantes. Before he could stop himself, he whipped about and caught the person's arm with all the mistrust of a spy under cover of darkness.

"Ouch!" his brother squealed, shaking his wrist as if it were sprained. "I use this hand to throw dice!"

"Did you find her?" Joshua demanded.

Frederick grinned at him. "I stowed your beloved away, so you'll need to rescue her before she expires from lack of air."

Joshua rolled his eyes, but his heart lifted. His brother led him out of the ballroom, through the wide entrance hall, and down the corridor that led to the back of the house.

Toward the end, Frederick stopped. "The duchess's sitting room—not the public one for receptions, but the one that Merry actually uses." He bowed low, gesturing to the door with a flourish. As Joshua stepped forward, Frederick straightened with a mad grin. "I have delivered my Adam to his Eve," he said, turning to walk back down the corridor with his hands in the air, "and thus, I'm off!"

Joshua opened the door and entered the room, which was small and messy.

To one side was a large, pale-blue wardrobe, the top worked with elegant scrolls in the French style. To the other, a table beside a lavish sofa held a stack of gardening books, although the sofa itself was piled so high with clothing that no reader could seat themselves. The single window had a velvet curtain on one side but not the other, so the candles burning on the mantelpiece reflected against the dark glass like far-off torches.

He frowned. Could she be hiding behind the sofa?

"Hello?" he called.

The door to the wardrobe swung open, and a slender hand beckoned.

Joshua, pushed the door closed behind him, walked across the room, and peered inside. The wardrobe was very deep, and empty but for a masked lady in a red domino and a masquerade hat, seated on the floor in a puddle of green velvet.

"Joshua?" she whispered.

He pulled the wardrobe doors wide-open, smiling down at her. "Indeed. What on earth are you doing?"

"Hiding, obviously." She patted the velvet. "Join me?"

Joshua crouched down just outside the wardrobe frame. "Hello, darling," he said. "Why are you hiding in the wardrobe?"

"I pretended to be Lady Regina's friend Petunia, so she is undoubtedly looking for me," she explained, a smile flickering at the edge of her generous mouth. "You ought to hide as well, given that she is considering marrying you."

"I can fight her off," he said wryly. "I'm trained in hand-to-hand combat." Joshua's heart was beating so fast that he could scarcely breathe, but even so, he could smell apple blossoms.

"Please join me?"

How was he ever going to control his body if one wide-eyed glance made him stiffen to the point of scandalizing onlookers? He cleared his throat again. "Might you remove your hat and veil, Lady Macbeth?"

She pulled off the hat, then untied her mask and put that to the side as well, lifting her chin and meeting his eyes.

Joshua had to swallow hard, seeing her face for the first time: the sum was so much greater than its parts. She had high cheekbones, hazel eyes fringed with dark lashes, and plump lips. It was a face he wanted to look at every day of his life. She was everything he ever wanted, with all the genuine sweetness that men on the battlefield dream about.

"Now come inside," she commanded.

If he joined her in the small space of that wardrobe, surrounded by her scent and her smile and the glow in her eyes, he might lose control: ease her backward onto velvet and ravish her. He stayed where he was. "I would very much like to learn your name, if I might."

"Livie," she answered. "Actually, Olive, but I prefer the diminutive."

"Livie suits you," he murmured, his voice husky. Against all his better—gentlemanly—instincts, Joshua leaned over the wardrobe's threshold and dusted his lips across hers, drawing back before the kiss deepened.

Her gaze went to his mouth; then she bit her plump bottom lip. The air between them ached with unspoken words.

Unspoken desire.

"Frederick says that the lock on the sitting room door is broken, so you must join me," she said, color rising in her cheeks. "Someone might enter at any moment."

Joshua registered that his brother seemed to know far too many details about the duchess's establishment; no wonder the duke had scowled. He pushed the thought away. His lady wanted him to climb into a wardrobe, so that was what he would do.

He straightened and stripped off his dress coat, throwing it on top of the pile of clothing on the sofa before he entered the wardrobe and sat against the wall opposite Livie.

"I'd be happy to offer you a softer seat," he said, holding out his arms.

Without hesitation, Livie moved forward.

"May I kiss you?" Joshua asked, his arms curving around her instinctively as her delicious weight settled into his lap.

"We ought to talk first." Her voice had just a trace of shyness.

He went directly to the only topic that interested him. "Are you going to marry me?"

When she blinked at him, her mouth forming a perfect *O*, he decided to kiss her again rather than wait for an answer. His lips lingered until hers opened.

Instantly the kiss turned hot, deep, and hungry. Joshua forgot that he was seated, somewhat uncomfortably, inside a wardrobe. His world narrowed to a honeyed parade of moments, interrupted only by his and Livie's occasional gasps for air before coming back together.

To his delight, she began experimenting, sucking in his bottom lip and giving it a little nip. Chuckling when he nipped her back. Blushing when a guttural sound came from his throat. Running her hands over his shoulders and then down his chest. Watching him from under her eyelashes.

Their kisses grew still deeper, almost frantic, until Livie pulled away again and sucked in a breath. Joshua waited, loving the dazed look in her eyes and her swollen, cherry-red lips. His fingers curled tightly around her hips, because he wouldn't allow himself to caress the soft breasts pressed against his chest.

Her hands ran through his hair before she came back to his mouth with new urgency, her tongue lapping his. They kissed until blood pounded through Joshua's body, and he could feel his control slipping. One of his hands slid down and wrapped around a plush thigh. With the other hand, he pulled the closest wardrobe door shut, casting her face into twilight.

"You're marrying me," he said hoarsely.

"I can't…Was that a proposal?" Livie's voice cracked as her eyes searched his face.

"Yes." He crushed his lips to hers, emerging from a scorching kiss to say, "My second proposal, because my first was within an hour of meeting you."

"You and I have different definitions of a request. Both of yours were commands."

"I can do better," he promised. "I could never have imagined going to my knees in a wardrobe, but I will if you wish."

She pulled him closer, licking his bottom lip before her tongue delved deep. A while later, she broke away and said with a gasp, "We haven't spoken yet. You may not wish to marry me after you learn more about me."

He growled, low and deep, into her mouth. "I don't kiss ladies in wardrobes. Or anywhere else. Of course I will want to marry you."

Her smile wobbled. "I still have to tell you the truth."

Joshua frowned, and then relaxed. "I already know."

Livie's brows knit. "You *do*?"

"My brother guessed."

"Your brother? He didn't say anything to me."

"He interpreted your first letter." Joshua let his lips drift along the line of her jaw. He felt ravenous. He wanted to push her backward in the pile of velvet, pull up her skirts, and kiss his way up her leg. The idea was dizzying. He could pleasure her until she didn't have a word in her head except his name.

His name and "Yes." *Yes, I'll marry you. Yes, I'll lie down in a velvet bed. Yes, I'll let you devour me. Yes, I'll let you keep me forever, and yes, I'll do the same for you.*

"Frederick interpreted my letter?" Livie sounded even more confused.

"He knows women."

"So everyone says." Her words had a sardonic edge, so presumably she had learned of Frederick's reputation.

"He'll quit drinking when he's ready," Joshua told her, meeting her eyes. "I'm not going to be an earl. My brother *will* stop drinking and marry—when he's ready. Just so you know."

"I don't care." Even in the dim light from the one open wardrobe door, he could see sincerity in her eyes.

"Of course, he may be gutted by an angry husband," Joshua added. "The Duke of Trent, for one."

"I know His Grace quite well. He growls, but his wife adores him and he knows it."

"You know the duke and duchess," Joshua said slowly. "Who are you, Livie?"

Chapter 27

Joshua's question echoed in Livie's head.

Who are you?

She was terrified to tell him the truth. "First, tell me what Frederick deciphered from my letter."

"That your father plans to marry you to a repulsive fellow," Joshua replied. Before she could reply, he added, "I'm sure that you wouldn't marry me just to escape an unwanted suitor, Livie, but if your father is going to marry you off before the next Season, I did need to know. I can make it clear to your father that you wish to wait for me—or I can take out the man your father has in mind."

His voice was rough and hard, which was incredibly...*erotic.*

A word that Livie had learned from that advice book for ladybirds she and Daisy read. "Erotic" referred to something that "arouses sexual desire." Obviously, it wasn't a word—or an action— that proper ladies were supposed to understand.

"The man in question is not a suitor," she told him. "I suppose he thinks he's a suitor, but he's my father's...my father's associate."

"He cannot have you," Joshua stated. "You're mine."

Livie's stomach clenched. Fear was sparking throughout her body. Joshua knew she was friendly with a duchess. He *didn't* know that she was the daughter of an accused traitor…that his own father…

The truth was terrifying.

Every lineament of his face proclaimed his honest and true nature. Without asking, she knew he would be repulsed by the idea of treachery.

Swallowing hard, she buried her face against his shoulder. "I will understand if you don't want me after learning the truth." Her voice was muffled by the thick fabric of his dress uniform.

After a momentary silence, he said, "I don't give a damn if you're not a virgin, but if, God forbid, someone forced you, I will *destroy* him."

Livie's head popped away from his chest. "Nothing like that!"

"Good." Joshua's smile was patently relieved. He brushed a kiss on her lips. "Nothing else matters."

Her heart swelled. "If that *had* been the case, I would have been so happy with what you said."

His brow drew together, confused.

"What you said was *so...*" She ran out of words. The only one that came to mind was that vocabulary word forbidden to ladies: erotic. His fierce defense of her was erotic.

"So...what?" Joshua asked. He leaned in, nipping her earlobe.

"*Erotic*," Livie breathed, turning her head enough so their lips met. "Not that I should say that word, or know that word, or—"

She stopped talking because he slipped his tongue between her lips and stole her fumbled explanation.

Ten minutes later, only a crack of light shone through the nearly closed wardrobe doors. Livie was on her back, her shoulders cradled in velvet. One of her legs was bent at the knee, and Joshua had a heavy leg thrown over the other.

"I refuse to take you in a wardrobe," he muttered. His eyes glinted at Livie in the half-light.

"I love this wardrobe," Livie whispered. She couldn't help rocking against the weight and the friction of his thigh.

A grin curled the edge of his lips. "I'll buy the wardrobe from the duke." He kissed her nose. "We can put it in a bedchamber or a sitting room. Even so, I won't make love to you in it." He kissed her jaw. "A wardrobe is not erotic."

"I shouldn't know that word," Livie said, wrinkling her nose.

"I didn't really understand what it meant until tonight. *Erotic*," he said, kissing her eyelashes. "*Erotic*," nipping her bottom lip. "*Erotic*," pressing his hips against her leg, the one he had pinned down. He watched her dazed face carefully. "*Erotic*," he whispered again, running his left hand up her leg, under her gown, biting back a groan.

Livie's mouth eased open into a little pant, her pulse beating frantically in her throat. He eased his fingers higher over the inner curve of her leg. "May I touch you?"

"*There?*"

Joshua nodded.

She gulped. "I suppose."

Joshua slipped his hand beneath the lace trim of Livie's fashionable drawers, his fingertips grazing the soft skin of her hip.

And then, when she bit her lip but didn't protest, he skimmed his fingers over delicate hair.

"This is so improper." Her eyes were glossy, *needy*.

"I love being improper with you." He dipped his fingers into her sleek, wet flesh, giving her a torturously slow caress. And another.

One of her hands curled tightly around his wrist. "Joshua, this is *wrong*."

But Joshua could see and feel pleasure building in her body. "No, it's not," he growled in her ear, as one thick finger eased into her tight warmth.

Livie squeaked and then arched toward him, melting into his touch, spinning out of control a moment later. Her whole body clenched around him, her eyes closing in bliss, her plump lips opening in a scream that he only just managed to stifle with a kiss.

When he eased his fingers away, she was chanting under her breath, "Oh, goodness, oh, goodness." Then she pulled him close, pasting her mouth to his clumsily but with great enthusiasm. "I'm so…but that was wrong."

"Because we're not married?"

"It's just *not done*. I'm certain of it."

"I'm sure of the opposite."

"Perhaps only in a secret place like this, where you're just Joshua and I'm just Livie," she offered. "A secret place doesn't count."

"In that case, I am definitely buying this wardrobe," he said, licking his finger. "Essence of Livie."

Her mouth fell open again.

"Essence of *my wife*." He licked his finger again, eyes still on Livie's face. "I'll buy this wardrobe, cut off the top, and make it into a bed." His blood was boiling. He longed to wrench off his pantaloons, thrust inside, fill her up.

Yet he'd been taught the order of things:

Marry a lady.

Then bed that lady.

Still, he let his hand stroke her thigh again.

This wasn't bedding; it was *wardrobing*.

It didn't count.

Chapter 28

In Which Everything Changes

Livie came back to herself slowly, as if waking from a dream.

She knew why "erotic" was a word that ladies were supposed to avoid.

Joshua had seen her at a moment when she had no defenses, blind and deaf to everything except bodily pleasure. Now she felt vulnerable and exposed, as if she had slid down a steep slope and could no longer see the top.

"We must talk," she said, sitting up, easing away and pulling down her skirts. She felt sweaty and limp. Her drawers were twisted around one hip, but she was too embarrassed to adjust them.

She scooted backward until her back was against the opposite wall of the wardrobe.

Joshua sat up as well, watching with a wry smile as she tucked her legs to the side and rearranged her skirts to cover her ankles. "Yes, let's talk about that suitor of yours. Specifically, whether I need to run a sword through him."

"Oh goodness," Livie exclaimed. "Of course not. Mr. Cassio is objectionable, but—"

"*Cassio?*" Joshua snorted. "He sounds like a lustful Lothario, one of those sleek Italian fellows who offer dance lessons."

Livie managed a crooked smile. "Cassio is not sleek, and he's English. But I don't wish to talk about him." She cleared her throat. "My last name is Tyron."

"Livie Tyron. Olive Tyron." Joshua's eyes glinted in the half-light. "I prefer Livie FitzRoy."

"You don't…you don't recognize my name?"

"No," he said, shaking his head. "I know nothing of scandals in polite society. What happened?"

"The scandal concerns my father." She stopped speaking, unable to find the right words.

"Is he alive?" Joshua asked.

She nodded.

"I gather he is famous?"

"Infamous rather than famous," Livie said. She cleared her throat. "My father is imprisoned in the Tower of London." The silence in the wardrobe was deafening. She reached out and pushed open one of the doors, letting in more light so she could see Joshua's expression clearly.

"Why was Mr. Tyron arrested?"

"An act of treason that he *didn't* commit. He's Captain Sir Tyron, commander of the *Royal Oak*."

Joshua nodded, accepting her firm avowal. She could see him turning over the situation in his head. He was the type of man who liked to solve things, rather like Lord Devin. "Is your family able to afford a solicitor?"

"Yes. My aunt is—Yes." She took a deep breath. "The case is being handled in the House of Lords." She hesitated and then blurted it out. "Your father is the presiding judge."

Joshua flinched, then paled, his cheekbones suddenly standing out from his face.

His expression fixed into…into no expression.

"My father is presiding," he said slowly, as if tasting the words.

She nodded. "Lord Devin informed us that Lord Paget is the Lord High Steward, presiding over the case. My father didn't do it, Joshua!"

Another silence. "You are very loyal," he said slowly.

"Yes." She had an instinctive, terrible feeling that everything was going wrong.

His brows drew together, and she saw his Adam's apple bobble as he swallowed. "I appreciate your concern for your father."

Livie's stomach clenched as tightly as his eyebrows; a "but" was clearly following. Her heartbeat thundered in her ears as she waited for him to speak.

"But you went too far."

She blinked. "How so?"

Joshua's eyes softened. "I do understand, Livie. I truly do. I would ferociously protect Frederick or my father. But this isn't...this isn't right. This country was built on justice."

She straightened. "No, that's not—"

"I do believe that your father is not a traitor."

"He is *not*."

"But as a man of honor, he would never wish to be exonerated in *this* way."

The sentence hit Livie like a kick in the gut. That, and the look in Joshua's eyes: the chiding look. The "you haven't been good" look. The look she knew down to her bones, because it was *exactly* the way her father always looked at her, no matter how docile and obedient she tried to be.

"Exactly what do you mean?" she asked, keeping her voice even.

He hesitated. "Obviously, you felt I could help by influencing my father's opinion. So."

Livie gaped at him before rage cracked open the armor she had grown to weather to her father's disdain. "You are suggesting I deliberately *targeted* you? May I remind you that you found me at the masquerade rather than the other way around!"

His eyes kindled. "You hunted me down at this ball, you drew your bow, and today you certainly hit the mark."

The images of their recent debauchery flooded Livie's mind, as the implications of his reproach became clear. "You think that I let you do that to me to persuade you to help my father?" Her voice cracked. "Some sort of payment in which I humiliate myself in order to entangle you?"

Joshua frowned at her. "No! You were not humiliated."

Just like a man: he thought he could tell her exactly how she felt. Livie stared at his strong jaw, the arch of his brow, his hair ruffled by her hands, that perfect nose. She was fairly certain he was furious, but not a bit of emotion showed on his face.

Her chest felt so tight that she found herself rubbing her breastbone. His eyes flickered to her fingers.

"You don't need to do that," he bit out, showing anger for the first time.

"Do what?" she gasped.

"Draw my attention to your charms. I will marry you, Livie, but you cannot expect me to help you with your father's case. I will not dishonor myself, or your father, for that matter."

"Oh, my God." Livie shoved open the closed wardrobe door and scrambled out. She shook out her skirts, grabbed her crumpled domino, and pulled it tightly around her. "I didn't—how could you think that of me?"

He followed, uncurling his tall body. "I think you are a deeply loyal woman who loves her father, and is desperately worried for him."

It wasn't untrue. She had recently begun to feel more loyal to Joshua than to her father, but she pushed away that thought.

"Think of your father," Joshua continued, the lines around his mouth seeming deeper than they had been an hour ago. "How would he feel if he knew that you'd met me here, for this reason?"

"He'd think I was a trollop," Livie said flatly. "But he already believes that, as must you, since I gather you imagine I attended the Rothingale masquerade planning to seduce the first lord I saw. Or was it that I knew of Lord Paget's role and deliberately searched for you? That would, of course, have been the most advantageous, but also implies the mysterious ability to recognize you at sight, not to mention predict that you could be found there."

"I have no idea why you attended that particular event," Joshua stated. His smoky brown eyes had darkened.

Clearly, he thought she'd gone there trolling for assistance from any man with a seat in the House of Lords.

Livie's cheeks burned with anger. "You know nothing of me, nothing of my father," she spat. "You call yourself a gentleman, but your imagination is—*disgusting*." She held up her hand when he opened his mouth. "Obviously, I knew nothing of you either, but I know more now."

"Then know this. I am not a man who would ever interfere with a fair and honest trial. My father raised me to be an honorable man."

"I would prefer that *my* father not believe that his daughter is a seductress," Livie said with scathing emphasis. "So I would be grateful if you did not inform your father of our brief acquaintance."

"*You* learned who I was, and *you* wrote to me. I fail to see why you take umbrage at the truth." He turned and picked up his dress coat.

Joshua was right.

Livie was abruptly flattened by that truth.

How could she confess that she thought he'd fallen in love with her? That her problems would become his problems?

What an idiot she had been.

She watched him shrug on his crimson coat, the epaulets of his rank swishing as they settled on his broad shoulders.

His honor came first, of course. Had she learned nothing as her father's daughter? How could Joshua have helped her father, anyway? She hadn't thought beyond a plea for support.

That was her first mistake. Why did she ever write to him? She knew that ladies could not write to gentlemen without being branded loose or worse. To be honest, she *was* loose, because no lady worth the name would crawl into a man's arms in a wardrobe and let him do...*that*.

Naturally, he had instantly jumped to the worst conclusion. She was a trollop, and it seemed that was a short step to prostitute, albeit with a payment that had nothing to do with money.

"I thought you might be able to help," Livie said. "I didn't think through the implications of my request. I apologize for my misperception." She fought to keep her voice from wavering. "You'll be happy to know that I am hereby refusing your proposal of marriage."

Joshua made an abrupt movement; she fell back a step.

"I made an error. I acknowledge my own foolishness." She nodded toward the door. "Won't you please leave first?"

"Next Season—" he began.

"Absolutely not," she cut in.

"Once your father—"

She cut him off again. "I have received a letter a day during most of my life from a man who thinks my every instinct is wanton at best and debauched at worst. I will *never* put myself in a situation where I marry a man who thinks me dishonorable."

"I don't!" He growled it.

She snorted. "Yes, you do. It was one thing when I played the hussy as your future wife, but when I was also asking for help? I fell from hussy to slut in one fell swoop. So, no, Major FitzRoy, I would prefer never to see or speak to you again, in this Season or the next. Now, *leave*."

When she met him, she thought he had molten brown eyes, the kindest, most passionate, most desiring, most *admiring* eyes she'd ever seen.

Now they were flat and ice-cold.

He bowed. "Miss Tyron."

The door closed behind him.

Chapter 29

After a few sustaining gulps of brandy, Frederick returned to the corridor and propped himself up next to the duchess's sitting room; if an amorous couple came looking for privacy, he would warn them off.

His location conveniently allowed him to avoid ladies who wished to dance, whether in the ballroom or the bedroom. He'd passed the point of being able to negotiate a quadrille at least an hour ago, and he wasn't interested in setting up a new mistress. He was hazily staring into space when a lady in a scarlet domino emerged from the ladies' retiring room next door.

She had to be Joshua's lady's cousin, the second lady in red.

When she neared him, he slid out a leg to block her way, risking tumbling on his arse.

"Sir?" The cousin drew herself up like an indignant hen about to fluff her feathers and squawk up a storm. Up close, she was small but luscious—a peach of a girl. That silly masquerade veil didn't hide her deep lower lip.

"I'm Major FitzRoy's brother," he said, without bothering to fuss about introductions.

"Oh." She scowled at him. "Where is Major FitzRoy?"

Frederick jerked his head toward the door to his left. "In there."

She started forward, so he caught her arm. "You *are* an innocent, aren't you? Never barge in on newlyweds."

His insouciant question ought to have sparked outrage; instead her eyes sparked with irritation. "They aren't married!"

"Close enough. Tell me your name and the details of your cousin's horrible suitor."

She squinted at him. "You're the major's brother?"

"The same."

"You reek of brandy."

"True," he agreed. "It's my preferred scent." He gave a loud sniff. "You smell of…something flowery."

"Orange blossoms," she said, giving in. "I suppose I'll wait here for Livie. You're certain she's inside that room?"

"I brought her there myself. *Livie*?" he said musingly. "Suits her. And you?"

"Daisy."

"Disturbingly akin to names for a pair of fluffy kittens." He slid away when she swatted him. "We might expire from boredom guarding this door while yon lovebirds coo at each other, so you'd better tell me everything."

Three minutes later he straightened and barked, "*What*?"

"You nearly fell over! You're intoxicated, aren't you?"

"Not quite. On the threshold of Bacchus, not in his very bedchamber."

"Bacchus?"

He sighed. "Listen, *very* young woman, someday you'll understand me, but I'm too old to play schoolmaster. We have a problem. My brother will be deeply offended when your cousin asks him for help."

"Why?"

"I don't answer foolish questions. Take it as a given. He's a man of honor."

"He's in love with Livie!" she protested. "His letter was daft, but Livie is never wrong about people, and she said he loves her."

"'*Daft?*'" he repeated.

"Like gilded mirrors," she said impatiently. "Better without all the false gold."

"I don't—"

The door opened before Frederick could set the girl straight about elegant correspondence. His brother strode into the corridor, pushing the door closed behind him.

"Hi! You!" Frederick called, but Joshua glanced at him, turned without a word, and walked off down the corridor.

Yup. That hadn't gone well.

"In a temper. What did I tell you?" Frederick said, slumping back against the wall.

"Distinctly unfriendly," Daisy agreed. "Are you certain Livie was with him?"

"I expect she's in a storm of tears. Believed herself in love, you said?"

Daisy nodded.

"She's better off without him," Frederick said bluntly. "He'll go to war again, after all. The problem is that *he's* not better off without *her*. He'll make his way to a battlefield and jump in front of a cannon. Shit."

"You're not supposed to curse in front of me," Daisy observed.

Frederick spared her a glance. "Save your missishness for someone else. Your face speaks for itself. I'd guess you have a bigger vocabulary of expletives than I do."

Daisy gave him a disarming grin. "Perhaps. So, if Major FitzRoy won't help with my uncle's case…what about you?"

"Me?"

"You are Lord Paget's son as well, aren't you?" She caught his arm and pulled him away from the wall. "Your little brother may be a swine, but you can make up for it. You can't tell me that your 'honor' matters, because from what I've heard, you don't have any."

"Bloody hell," Frederick muttered as Daisy yanked open the sitting room door.

She grinned at him over her shoulder. "That's one of my favorite curses."

Livie was not crying.

She was too furious to cry.

When Daisy walked in, Joshua's brother in tow, Livie didn't even blink, just informed them both, "Major FitzRoy is a nonentity whom I never met." Her voice allowed no disagreement.

Daisy raised her eyebrows, but Frederick grinned. "Understandable. There's been many a time I've wished that I had never met my relatives. If we're going to get specific, I would prefer that my parents had never met."

"I want to go home," Livie said stonily.

"Frederick is going to help us with your father's case," Daisy said.

Looking at Joshua's brother, Livie thought he was even more unsteady than he had been earlier in the evening. His eyes were red-rimmed, his neck cloth crumpled, and the air around him so thick with brandied fumes that it could have been set aflame.

"I will try, but my father is as stiff-rumped as my brother," he said. "God knows the earl wouldn't take account of my opinion if I offered it. Before you ask, Lord Paget wouldn't take a bribe either, even accompanied by a heap of coins. So, what can I possibly do to help?"

"We don't have any extra money," Daisy said, picking up an armful of clothing from the couch and dropping it on the floor, followed by another.

"The duchess might be a trifle peeved by that," Frederick remarked.

"Her Grace shouldn't leave piles of clothing on the only seating in the room!"

"She didn't. I did," Frederick said, shambling over and dropping onto the now-empty sofa. "I had to clear out the wardrobe so the lovebirds could hide from evil Regina."

"Regina!" Daisy exclaimed, sitting down. "What does she have to do with it? Oh, never mind. Livie, come over here!"

Livie walked over slowly. She was trying to hang on to the coal of rage in her heart. She'd put so much faith in Joshua, and the pounding beat of "*stupid*" in her head only compounded the blend of sorrow and shame she felt at the thought of his chilly disapproval.

"I appreciate your willingness to help," she told Frederick. "Your brother was less gracious."

"Got on his high horse, I expect," he said, nodding. "Joshua's chockful of honor. It's like a sludge in the blood that he inherited from my father. Needless to say, the trait skipped me."

"I didn't expect him to bribe your father," Livie said. "I just thought…" Her voice trailed off.

"You wanted him to listen and to *try* to help," Frederick said, his voice softening, one side of his mouth crooking up. "Believe me, I understand. So tell me."

Livie sank down between them and blurted out the whole. "Mr. Cassio is an obvious suspect," she finished.

"Whether he is or not, better for you to see him thrown in the Tower than waiting at the altar," Frederick remarked. "We need proof." He slid down until his head was supported by the back of the sofa, legs stretched out before him.

"I have no proof," Livie said unhappily.

"What about your father's letters?" Daisy asked. "Perhaps there's a clue in the captain's reports. We can take his correspondence out of the trunk, arrange it by date, and scan each one!"

"Excellent idea," Frederick said sleepily. "The clue is in the library."

"Not the library, the letters!" Daisy said.

His only response was a faint snore.

Daisy jumped up. "Come on, Livie. Time to go home and start reading."

Livie looked up at her. Despite herself, her eyes filled with tears.

"Oh, honey," Daisy sighed, sitting down again and giving her a hug.

"He kissed me as if he loved me," Livie explained, her voice wobbling. "I believed it, which was idiotic. No one falls in love at first sight."

"No one except people with big hearts, like you and Romeo," Daisy said, rocking her back and forth. "I am in awe of you, Livie. You still love your father, when—to be blunt—so many other women would have run away from home rather than read another of his windy reprimands."

"He means well," Livie said, blotting her eyes with the corner of her cloak.

Daisy's expression suggested she didn't agree. She got up again. "Where's your mask?"

Livie pointed at the wardrobe. "Joshua didn't even *like* me, let alone love me. Why did he consider marrying me? Why was I so stupid as to think it a good idea to marry a stranger?"

"He was very, very pretty," Daisy pointed out. "I suppose he thought the same of you."

"I feel so ashamed," Livie admitted. "I asked him for help thinking that…thinking that he would somehow magically *solve* the problem. I thought he was a problem-solver."

Daisy fished Livie's mask from the depths of the wardrobe. "Male honor," she said, sighing. "It's all so relative, isn't it?"

"What do you mean?"

"Lord Devin would claim to have honor, wouldn't he? But he went to the Rothingale masquerade to buy a woman with a coin or two."

"Joshua was there too," Livie said, scowling. "He *said* he didn't mean to be there."

"Lying, no doubt," Daisy said.

"Just now he looked at me precisely the way my father does."

"That's the flip side of this honor business," Daisy said. "A woman can't look sideways at a man without being labeled a strumpet. She can't ask a man for help without being accused of using her womanly wiles to seduce him into dishonoring himself—when he'd already have been dishonored, if the standard applied equally to both sexes!"

Livie looked around for her masquerade hat and plopped it on her head, twitching the veil. "Let's go home."

"Hopefully without encountering Regina… Just what did you do to her?"

"I behaved in a very unladylike fashion," Livie confessed, thinking that the statement applied to her entire evening.

"Tell me everything!"

Chapter 30

Joshua didn't sleep the whole night. Staring into the dark, he registered the hours bellowed by the night watchman; he listened as the night soil cart rumbled around to the back of the townhouse; he heard the milkman deposit clinking bottles at the kitchen door.

How had Livie imagined that he would respond to her request?

Livie. The name was still sweet to his tongue, like a dream he longed to fall into again—the dream of finding a woman who would make the dangers of war worth facing.

Until he remembered that she wanted him to obstruct the due process of law. To interfere with his father's judicial duties.

That dream veiled the biggest betrayal of his life.

He had grieved when his older brother shaped a life punctuated by brandy bottles and sardonic remarks. He had wrestled with scorn when his father embraced his new nobility and abruptly transformed into the lordliest of lords.

This felt worse.

Joshua knew his place in the world, and no title—or woman—could change it.

For good or ill, he was a warrior. The wound he suffered fighting against Napoleon's army was a badge of honor. He would never pervert the course of justice, not even by asking his father to show mercy.

Even so, his heart grieved for what could have been.

When his valet entered, thinking to draw open the curtains and wake him, Joshua was already standing at the window, staring out at a gray, rainy London. Once he descended the stairs, Oates-Plagitt welcomed him to the breakfast room with a bow.

His father was seated at the head of the table reading a precisely ironed newspaper, a footman hovering at his shoulder waiting to turn and refold the page so that the earl's fingers wouldn't be soiled by ink.

"Lord Paget," Joshua said, bowing before he seated himself. "Good morning."

His father nodded. "Good morning, son."

They sat silently until Lord Paget finished reading and waved away the newspaper.

"I learned last night of a case put before you in the House of Lords," Joshua said, unable to stop himself.

"I have two on the docket," his father said importantly.

"This one pertains to a sea captain by the name of Tyron."

"Ah, Captain Sir Tyron." His father grimaced. "An unpleasant incident involving a treasonous attempt to take His Majesty's life. Failed, of course. A group of feckless French insurgents thought they had a captain in His Majesty's Navy at their back."

"And was he?"

"The evidence has not yet been presented, but I gather it is substantial. However, Lord Devin has indicated there's another suspect. Tyron's first mate, a man by the name of Cassio. I remember the name due to the Shakespearean character."

Joshua froze.

Cassio...Livie's admirer. The mere thought of her with another man sent a jolt down his spine. But he had given her up; he could hardly—

Abruptly, his mind cleared. This wasn't the moment to consider Livie's future. Cassio was suspected of treason. Surely Lord Devin wouldn't name the fellow unless he had strong suspicions.

"How is Lord Devin involved?" he asked.

"He's leading the defense," the earl said. He raised an eyebrow. "Your questions are pointed."

Joshua shrugged. "One tries to take an interest when a case is discussed in the ballroom."

"I expect there is a great deal of gossip about the matter," his father conceded, picking up a piece of wafer-thin toast. "Captain Sir Tyron's sister, a noblewoman and leader in society, is agitating for his release. I gather she is currently in the country, petitioning the Duke of Lennox's aid, though it's an effort undertaken in vain. I need hardly state that not even a duke could influence my judgment."

"But Lord Devin feels the culprit might be this Cassio?" Joshua asked.

"Without proof. I sympathize with Lord Devin's wish to clear Captain Sir Tyron's name, but justice is particularly important in cases involving the nobility. We owe it to ourselves to maintain an example for those lower in standing."

He raised a white hand. "Oates-Plagitt, I will have that bitter infusion now." He turned to Joshua. "Orange peel, lemon, and gentian root. The Duke of Marlborough drinks it every morning without fail. Oates-Plagitt, give my son a cup as well."

"No, thank you," Joshua said.

"It's excellent for plethoric inflammations, and you are still healing. I was pleased to learn that you are no longer pressing to return to the battlefield."

Oates-Plagitt placed a steaming cup before the earl. *"Infusum Amarum Simplex."*

Behind the earl's back, the butler poured a cup of breakfast tea and placed it before Joshua's place.

Livie had defended her father fiercely—as would any child—but what if her fervor was owed not to blood, but to her deep understanding of the captain's character?

What if she was telling the truth? What if the captain was sent to the gallows for a crime committed by his first mate? Joshua had been so blinded by the thought that Livie wanted him to forsake his honor that he hadn't stopped to consider that she may be right.

But did that make a difference? She had asked him to intervene, and whether *her* father was blameless or not, it would still be dishonest to try to influence *his* father. Joshua couldn't ask the Lord High Steward to overlook the possibility of a man's guilt, even if that man had the potential to be his son's father-in-law.

Livie relied on instinct when deciding her father's innocence, but the court would require a compelling argument to reverse the charges.

It seemed that Lord Devin suspected Cassio but had no evidence. Perhaps Joshua could help gather evidence of Cassio's treachery. He pushed away the uncomfortable fact that he'd be happy to skewer the man, guilty or not.

"Our excellent Oates-Plagitt asked His Grace's butler for this recipe," Joshua's father commented, though he couldn't suppress a tiny shudder as he sipped. "Surely the recipe called for honey?"

Their butler stepped forward, honey spindle at the ready. "A glaring omission, but one easily amended." He stirred a generous amount of honey into the bitter drink.

Joshua watched silently as his father forced himself to swallow the loathsome brew.

No appeal he could make would ever sway his father's judgment—not without evidence. Lord Paget was punctilious in that respect; he would be influenced only by sound logic and documented facts.

Joshua would never hinder a fair trial—his honor wouldn't allow it—but that same integrity wouldn't let him sit by idly while the pursuit of true justice failed.

Which meant that he had work to do.

He waited until his father left the breakfast room before he said, "Oates-Plagitt, if you would please join me in the library."

The butler had barely closed the library door before he said, "Your lady's father, I gather?"

Joshua nodded. He'd learned years ago that there was no point in keeping secrets from Oates-Plagitt. The man ran the household—and the family. Joshua was fairly certain that their butler had somehow arranged for his father's new title.

"A tricky proposition," Oates-Plagitt said after Joshua explained. "Several methods of quickly clearing Captain Sir Tyron's name come to mind, but most are a touch illegal."

Joshua shook his head.

"Right. We'll need to locate Cassio. The boot boy is quick and clever, so I'll send him to the Tower to learn what he can."

The butler's brows drew together as he glanced at Joshua's hand, clenched as if he had wrapped it around Cassio's throat. "*Not* a good idea," Oates-Plagitt remarked. "Your direct interference would be prejudicial to the defense."

"It's not interfering to persuade a suspect to tell the truth."

"Killing a suspect is generally interpreted as meddling. You'd better leave it to me."

* * *

Livie couldn't remember ever feeling this tired or this sad. The night before, after she and Daisy returned home from the masquerade, they had pulled every letter out of her trunk and organized them by date.

Merely looking at the tall piles made her feel sadder than she had already felt: she was surrounded by men waiting for her to prove herself unworthy by one mistake or another.

At breakfast, Daisy seated herself opposite Livie, eyes shining, certain that they would find evidence to clear Captain Sir Tyron.

Livie was not hopeful. After all, she'd been reading her father's missives for years. They were all the same: dispiritingly moralistic and accusatory. Even back when the captain's ship was directly engaged in the war against Napoleon, he had scarcely mentioned it.

She was listlessly eating a piece of toast and marmalade when the door opened, and Frederick walked in.

"I told your excellent butler that I would announce myself," he said. "Lord FitzRoy-Paget, future earl," he said over his shoulder to their affronted butler.

"Good morning," Livie said, summoning up a smile.

"I never drink tea," Frederick remarked, waving away a footman.

"Why did you come to breakfast, if not for a cup of tea?" Daisy asked.

"Letters," Frederick said promptly. "I have an enduring interest in 'em. The letters we write today will be the museum exhibits of tomorrow. It's one of the reasons I nurture a flowery style, the better to flummox the future."

"I knew someone other than Major FitzRoy wrote that absurd letter!" Daisy exclaimed.

"It was *not* absurd, but an excellent example of a nineteenth century aristocratic missive," Frederick retorted. "Are you both ready to begin reading?"

"This is a losing proposition," Livie said as she rose from the table.

"We brought all the letters to the library," Daisy said, ignoring Livie's pessimism.

"Excellent choice," Frederick said. "Libraries usually house brandy decanters, and I haven't had breakfast yet."

"I, for one, am glad you're joining us," Daisy said to Frederick, as they walked out of the room. "Captain Sir Tyron's writing style is frightfully grim. Now that Livie is disappointed in love, rereading them might send her into a decline."

"Can't have that," Frederick said.

A few hours later, they were *all* in a decline. The library table was piled high with letters, battered and salt-stained after making their way to London from various seaports. They had managed to read through four years of them.

"Bloody hell," Frederick said, getting up to pour himself another brandy.

"I agree," Daisy murmured, her head bent over a three-page, closely-written letter. "In this one, the captain is talking about Cassio again, predicting that one day he'll captain his own ship and help Britannia rule the seas. How on earth could you have overlooked your father's adoration of his first mate, Livie?"

Livie looked up from the letter she held. "I never read them very carefully."

"I wouldn't have either," Frederick said, returning with a full glass. "They remind me of a nasty old gull at Eton who called himself a minister."

"You can't have that brandy unless you eat something first," Livie said, dropping her letter and taking the snifter away.

Frederick grumbled, but Livie didn't give it back until the butler brought him bread and a slice of meat.

"Honestly, Livie, if someone in the future happens to read these letters, they'll believe the captain's daughter was an accomplished strumpet," Daisy said, an hour later. "Maybe we should destroy them."

Livie choked back the foolish confession that she *was* a strumpet. More relevant was the fact that her father had castigated her for sins she hadn't yet committed.

"Let's each read aloud a favorite sentence," Frederick said, picking up a letter he'd just dropped. "Here's mine: 'She that walks in slippery places is every moment liable to fall, and when she does fall, she falls at once without warning.' Did you know, that happens to me regularly? Usually when I'm on my fourth bottle."

"I can't mock my father's letters," Livie protested. "There's a line in this one, for example—" She broke off. "Here—" She broke off again.

"What is it?" Daisy asked.

"Have you noticed ink blots above certain words?"

Chapter 31

Livie slapped the letter she was holding down onto the library table. "There!" she cried, pointing to a dot over the word "for."

Daisy squinted at it. "So?"

"There's another ink blot, a few lines down," Livie said. "A big one over 'the'...'for the!' For the *what*?"

It took several hours, but finally seven letters were discovered to have round ink blots, all seven dating to the year before the meeting in France when a traitor met his regicidal band on the shore. At a careless glance, they looked as if the author had raised his quill in thought without carefully tapping away his ink.

Livie snatched up a piece of foolscap and began taking notes. If a large dot topped a small word like "for," the entire letter was part of the cypher; larger words were spelled out with tiny dots over individual letters.

"This letter spells out 'May fourth,'" Daisy said, putting down the sheet she held. "I suspect that's the date of the incident." She picked up another. "This letter spells out 'Trouville,' presumably the town on the French shoreline near to their landing. These two were likely sent together, because with 'dark shore' the traitor's plot is outlined. He was telling his confederates that the boat should land under cover of darkness."

"Must be," Frederick said. He was turning over the discarded letters, making certain that no other missive contained dots.

"But why send the messages here? To me?" Livie asked. "The information would only be useful to the plotters, and there's no one here but family and staff!"

Daisy jumped up, ran to the library door, and locked it. "Someone in this house decoded those messages," she hissed, when she got back to the table. "Some treacherous double-crosser infiltrated our household!"

"Actually, I think I know who it was," Livie said. "Remember our French chambermaid, Bernadette?"

Daisy nodded, eyes huge. "She was a *spy*? Impossible! My mother prized her expertise with curling tongs! I thought she might weep when Bernadette left our employ."

"Bernadette cleaned my bedchamber every day," Livie said hollowly. "She had all the time in the world to find the newest letter in the trunk and decipher it. When letters arrived in a bundle, she could have taken it up to the attic and read them at her leisure without my noticing."

"Crucial question," Frederick put in. "When did she leave your aunt's employment?"

"She left without a word of warning the day after my uncle was arrested," Daisy replied. "Mother was furious, thinking that Bernadette had decided she was too good to work for us. My goodness, I've had my hair curled by an enemy agent!"

Livie bent down until her forehead rested on the library table. "Oh, Daisy, what am I going to do? My father's private letters spell out the traitors' plot to the last detail. If anything, all we've uncovered is evidence against him!" The aching words sank into the empty room. A sob broke free in her chest.

Frederick pushed back his chair, strode around the table, scooped up Livie and sat back down, awkwardly patting her back.

"Don't misinterpret my gesture," he warned. "Think of me as your future brother-in-law."

"You're not," Daisy said, pushing a handkerchief into Livie's hand. "I'm so sorry, dear."

"It's not just me," Livie sobbed. "It's you, too, Daisy. It's all of us. Lady Wharton, too. And my…my *mother*! It will likely kill her."

There was silence in the room.

"Perhaps we could move to France," Daisy offered. "I, for one, could not bear to see Lady Regina's triumphant face next Season."

"You won't see her, because we'll be pariahs, more than we already are." Livie sat up straight. "They'll execute my father, won't they? They kill traitors."

Frederick shook his head. "I don't know. I don't think we should jump to conclusions."

Livie slumped back against his shoulder.

"These are his personal letters," she said drearily. "Who could possibly have access to them besides the author?"

"His first mate?" Daisy asked. "The revered Cassio?"

"The captain dictates formal letters, but he wouldn't…They are private…"

Her voice trailed off.

"But he would, wouldn't he?" Frederick put in. "Because these letters are not very intimate. They resemble communal sermons more than private missives."

"He does dictate his letters to Cassio," Daisy said. "I saw him do that last summer."

"Cassio might have added the dots," Livie agreed, with a flash of hope.

"It didn't have to be Cassio," Frederick pointed out. "The quartermaster was likely in charge of posting the captain's mail. Or there might have been a cabin boy with access. Presumably, if the captain was writing to you every day, some letters sat on his desk for weeks."

"They often arrive in bundles," Daisy said, nodding.

"Were these seven a bundle?"

"Perhaps. I don't know."

Daisy picked the seven letters up and began folding them again, trying to see whether they shared dents from being tied together with string.

"The simplest solution is often correct," Frederick said.

"The simplest solution is that my father is a traitor," Livie stated. Her mouth was sour with fear.

Frederick shook his head. "I vote for Cassio. Quite likely he suggested wording or altered what your father had dictated. What if your father concluded the letter before Cassio had managed to include everything he needed?"

"Some letters are distinctly awkward," Livie said, sitting up. Feeling a stab of embarrassment, she rose and patted Frederick's shoulder. "You are not my brother-in-law, and you never will be, but I appreciate your kindness."

None of her father's harangues were elegant, but one of the seven missives had struck her as odder than most. For one thing, it was short: only a single page rather than two to three. For another, the dots were clustered toward the bottom of the sheet.

"Listen to this," she said, picking up that letter. "He bids me farewell and then he adds an addendum: *The dark shore of the heart may engender fornications, murders and thefts.*"

"I have the oddest feeling that your father wouldn't approve of me," Frederick muttered.

"There are two large dots over 'dark shore,' as well as one over 'May' and then, spelled out, 'f-o-u-r-t-h'. My father is not poetic. 'Dark shore of the heart' doesn't sound like him."

"Mr. Cassio reveals untold poetic depths," Daisy cried.

"Right! He is guilty of bad poetry *and* treason, both hangable offenses. Is hangable a word? In any case, Frederick can let his father know, and this nightmare will be over."

"No!" Livie said. "I have to tell my father first."

Frederick raised an eyebrow. "Having spent the better part of a day reading your father's tender missives—while remaining woefully sober—I agree with Daisy."

"I can't turn over private letters that my father wrote to me to a judge without informing him," Livie said. "He'd never forgive me." She didn't say it, but she was a little afraid that he wouldn't forgive her anyway.

"The captain likely won't believe you. You'll have to bring the letters as evidence," Daisy said, tactfully avoiding the question of whether her father placed the dots himself.

Livie nodded.

"Lord Devin must accompany you," Daisy continued. "You'll never get into the Tower without him, Livie. Besides, his lordship obviously needs to know about the coded letters."

Livie winced. The idea of Lord Devin reading her father's letters was embarrassing to her personally—but not as terrible as having one's father executed for a crime he didn't commit.

Daisy hopped up. "I'll write Devin a note."

After the door closed behind her, Frederick asked, "Do you think that your cousin is alarmingly enthusiastic about carrying on a clandestine correspondence, or is that just my imagination? I'll admit to having a filthy one that frequently sees tupping where there's none going on."

"Tupping?" Livie asked.

"Intercourse," he said flatly. "You need to know the meaning of that word, whether you marry my brother or not."

"Not," Livie said, equally flatly.

After a moment's silence, Frederick said, "Joshua doesn't mean to be so rigid."

"Actually, I think he does," Livie said. She discovered she was rubbing her chest again and dropped her hand. "Don't you dare think that I am drawing attention to my chest!"

Frederick gaped at her. "Why would I?" His eyes dropped. "Now that you mention it, it's a very nice bosom."

"Your brother did," she snapped. "I gather that's what a swindler like me would do. A ladybird bent on seducing him into saving my father's life through…through nefarious means."

Frederick sighed. "Would you like to marry me instead?"

"Absolutely not."

"Oh, good. I felt that the family honor required that proposal but honestly, I'd rather not."

"I shall find a husband who respects me and doesn't think I'm a strumpet," Livie said, struggling to hold back tears.

In the end Frederick hauled her back onto his lap and took up awkward patting once again.

Not, he informed her this time, in a brother-in-law fashion, but like an uncle.

"A very, very sober uncle."

Chapter 32

Of Traitors and Gentlemen

"I haven't been in your bedchamber since you had spent two days in a fever, and the doctor instructed us to bid you farewell," Frederick observed, strolling into Joshua's room without knocking.

Having requested to meet with Lord Devin the following morning, Joshua was trying to pass time reading dispatches from the British Ordnance Department. "Good evening."

His brother threw himself onto the bed.

"You might remove your boots."

Frederick ignored that, crossing his arms behind his head. "So, little brother, would you please recount your conversation with the delightful Livie, who informs me that she will never be my sister-in-law? I'd like to know just how much of a sapskull you are—for my own amusement, naturally."

"When did Livie tell you that?" Joshua growled.

"After you left her in the duchess's sitting room in a puddle of tears," Frederick replied. "Moreover, I just spent the day with her. Would you like to know what we were doing?"

Violent impulses rocketed through Joshua's mind: red, ferocious, bloody urges. Every muscle in his body tensed.

Frederick rolled his eyes. "For God's sake, you know I don't go near women who aren't wearing wedding rings."

"Just what were you doing with Livie, then?" Joshua asked through clenched teeth.

"Reading letters."

"*What?*"

"Letters written by Livie's father. Letters that evidence treachery. Letters that plan a nefarious act that apparently involved regicide."

Joshua let out a short, blunt curse.

"The correspondence between sweet Livie and her father was a cover. The captain regularly posted letters that disguised treasonous messages spelled out in ink blots. A spy in her household decoded the messages and presumably added replies to letters she sent in return."

Joshua's mind reeled. The captain's guilt was a shock. He'd felt certain that Livie's father would be found innocent by the trial's end. How could this be?

Suddenly he realized that when Livie pleaded her father's case, he had believed her absolutely. He had trusted that the captain was innocent—and still he refused to help. Where was the honor in that?

The image of her looking up at him when he first opened the wardrobe door popped into his mind. Livie, beautiful Livie, would never marry. Her father would be executed. She would never have a place in society again; there would be no second Season for her.

"Captain Sir Tyron is a traitor," he said, dumbfounded. "Livie's father plotted against the king and crown."

Frederick nodded. "Guilty as the day is long."

"She thought…"

"She thought wrong." Frederick smirked as he raised an eyebrow. "Of course, Livie also thought you loved her, so it's been quite a week for misapprehensions, hasn't it?"

"I do love her," Joshua snapped, without a second's thought.

"Indeed?" His brother pushed himself to a sitting position against the bed board. "Do tell. Though I have to say, your revelation is as unlikely as the conclusion to Miss Austen's masterpiece. No one will ever convince me that Darcy gave a damn for Lizzie Bennet."

"Livie asked me—" Joshua bit off the sentence. He was a fool. Had she actually spelled out what she wanted, or had he leapt to the conclusion that she wanted him to influence his father's judgment?

"Livie believed that her father was innocent. She knows better now. She also believed you a gentleman, yet a gentleman never deserts his lady in her hour of need. A gentleman places her before all others."

Their father had taught Joshua everything he knew about being a gentleman, back when the earl was plain Baron FitzRoy, more interested in honor than rank.

A gentleman was *gentle* toward a lady. He didn't find her in a wardrobe, pull up her gown, and pin her to the floor with his weight, allowing her breath to escape only in sighs.

The only time a gentleman pictured himself on his knees before a lady was with a ring in hand, not pushing up her gown to perform intimate acts that would scandalize most ladies.

A gentleman wasn't possessive and half-crazed.

Shakespeare had it right after all. Romeo saw Juliet, and that was it. She was in his heart—no, she *became* his heart. In fact, she became the center of his universe.

The truth dawned on Joshua slowly.

If Livie was the center of his universe, then she was more important to him than anything else.

If she was the still center of his world, then he had to fight for her with all the ferocity with which he fought any other battle. She hadn't asked him to dishonor himself.

She had only begged for help.

"I asked her to marry me," Frederick said casually.

The words clicked in Joshua's mind like the hammer of a flintlock. He started to his feet.

"Merely for the sake of family honor," Frederick added lazily, waving one hand in the air. "I hoped to salvage a bit of our dignity lost by our father's embarrassing adulation of his new title and your equally embarrassing—and prudish—adulation of your so-called honor."

Joshua's hands curled into fists. "You asked Livie—*my* Livie—to marry you?"

"Even a drunk doesn't like to see a woman crying," Frederick said. He sat up, swung his legs over the side of the bed, and rose to his feet. "Naturally, I was rebuffed. One has to assume that she has more discerning taste in bedfellows than I."

"She refused," Joshua exclaimed, relief flooding his body. "She wants me."

"Not any longer. Not after your pusillanimous—that means 'cowardly,' by the way—pusillanimous rejection of her plea for assistance."

"I was wrong," Joshua said. "I'll marry her before her father is convicted and take her with me to battle. Major-General Sale takes his wife everywhere. The Lady Grenadier, they call her."

His brother raised an eyebrow. "*You*? Marry a traitor's daughter? That bright military future of yours would be destroyed. No 'Major-General' rank for you."

"I don't give a damn," Joshua said. "Actually, I do care, but not as much as I care for Livie. I will not leave her alone to face the grief and shame that lie ahead."

"What if you're forced out of the service? You've played with tin soldiers from the age of four," his brother pointed out.

Frederick was leaning against the wall, but miraculously, he didn't appear to be drunk.

Joshua shrugged. "I'll buy some land and farm it."

"And how will you convince Livie to give you a second chance? She doesn't spit on hearing your name, but I reckon that's only because she was raised a lady."

"I'll give her the diamond that Mother—"

His brother interrupted. "She doesn't want a diamond, you fool."

"I'll beg," Joshua said, "I'll promise to put her before all others, in sickness, in health, in happiness and grief—"

"In spite of treachery," Frederick put in. He gave Joshua a wry grin. "And so goes the story of my brother who sacrificed all for love. Bound to be a bestseller with the ladies. One day our hero is slaying foes in thrilling acts of derring-do, and the next he's raising potatoes. Our father, by the way, will disown you for that marriage."

"I don't need him or his money," Joshua said. He and Livie faced huge challenges, and yet his heart was suddenly filled with joy. "I'll take Oates-Plagitt."

"Absolutely not!" Frederick snarled.

Joshua grinned. The moment he chose Livie over his job, over the polite world, his melancholy fell away. "I need him more than you do."

"That is true," Frederick said. "He's waiting for us downstairs, by the way."

"Why?"

"I prevaricated a trifle. Looks like the traitor may be a man named Cassio—quite Shakespearean, though I believe it was Iago who betrayed his general, Othello."

Joshua's brows drew together.

"You just said that the captain was—"

Frederick slapped him on the back. "My wedding present."

"*What?*" Joshua shouted it.

"You're as stubborn as our father, and every bit as wedded to black-and-white morality over the nuanced grays of real life. You needed to be shocked into sensibility."

Joshua shook his head. "You lied to me? The captain is innocent?"

"I think so," Frederick said unrepentantly. "I didn't have had the time to politely shake you out of your fixed belief that your honor is more important than your wife."

Joshua let the words sink in. "Thank you."

"Livie will come to you unmarred by this charge of treason, as long as we can convince Cassio to confess. Somehow I feel certain that we can—or rather, that *you* can."

"Did Oates-Plagitt tell you that I asked him to find Cassio?"

"Only after I asked the same thing," Frederick said. "He's waiting for us, just having let me know that he has rooted out Cassio's abode with the help of our boot-boy, who is apparently a gifted spy. Perhaps you should take the lad off with you to war. *And* perhaps you should bring your sword."

"You should have told me immediately!" Joshua caught up his coat from a chair and pulled it on. "Are we anticipating violence?"

"Hopefully not, but its blade does look as if it has whipped off many a head. Perchance Cassio will recognize he's a character in *Othello* and disembowel himself. Though, again, I think it was Othello who took his own life, not Cassio."

Joshua ignored his brother's foolishness, walking to the corner of the room to pick up the sword he hadn't touched since being wounded. Its hilt had a lion's head appended to the body of a serpent; the blade itself was Spanish, with a slight curve. It settled into his palm with the comforting ease of familiarity.

He buckled on the scabbard, his sword's reassuring weight settling on his right hip.

"Off with his head!" Frederick cried, with all the blithe cheer of a man who has never walked onto a battlefield.

Joshua nodded.

If this Cassio had committed treason, he deserved to lose his head.

Chapter 33

Rank Treason: In Novels or Real Life?

Livie collected herself enough to offer a polite greeting to the
two elderly yeomen guarding the Tower, but it was left to Lord
Devin to announce they meant to pay another visit to Captain Sir
Tyron.

A light rain hung in the air, misting Livie's face as they
walked through the courtyard toward Beauchamp Tower. She
readjusted her bonnet to make certain that no rain touched her hair;
that morning her maid had ironed her curls and then scraped them
back from her forehead in a sleek line with no fashionable ringlets to
be seen.

She was wearing an elegant yet somber gray carriage dress.
Her fichu was snowy white and so modest that it brushed her chin.
Hopefully, her appearance wouldn't affront her father's sensibilities.

She couldn't help thinking that the captain would be furious
on hearing her news. Rereading his letters had revealed a fact she
had overlooked: he considered Cassio the son he wished he had.

He would be devastated by the man's treachery.

He might not believe it, even given the evidence tucked in her reticule.

"If Mr. Cassio is in the chamber, I shall expel him before you enter," Lord Devin told her as they approached Beauchamp Tower.

Following his lordship up the stairs, Livie couldn't catch her breath. The dripping stone walls seemed closer to her shoulders than they had been on her first visit, the miasma of sewage and mildew even more stifling.

"Is Mr. Cassio in attendance?" Lord Devin asked the guard outside her father's cell.

"No, my lord," the man answered, unbarring the door.

Lord Devin gave a brisk knock and then strode into the chamber. Livie remained outside and out of sight, listening through the open door as her father issued a cheerful greeting.

"I have brought news of a significant development," Lord Devin said, "news that, I am happy to say, is likely to exonerate you."

"I am unsurprised," Livie's father replied, confidence resounding in his deep voice. "I suppose you caught the miscreant who took advantage of my name and seal?"

"I believe we have," Lord Devin said. "With your permission, I shall ask our chief investigator to join us."

"Certainly," the captain said.

Livie took this as the signal to join her father and Lord Devin. The two men were standing in the center of the room; both of them turned as she entered. Her hands were wound together so tightly that she had to force them apart in order to drop into a respectful curtsy. "Good morning, Father," she murmured, bowing her head.

She straightened to see her father scowling. "If you'll forgive me, Lord Devin," he said with icy precision, "I previously explained my reluctance to have my daughter placed in invidious proximity to a bed."

"Your daughter has discovered that your letters to her had been used to plan treason," Lord Devin said, his voice just as cold. "Wouldn't you like to hear how it happened?"

"*My* letters to *her*?" The captain drew himself up and turned to Livie, his face turning dull purple. "What did you do to my letters, you fool girl?"

Livie swallowed hard. "I did nothing to them, Father, other than discover that your letters had been modified to communicate a plot to meet with revolutionaries on the French shore under cover of darkness."

"Modified?" He snorted. "What are you talking about?"

"The letters were adulterated, marked in a way that translated to a coded message," Lord Devin explained.

The captain gaped. "Impossible."

"It may be that these communications were added by the man who transcribed your letters," Lord Devin continued.

Captain Sir Tyron snorted. "Do I understand that you think that Mr. Cassio, my devoted, nay, my *beloved* right hand, used my correspondence to plan treason?" A rough bark of laughter erupted from his throat. "I can only suppose that the idiotic chit who calls herself my daughter has influenced you in this preposterous idea, likely because she thinks herself too good to marry Mr. Cassio."

Livie didn't know Lord Devin terribly well, but even so, she could read his expression. Lord Devin didn't approve of the way her father was shouting at her. The captain's eyes were screwed to the size of currants. Angry currants.

Was it possible for a raisin to be angry?

Once again she felt as if her lungs couldn't expand enough to gulp air. "Mr. Cassio is a suspect," she said haltingly. "But perhaps you can point to another who had access to your letters?"

"If we do not find a culprit, the Lord High Steward will come to an obvious conclusion," Lord Devin remarked.

Her father's eyes bulged. "Do you *dare*?"

"The letters are yours, so Lord Paget will conclude that the coded messages are yours as well," his lordship replied without flinching.

For her part, Livie felt ill with anxiety. Had her father no understanding of the danger in which he stood?

"I shall inspect these supposed markings myself," her father snarled. He cast Lord Devin a withering look, wheeled about, and walked to the chairs before the fire.

Lord Devin took Livie's elbow. "Steady," he whispered, drawing her over to the hearth.

Once they were seated, the captain turned to Livie with a ferocious scowl. "Am I to understand that you shared our private communications with his lordship?"

The scorn in his eyes was familiar; she had again stepped over the invisible line demarcating ladylike behavior. "Only after I discovered that someone had employed your letters for treasonous means," she offered in her defense.

"For which you, Captain Sir Tyron, are currently imprisoned and at risk of execution," Lord Devin remarked. He was no longer making the slightest attempt to hide his dislike, if not contempt.

Livie drew the shortest letter from her reticule and handed it over.

Her father scanned it quickly. "This is one of the letters I sent you, with advice that I sincerely hope you took to heart. I note here that novels '*are in their nature shameful, in their tendency pestiferous, and contain rank treason against the royalty of Virtue and horrible violations of all decorum.*' I stand by that judgment."

He put down the letter. "I gather that you are implying that my mention of 'treason' is tantamount to a plot against His Majesty." He brayed with laughter again, the sound filling the stone-walled cell.

"Please look at the postscript," Livie said.

His eyes dropped to the bottom of the page. She watched closely as he read it once, blinked, then skimmed it again. "Rather more poetic than my usual vein, but certainly my own."

"'*The dark shore of the heart may engender fornications, murders and thefts,*'" Lord Devin quoted from memory. "You recall the words, Captain Sir Tyron?"

"Certainly."

"Do you remember dictating that sentence specifically?"

"I agree with the sentiment," her father said hotly. "These wretched novels consumed in the hundreds by young women must be condemned as inspiring lewdness—and yes, criminality as well."

Livie couldn't tell whether her father didn't grasp the stakes of the conversation, or if he was bull-headedly intent on saving his would-be son.

"The hand that wrote the letter is that of Mr. Cassio," Lord Devin stated. "This morning I compared it to a letter you sent to Admiralty, similarly scribed by your first mate."

"Cassio faithfully transcribes my words," the captain said sharply. "You hate him due to the enmity of your nature," he said to Livie.

"I do not hate Mr. Cassio, Father."

"Like Cain, you are jealous of him because I've deemed him worthy, and you are threatened by my pride in him. You hate the man who is as dear to me as a son.."

Livie cleared her throat. "No."

"A woman instinctively rejoices in pride, avarice, and luxury. Therefore, you seek to cast blame upon the virtuous young man whom I have chosen to be your husband. Driven by the flippant impertinence of ambition, you want more. You think Mr. Cassio is not good enough for you?"

"Father…" His voice had risen to a bellow, and Livie couldn't stop herself from shrinking back.

"You are naught compared to him!"

"Your daughter's future is irrelevant at the moment," Lord Devin said. "It is your own that is in question."

The captain didn't spare him a glance. "Unable to please me in any respect, you have set your sights on a title and fortune. You think that Mr. Cassio, despite his sober mind and steady attachment, is insufficient on the grounds that he isn't wealthy enough to buy the fripperies you lust for!"

"It isn't that!" Livie cried. "Father, whoever wrote that line committed treason—*and framed you for their crimes!*"

"Nonsense! The line is a mere bagatelle, an admonishment in my ongoing and endless attempt to steer you away from vanity and levity!"

"But there are ink blots—" Livie began.

Her father sprang from his seat. "I have spent my life trying to guide you toward chastity and dignity, only to fail again and again. Do you think that I don't know your many crimes?" He crumpled the letter. "I wrote this after my sister revealed your love of novels!"

Livie blinked up at him. "'Crimes?'" she repeated.

"My sister unwittingly revealed the way you got around my injunction by having your cousin read aloud works I had banned." His mouth twisted with distaste.

Lord Devin folded his arms over his chest with the air of a man watching the fifth act of a tragedy he'd seen before.

"Father, won't you please consider the situation?" Livie pleaded. "That final sentence is marked with ink blots that spell out the very plot for which you are imprisoned."

The captain crumpled the letter in his hand and began to turn toward the burning fire when Lord Devin lunged forward and snatched it from his hand. "Evidence to be submitted in court," he said calmly.

"Poppycock!" The captain leveled a long finger at Livie. "This so-called evidence is spun from a woman's mind. From her shameful, pestiferous imagination!"

"Your daughter's imagination had nothing to do with it," Lord Devin stated. He folded the sheet, tucked into his coat, and reseated himself. "I have long been bothered by the fact that two years passed between the events on the shore and the trial you face."

"I reported the event promptly, but I'd been at sea in His Majesty's service," the captain said impatiently. "I have had enough! I don't want to hear another word from either of you."

Out of nowhere, Livie realized that if her father had had enough, so had she. She came to her feet, proud to find that her knees were not shaking, and that her breath was even. To her side, Lord Devin automatically rose, as a gentleman must.

"Mr. Cassio committed treason, and you would go to the gallows in his stead, from a pig-headed belief that I made up the evidence?" she asked.

"*Pig-headed?*"

"I'd agree with that assessment," Lord Devin put in. "I would content that Cassio stayed in your service planning to hatch another plot and use your letters to send messages to his conspirators."

"*She* has nourished this ridiculous idea and thrust it upon an innocent man," the captain said.

"The letters contains a code," Livie stated.

"If there is a code, *you* added it!"

Livie wasn't even surprised. "What could I possibly gain by that?" she inquired. "After assuring me of my own stupidity time and again, now you think that I am clever enough to frame Cassio for a crime he didn't commit in order to avoid marriage to him?"

"Nothing would surprise me," her father said grimly. "You added those supposed dots after the letters were delivered."

"The plot is spelled out in mail that was sent from *your* ship, written in *your* personal letters. I did not add the line in question. Cassio did."

"May I remind you that the conspirators swear that your seal was used to in traitorous communications?" Lord Devin inquired. "Who has better access to it than your first mate?"

"You don't want to marry him because you consider yourself his better!" the captain said, ignoring the question of his seal.

Lord Devin cleared his throat.

"*You* are too low for Cassio. I'd have to give him my estate to make *you* an acceptable wife!"

"I am virtuous!" Livie cried. "I have been a dutiful daughter to you."

"Ah, but there's the problem!" her father barked.

Lord Devin moved closer to her.

"You are no daughter of mine!"

Chapter 34

He Who Denies All, Confesses All

"Michael Cassio lives in rented lodgings in Hammersmith," Oates-Plagitt told Frederick and Joshua as their carriage rumbled down the street. "And you know what they say about Hammersmith."

Joshua was obsessively revisiting the moment when he refused to help Livie prove her father's innocence. She hadn't searched him out at the masquerade, knowing who his father was. The very idea was absurd. Equally absurd was the notion that she had attended the masquerade hoping to meet some random lord who could sway the court in her father's favor.

"I know nothing of Hammersmith," Frederick replied, pulling a flask from his pocket and taking a healthy swallow. The fruity smell of brandy quickly filled the carriage.

Joshua noted that Frederick's coat bulged as if he had stuck flasks in every pocket, but he turned to stare out the window rather than comment.

Fate had led him to the perfect woman, and his own idiocy had caused him to throw her away. He was such a fool. He deserved to lose Livie. Yet some stubborn part of his soul refused to give up. Perhaps he could force Cassio to his knees before her, prying an admission of guilt from the wretch. Then he would go to his own knees in turn and beg her to forgive him.

"Hammersmith is the heart of the French community in London," Oates-Plagitt explained. "I understand that the Crown's witnesses—the two enemy agents who assert, based on use of the captain's seal, that he was instrumental in a plot to kill the king—both lived covertly in Hammersmith for some time."

"How on earth do you know the identity of the witnesses?" Joshua asked, his attention snapping back to the conversation.

"I have my means," the butler said airily. "The two men maintain that initial information came in correspondence sealed with the captain's mark. They also saw Captain Sir Tyron on the shore in the midst of the confused battle that ensued once the boat landed. But here is my question: What was the point of that battle?"

Frederick scowled. "What do you mean?" He took another swig.

"What did they gain from that skirmish?" Joshua asked, his mind racing. "The coded letters detailed a time and place. A boat was sent to the French shore, supposedly to rescue an Englishman deserted in enemy territory. Why would the conspirators attack the British men who arrived in that boat? How would it further their plot?"

"The King's investigators have concluded that they hoped to infiltrate the boat's crew," Oates-Plagitt said. "In their scenario, Captain Sir Tyron took the boat to the shore to rendezvous with his confederates. Then, under the cover of the supposed battle with enemy forces, one or more sailors would be replaced by imposters following a plan to assassinate the king."

"That is most unlikely," Joshua said.

"If it were me, and I wanted to assassinate the king," Frederick said, with a faint slur in his voice, "I would walk into the throne room, take out a pistol, and get the job done."

Joshua and Oates-Plagitt looked at him.

"The captain is a nobleman. He could have requested an audience with His Majesty. Why the hell not? Why all the subterfuge?"

"If the captain didn't want to personally kill the king," Joshua said, working it out in his head, "an assassin could have boarded that boat in order to reach London."

"I don't like it," Oates-Plagitt said. "Coordination of both allied and enemy forces, short window of time in which to execute the switch, not to mention the close proximity to one's superior officers, makes for too many moving parts. Not how I would have done it."

"You!" Frederick said with a bark of laughter. "I'd hope you never get it in your head to become an assassin, because no one under God himself would be safe."

"I'll take that as a compliment," the butler said primly. He looked to Joshua. "I don't wish to shock you, Major, but I am convinced that Mr. Cassio will be a hard nut to crack. One doesn't attempt assassination without having the wherewithal to deny the crime."

"I think that violence is the answer—in short, threaten to skewer him with your sword," Frederick told Joshua. "Oates-Plagitt has a less bloody idea. Not entirely legitimate, nor—ahem—noble."

Their butler met Joshua's eyes with unrepentant calm. "Rather than threaten him, we arrest him. If Mr. Cassio is innocent, he will be released from the Tower in due time. If he is not, imprisonment will ensure that he remains in this country until he can be further questioned."

A crossroads lay before Joshua, but he had no doubts about his response.

He nodded.

Michael Cassio was a short man wearing a plain, black suit that showed no signs of wear, but certainly couldn't be described as being of good quality. Upon greeting him, Joshua immediately realized that he was not French: his scouse accent suggested that he grew up in Liverpool.

He ushered them into his living room without any signs of concern at their unexpected arrival. The room was furnished with drab, serviceable pieces. The only indications of the occupant's personality were a portrait of a sailing ship hung over the mantelpiece and a double-framed brass sextant on a side table.

"Nice lodgings," Frederick said, glancing around. "Shipshape, wouldn't you say?"

Oates-Plagitt strolled over to the table and picked up the sextant. "A beautiful instrument. A silvered scale, signed by Edward Troughton."

"That is very delicate," Cassio said sharply. "I treasure it as a gift from Captain Sir Tyron."

Oates-Plagitt put the piece down with a click.

"Won't you please be seated?" Cassio asked, leading them to the other side of the room.

Joshua and Oates-Plagitt took the chairs, leaving Frederick and Cassio to share the couch.

"You must be wondering why we have paid you this visit," Joshua said to Cassio.

"I haven't had many lords under my roof," Cassio acknowledged. "I must suppose that you are here with regard to my imprisoned master, Captain Sir Tyron."

"There's a matter of some letters that we think you could help us understand," Frederick said.

Joshua was watching carefully, but Cassio didn't show the faintest reaction. "Letters, my lord?"

"Letters you wrote," Frederick confirmed. "On behalf of the captain. You don't mind if I drink, do you? I brought my own refreshments." He pulled out his flask, took a sip, and tucked it away again.

"I transcribe the captain's missives on a regular basis." Cassio folded his hands in his lap.

Joshua noticed that the man's nails had been polished. That was hardly the sign of a traitor, though unusual for a Liverpool lad.

"Did you add to those missives?" Frederick asked. "That's the question." He took out his flask again. "Can I offer anyone a drink? This investigation business is taxing."

"You see," Oates-Plagitt intervened, "the letters you forwarded to England, Mr. Cassio, show evidence of being altered in order to transmit treasonable messages."

"Altered? The letters I transcribed?" Cassio's brow drew together. "I should note that *I* did not forward them myself. The quartermaster was responsible for collecting the captain's letters and posting them when possible. The captain maintains a very large correspondence, and bundles of letters often accumulated between postings."

"The letters in question were written to his daughter," Frederick announced.

Now, finally, Joshua thought he saw a reaction. Cassio's eyes narrowed slightly.

"I have no idea what you are talking about. I take the captain's dictation, including letters addressed to his daughter, Miss Tyron. That is all."

"You take the dictation and alter it," Frederick challenged.

"You are incorrect, my lord." His voice took on a faint edge.

Oates-Plagitt leaned toward him. "You do understand the danger you are in, Mr. Cassio? We are doing you a great service by visiting you at home rather than simply bringing you into custody."

"A service?" Cassio inquired. "What service is that? I would remind you that the captain authored those letters. I am merely the scribe. If his words contained a coded message, then they were dictated as such unbeknownst to me. I could not change his wording to…to create a code."

"Why couldn't you?" Joshua asked.

"Because the captain looks over every letter I transcribe before he signs his name to them," Cassio said flatly. He rose to his feet. "I must ask you to leave, gentlemen. I have an appointment at Beauchamp Tower to aid the captain."

Frederick deliberately stretched out his legs and crossed them. "Yet letters sent to Miss Tyron do include a code. Who did it, if not you?"

After a moment of silence, Cassio replied, "It is not for me to say."

"Oh?" Joshua said, standing up. It was hardly evidence of treachery to characterize Cassio as *too* calm, almost uninterested. "Say it anyway."

"I have come to terms with my master's traitorous activity," the man said. "I wish it weren't the case, for the sake of my country as well as my own career. I came to shore that fateful night and saw with my own eyes the captain engaged in fighting against his own men. Thankfully none were killed."

"It was dark," Oates-Plagitt said, rising as well. "The captain maintains that it was too murky to identify one man from another."

"He is my *captain*," Cassio said. "I had an eye on him from the moment the ship ran aground. At the time, I thought he had been confused by darkness. But in retrospect, after I learned of the witnesses who had confessed to treason, I understood the truth."

"Yet you have continued to visit the captain in the Tower and transcribe his letters," Frederick said, squinting up at him.

"Until Captain Sir Tyron is convicted of treason, he is my lord and master," Cassio said. A tired note crept into his voice. "If you have discovered the means by which he organized this plot, perhaps the Admiralty will reassign me to a different ship and captain."

"Or promote you to captain of the *Royal Oak*?" Joshua asked.

Cassio glanced at him indifferently. "I doubt that very much. Captains in the Royal Navy have wealth and birth to match their power and influence. I have neither."

Joshua had to admit that Cassio's points were sound. His heart sank.

Frederick got up, steadying himself on the couch, just as Oates-Plagitt walked over to Cassio, caught one of his wrists, twisted it behind his back and caught the other.

"What in the hell are you doing?" Cassio barked. He began to struggle, but Oates-Plagitt deftly pulled his arms higher, and the prisoner subsided.

"If you please, Lord Frederick FitzRoy-Paget," the butler said.

Frederick pulled a pair of handcuffs from one of the pockets Joshua had assumed contained a flask of brandy. "Right," he said cheerfully, without the faintest slur in his voice. He clicked them shut around Cassio's wrists.

Cassio glowered. "As a British citizen, I have rights. You have no authority to arrest me. I have done nothing wrong in transcribing the letters of a traitor. I had no way of knowing what he was writing."

"It's not that," Oates-Plagitt said cheerfully.

"Then what?"

The butler pulled a small brass seal from his pocket. "Perhaps you would like to explain why Captain Sir Tyron gave you a sextant that was clearly made for him alone, with his personal seal incorporated in its design?"

Cassio gaped. "I didn't—I've never seen that before!"

"The seal slots into the index arm," Oates-Plagitt said informatively. "I could demonstrate but I think it's best we simply turn you over to the judiciary. I expect the sextant is stolen. Certainly this seal was used to convince French traitors that an English lord backed their plot."

"The sextant is *not* stolen!" Cassio said, losing control for the first time. "The captain gave it to me. I had no idea there was a seal attached!"

"Why would he give his first mate such a valuable instrument, obviously designed for his family?"

"I am part of the family!" Cassio snarled. "He had no son, and he has offered his daughter as my wife!"

Joshua stepped forward, his hand instinctively going to the hilt of his sword. "*You*, who just described yourself as having neither birth, power, nor wealth?"

Cassio smirked. "Her father promised me an estate along with her hand in marriage."

The sword slid from its sheath with a dangerous sound. Cassio's eyes widened, but he held his tongue.

"You will *never* marry Miss Tyron," Joshua growled. "Do you understand me?"

"I understand that you don't know who she is!"

"What in the hell are you talking about?"

The first mate's smirk deepened. "She's not good enough for me, but I'll take her." He leaned forward, his chin jutting. "You ask the captain about that sextant, and then I'll have an apology when you set me free."

Joshua had control of himself; he allowed his sword to slide into its scabbard. "If it's an apology you want, I'll leave it to the hangman. I believe he apologizes before doing his work."

Chapter 35

Parental Sacrifice and its Repercussions

Years ago, Lady Wharton had told Daisy and Livie about the moment she learned of her mother's death: she had "turned to ice" on hearing the news. Livie had nodded sympathetically, but now, as a chill shot down to her toes, she truly understood the emotion. She felt cold, small, and pathetic.

A hailstone. A useless bit of ice, cast to the side.

Beside her, Lord Devin made a rough noise and edged sideways until his shoulder brushed hers.

"What do you mean?" Livie managed to ask the man glaring at her. The man married to her mother. The man who had never shown any signs of loving her.

The man who was apparently not her father. Her heart hurt as from a blow, and she wanted—she couldn't stifle it—she wanted *Joshua*. She scarcely knew him, and yet she wanted Joshua beside her rather than Lord Devin, for all his kindliness.

"I've always known," Captain Sir Tyron stated. "You're none of mine." Her expression must have made him feel guilty because he looked to the wall rather than meet her eyes.

Lord Devin cleared his throat. "You suspect your wife of adultery?"

Livie turned her head and found his lordship was regarding the captain with the disgusted air of a man who's turned over a cobblestone and found a writhing earthworm underneath.

That disgust would be directed at her from all sides soon enough, Livie thought numbly. Perhaps not from Lord Devin, but from the rest of the world. If she understood her father—no, the captain—correctly, she was illegitimate. A bastard.

No wonder her mother showed so little interest in her, never bothering to visit. No wonder she had grown up in her aunt's nursery. She, Livie, was living proof of infidelity.

"I was at sea for a year and came home to...*her*," the captain told the wall. "Not my heir, never my heir, though I gave her a dowry out of Christian charity."

Color had mounted in his cheeks. Livie thought he regretted blurting out the truth—not for her sake, but because he didn't want anyone to realize he had been cuckolded.

Still, he couldn't be the only one who knew. Her aunt, Lady Wharton, would certainly have recognized that her brother was at sea when his daughter was conceived.

And yet Livie's aunt had never indicated by the slightest gesture that she considered Livie less precious than her own daughter.

"I never went near the strumpet's bed again," the captain continued, turning to Lord Devin. "I didn't forsake her, though. I made a vow in God's church, even if my fidelity meant I'd never have an heir, nothing other than a bastard child. I did my best to fashion what I had into something better than her mother."

"That's why you always assumed I was a strumpet," Livie said. She was rather proud to discover that her voice was clear and calm.

Not friendly, though. Icy.

"Like mother, like daughter. I did my best," the captain repeated. He was still looking at Lord Devin. "Still, I couldn't allow her to marry a man of rank, could I? Not coming from…*that.* Not with her stained soul. Cassio comes from nothing, but he's made something of himself."

"He's made a traitor of himself," Lord Devin stated.

"Nonsense," the captain spat, pivoting and walking over to the mantelpiece. "Slander, mere slander."

"Treasonous letters exist. The crucial, flowery sentence could have been written by him. Likewise, the ink blots could have been added while inscribing your letters or directly thereafter. He had access to your seal, which he could have stolen."

"The seal?" the captain said, rolling his eyes. "First you allege a hidden code, and now you cry theft over my missing seal? Why would he need to steal the seal? He had use of it whenever he wished."

"The two French witnesses who will speak against you at trial disclosed that the letters convincing them to join the plot were signed by you and impressed with your seal," Lord Devin said.

"Obviously, my seal was stolen, but not by Cassio!" The captain was furious, the words spurting from his mouth.

"We have been over this ground before," Lord Devin retorted. "The person most likely to have written the letters and sealed them is, of course, you."

The captain snorted.

"He didn't," Livie said, feeling bitterness in the back of her throat, but forcing the truth out. "Captain Sir Tyron is not a kind man, but he is an honorable one." She turned to her father. "It seems that I owe you thanks for my keeping and education."

"Lady Wharton," he bit out.

"My aunt paid for everything? You never repaid her for my expenses?" The words fell sharply from her tongue. For the first time, she let herself understand that her "father" was a miserable person, a hollow man in a red coat.

"I did not agree with her desire to present you to society. It would have been better to bring you up in the country among your own kind," the captain said. His gaze finally settled on her, but his eyes slid away as though her face was disfigured. "I told Lady Wharton that it would break your heart to debut like a young lady and then be unable to marry. She argued with me, thinking that the truth could be hidden, but I warned her that honor demanded I tell your suitors the truth, no matter what it cost me. No man would take her after that."

"I think you'll find you're mistaken," Lord Devin said.

The captain snorted. "Is that a proposal?"

"It is not," Livie said, cutting in. "I suggest we put this revelation to the side and discuss Mr. Cassio."

She couldn't help herself; even after all Livie had learned, she didn't want the captain to be executed for treachery. He wasn't worthy of her trust, but she knew him better than anyone else.

"You think Cassio will still take *you* as a wife after you have tried to have him imprisoned for treason?" His voice dripped with disdain.

The captain was prideful, obstinate, mean-spirited—but he was law-abiding. A rule-follower. All those years of letters had been directed at teaching her the conduct required of a lady; he would never break those that applied to his own behavior.

It hurt to recognize that both men whom she had loved—and still did love—rejected her in order to protect their honor. "Captain Sir Tyron, do you refuse to consider the possibility that Mr. Cassio altered your letters?" she asked, her voice rasping.

His lip curled. "Perhaps you'll become a solicitor. Makes as much sense as a whore's daughter circling Almack's dancefloor."

"Do *not* speak of my mother—and your wife—in such an ill-bred manner," Livie snapped.

His cheeks turned from red to purple, and his eyes bulged. Like a frog's, Livie thought uncharitably. He was no longer her father—in fact, he had never been. She owed him nothing, not even respect.

"If not Cassio, and if not you, then who altered your letters?" Lord Devin demanded.

The captain turned his protuberant eyes toward him. "Some ruffian on board my ship, someone below my notice. Cassio is a good man, a loyal man." He hesitated for an infinitesimal moment. "Every word of those letters is mine," he added.

"I had hoped you would corroborate our suspicions. Even so, I shall call a meeting of the Special Commission, as we have enough evidence to move forward with Cassio's arrest," Lord Devin said with a jaundiced tone. "I can domicile him in the cell next to yours, if you wish. Though normally prisoners of his status would be housed in the common cells, underground."

As the captain broke into an outraged bellow at the mention of Cassio's arrest, Livie turned and walked to the door, knocking to be let out. She tried to ignore Captain Sir Tyron's furious protest as the guard slid back the deadbolt.

This time, when she walked into the courtyard, Daisy wasn't waiting in the sunshine. The air was gray and hazy with rain. Pools were forming between uneven cobblestones.

Her mind had gone numb.

She had lost everything. Her father—no, the captain—seemed likely to go to the gallows protesting Cassio's innocence. Her dearest friend in the world, Daisy, would be disgraced by the court case, but not nearly as disgraced as Livie would be as the daughter of the traitor.

Not to mention she was a bastard.

Lord Devin would never tell. Yet the truth changed something deep inside her. Never again would she walk into a ballroom, feeling free to smile at whomever she met. Feeling like an equal to a woman such as Lady Regina, even if the lady considered her position as a duke's daughter to be far above a captain's daughter.

What could she do? Where could she go?

An image of Joshua seared through her heart, but it wasn't longing she felt this time. It was relief. Thank goodness he threw her to the side. What if they had married, and the truth had emerged at a later date? He would have been ruined, his career in shambles.

His honor would be more than tarnished; it would be abolished.

There could be no second Season, no time in which he would calm down and return to her. Because Joshua *would* calm down. She knew it deep in her heart. He had reacted from fury, but he wouldn't remain angry.

Lord Devin stepped out of the threshold of Beauchamp Tower and wrapped one arm around her shoulder, turning her as he drew her against his chest. "You are still the same person you were an hour ago."

Livie leaned against him. He was warm and smelled comfortingly like starched linen.

"I'll bring you home to Daisy," he added, one wide hand making circles on her back.

After they reached the house, Livie had told her cousin everything.

"Impossible!" Daisy cried, throwing her arms in the air. "The man's insane! Well, of course he's insane." She paced to the end of the library and then wheeled about. "*He's* the traitor, isn't he? The captain claims Cassio's innocence, but obviously the crime is his. He's a devil, lying to distract everyone from the truth!"

Livie rested her head against the back of her chair and tried not to listen as Lord Devin and Daisy went in circles. A cuckold was not a traitor. Meanness of spirit was not indicative of treachery.

"My aunt would never have an *affaire* with another man!" Daisy cried. "She barely rises from her couch!"

"I've been thinking about that," Livie said wearily. "I believe that my mother's illness is a pretext, Daisy. I have long suspected, but I thought she—well, I thought she disliked my father so much that she couldn't bring herself to spend time with me."

Daisy rushed across the room, dropped to her knees, and caught Livie's hand. "No, love, that's not it. She's *ill*."

"I don't think so," Livie said. "In fact, it may be that I am lucky not to have siblings."

Daisy's frown deepened, but Livie shook her head. "I still remember when your mother came to the nursery and took me away to live with you. In light of my father's revelations, I believe that Lady Wharton decided not to allow me to grow up in proximity to my mother, even though she and I weren't blood relatives."

"*What?*"

"Your mother's moral values are as strict as my father's," Livie said. She leaned forward and put her arms around Daisy's shoulders. "Though Lady Wharton is far kinder and a much better person. She didn't hesitate to raise me herself, even given my ignominious birth."

"Of course, she didn't!" Daisy said indignantly. "She loves you!"

"May I assist you to rise, Miss Wharton?" Lord Devin appeared at Daisy's side and held out a hand, which she took and then seemingly forgot to let go once she was on her feet.

"If you'll forgive me, Miss Tyron," he said to Livie, "the circumstances of your birth are known only to the three of us and are irrelevant to the current moment. Your father has vehemently denied

Cassio's involvement. He seems to have little sense of the peril in which this disavowal places him."

"He thinks of Cassio as his son," Livie explained. "Like any parent, he will sacrifice himself for his child." Her eyes felt hot, but she refused to cry. The fact that *her* parents didn't fall into that camp was irrelevant.

"I'll have Cassio arrested this evening," Lord Devin said grimly. "The captain may wish to sacrifice himself, but I won't stand for his sacrificial idiocy affecting his family."

Livie opened her mouth to point out that she was no relation to Captain Sir Tyron, but then she caught something in Lord Devin's eyes as Daisy dropped his hand and seated herself beside Livie, putting an arm around her waist.

"Let the captain sacrifice himself," Daisy said confidently. "We can prove Cassio's guilt without him. For one thing, we know about Bernadette!" She turned to Lord Devin. "She was our chambermaid and transcribed the coded letters."

"What do we know about her, other than that she's French?" Livie asked.

"I know where she is!" Daisy cried.

"You do?"

"We all agreed that she had a rare gift for curling hair," Daisy reminded her. "Who always wants the best, all the time? And whose house often welcomes powerful men—and therefore might house secrets that could be stolen by an energetic spy?"

"Who?" Lord Devin inquired.

Livie gasped. "Lady Regina! Lady Regina, the sister of the Duke of Lennox."

Chapter 36

Rejected.

At breakfast the next day, Daisy was full of plans to capture Bernadette and force her to confess her traitorous actions. "Nay, her treacherous nature!" she cried, waving a piece of toast in the air.

"After Lord Devin schedules a Special Commission meeting," Livie said, not for the first time, "he will arrest both Cassio and Bernadette."

"Setting up a meeting may take *days*," Daisy said. "She'll discover we're on her trail, and slip away to the port and be gone." A blob of blackberry jelly fell to the tablecloth. "Don't you see how crucial it is to accost Bernadette immediately, Livie?"

Livie had been up all night thinking about the fact that her not-father may be executed in lieu of his not-son, her never-husband. She had recognized the stubborn look on Captain Sir Tyron's face when he insisted that he had written every sentence of his letters.

He *knew* Cassio wrote the crucial sentence. He had to know. He was infuriating, judgmental, and moralistic. Sacrificial as well, it seemed.

Still, she loved him.

It wasn't easy to dismiss all those years when she wrote him near daily, yearned for his attention, looked forward to his letters no matter how critical…

He wasn't the only man she loved, either. "I'm going to ask Joshua for help," she announced.

Daisy's mouth fell open. "*What?*"

"Not for help convincing his father. I'm going to ask him to pay a call on Lady Regina and use a pretext to talk to her maid."

"What good will that do?" Daisy asked, frowning over her toast.

"Joshua will be able to ascertain whether Bernadette is a traitor," Livie said with conviction. "He is a major in the army, after all."

"There's no evidence that rank brings insight," Daisy retorted. "I'd offer Captain Sir Tyron as evidence."

"Actually, in my opinion, the captain realizes Cassio is guilty."

Daisy's toast fell face down on the tablecloth in a splatter of jelly, but before she could speak, their butler entered the breakfast room and said, "Lady Wharton sent a groom ahead of her carriage. She should arrive home tomorrow afternoon."

"Thank you," Daisy said. She waited until the butler left the room before she asked, "The captain *knows* that Cassio is guilty? How is that possible—unless he too is a traitor?"

"The captain is not a traitor. I thought about it all night, and I believe he knew nothing of the plot. Still, he intends to stand behind Cassio." Livie refilled her teacup herself, since Daisy had banished the footman who usually waited on the table.

"That's madness," Daisy breathed. "He plans to sacrifice himself?"

"You read those letters," Livie said. "You know how much he loves Cassio. He talked of him in every letter for the last year. The captain values loyalty and, equally important, he seems to have no real sense of how much danger he's in."

"Loyalty—to someone who planned to kill the king? That's aiding and abetting the enemy, Livie!"

"The captain won't see it that way."

"The Lord High Steward *will* see it that way," Daisy stated. "We must pay a call on Lady Regina immediately and force

Bernadette to disclose the plot. If the woman escapes to France before the Commission can meet, no evidence will confirm the captain's ignorance of the plan."

"Unless Cassio confesses. Unless he cares for my father as much as my father cares for him."

Daisy scoffed, and Livie had to agree.

"Lady Regina would refuse to see you and me," Livie predicted. "I shall write to Joshua."

As it turned out, Livie didn't need to request Major FitzRoy's assistance: as she and Daisy left the breakfast room, they learned that the major had paid them a morning call. "I've asked him to wait in the drawing room," the butler reported. "Shall I ring for your maid, Miss Tyron?"

"Nonsense, I shall chaperone Livie, and she will chaperone me," Daisy said, marching directly to the drawing room door.

Just outside, she turned and caught Livie's hand. "He's here for you," she whispered. "He loves you. You don't have to ask him to put aside his honor. He decided *you* matter more."

Livie managed a crooked smile. She had guessed that Joshua would change his mind and admit that he had spoken rashly. He may have been angered, but after calming down, he would realize she hadn't asked him to do something as nefarious as bribe his father.

But at the same time, Joshua didn't know who she was. Who she *really* was. He had no idea of the damage she would do to him by becoming his wife.

Captain Sir Tyron would inform the major of her birth, warning him away from marrying her. And Joshua would marry her anyway, even knowing that the revelation of her illegitimacy would destroy his career.

"Major FitzRoy, good morning," Daisy said, trotting into the drawing room and dropping a curtsy.

Livie murmured a greeting as her knees bent in the familiar gesture. The sight of Joshua seared her heart like a flame. Of course, he was handsome, but it was his somber, loving expression that drew her to him.

In direct opposition to the way he last regarded her, now Joshua was looking at her as if she were *perfect*.

Not flawed, not deficient, not immoral, but precious.

Yet he didn't know the truth.

He bowed and kissed both of their hands, his lips lingering on the back of Livie's as he flashed her a look from under his thick lashes. She knew what he was thinking. In fact, if they'd been lucky enough to marry, she would probably have always known what he was thinking.

He wanted her. *Needed* her, even.

Daisy bounced over to a chair. "Sit down," she commanded. "We'll discuss Bernadette, and then I'll leave the two of you alone."

Livie looked up to find Joshua's lips quirking in a wry smile.

"Is your cousin always this blunt?"

"Almost always." She realized that he was still holding her hand and tried to tug it free, but Joshua drew her over to the sofa and sat, pulling her close so that their legs were touching.

"Improper!" Daisy chortled. "But I suppose it's to be expected."

Livie pulled her hand away and edged to the side.

"We need you to pay a call on Lady Regina," Daisy told Joshua, without preamble.

He frowned. "I'd rather not."

"You have to seduce her!" Daisy said enthusiastically.

A look of deep disgust crossed his face. "Absolutely not."

Livie intervened before Daisy could issue any more commands. "Major FitzRoy, I must explain that coded letters were sent from my father on his vessel to me, here in London. We think they were sent by Captain Sir Tyron's first mate, Mr. Cassio."

"I am aware," Joshua replied. "Frederick and I paid a visit to Cassio's chambers, but the man denies responsibility for the ink blots and added sentences."

"*We* should accost him!" Daisy burst out. "Cassio couldn't lie to you, Livie!"

"Actually, Cassio is presently in custody," Joshua said.

Livie leaned back against the couch, relief flooding her body. "Oh, thank goodness! The letters proved strong enough evidence without his confession?"

Daisy clapped her hands. "Of course! They were in his handwriting, after all."

Joshua shook his head. "He is in custody on the charge of stealing the captain's seal." He held up his hand when Livie's mouth fell open. "While he may well have done that crime, after we determined that he could not be allowed to flee, my butler planted the seal, and we arrested him on the grounds of its theft. In fact, the seal in question belonged to my father, not to the captain."

"What a fantastic idea!" Daisy cried. "I like the sound of your butler."

"I do not," Livie said, her voice emerging shakily. "You are so attentive to your honor," she told Joshua. "But you've deliberately arrested a man on false grounds? I gather you knew of this plan before your butler enacted it?"

Joshua turned rather pale, but he said, "My honor is less important than you."

"That's my cue to leave," Daisy said, jumping to her feet. "Don't forget to dispatch the major to Lady Regina, Livie. After you're proposed to, I mean." With a giggle and flip of her skirts, she headed for the door.

Joshua reached out and gathered Livie's hands. "I owe you an apology. I lost my temper and misjudged you. But more importantly, I made the wrong choice. You are the woman who will be my partner—my life. I should have listened to you and helped you, above all others. Will you still marry me, Livie?"

Livie drew in a shuddering breath. She couldn't marry him. Not now. "I understand why you felt angry." Her eyes searched his strong jaw, clenched and tense, before she finally met his eyes. The blaze there was purely masculine—and possessive.

He wouldn't accept a flimsy excuse. He had been wracked by a conflict between his honor and his future wife. Now he had chosen her, and he would never turn back.

"From this moment forward, I will always support you and take your feelings into account before anything or anyone else," Joshua said, his voice deep with passion. He brought her left hand to his lips and kissed her palm.

Livie could feel a flush rising in her cheeks. "No."

His eyes locked on hers. "No, you refuse to marry me?"

She freed her hands. "Yes." Tears were threatening to close her throat. "I will not marry you."

"Because of your father's possible crime? I don't care, Livie. If the military doesn't approve of you as my wife, I'll leave the army. I have an inheritance. We can go—"

"No," she bit out. "I don't *want* to marry you."

Savage incredulity crossed his eyes. Some small part of her registered that Major FitzRoy was not used to being denied. His eyes darkened like a storm, and his jaw clenched. "Because I lost my temper? I realize that I acted like an ass."

Livie cleared her throat, telling herself again that she couldn't allow him to sacrifice himself. He would. He would throw away a brilliant career to marry an illegitimate woman, simply because he had made a promise to her.

Oddly enough, she saw a parallel: Captain Sir Tyron had promised his loyalty to the treasonous Cassio and would go down with the ship—metaphorically. Joshua had promised his loyalty to her, and would likewise be true to his word despite the consequences. But she'd be damned if Joshua would lose everything he loved to be with her. He wasn't a man who could be happy growing potatoes.

"Our behavior at the masquerade was shocking," she managed, her heart banging against her ribs. "I will not marry you."

He cleared his throat. "I cannot excuse my actions at the masquerade. I took advantage of your innocence."

"And *then* you claimed that I dishonored you," Livie pointed out. "After *you* had discarded the rules of gentlemanly behavior. I cannot marry with the knowledge that my husband will not only abrogate his own honor on occasion, but accuse me of the same. I did not ask you to dishonor yourself when I told you of my father's plight. I merely asked for help...for your advice."

"I understand," he said evenly. "Is there any chance I can change your mind?"

She shook her head, swallowing hard.

"Perhaps with greater acquaintance?" he suggested.

"No," she stated. "I ask you to honor my decision, Major FitzRoy. I have given it much thought, and we both lowered ourselves that evening. I shudder to think what my...my father would think of my behavior. He has often warned me that when a woman stoops to indelicacy, she risks falling to the depths of depraved behavior. I have concluded that I must seek a spouse who will be a prop to righteousness."

"Livie—" But he stopped.

"I never want to give another man the right to accuse me of impropriety," she added. "You and my father set out a pattern that I am determined to break."

A heavy silence hung in the room as Livie forced back another sob. She actually saw Joshua withdraw behind a front of immovable chill.

"If that is your decision, I cannot gainsay it," he said. "To tell the truth, I would spend my life kissing you in every room or wardrobe in our house, Livie. I do not believe that 'depravity' applies to the behavior of a man and woman who love each other."

Unable to meet his eyes again, she looked down at her hands, shaking her head.

"Nonetheless, I request the honor of helping you," Joshua said. "Why did you wish me to visit Lady Regina?"

Livie lifted her head. Joshua's gaze was that of a military man, a mere acquaintance.

"She employs Bernadette, the French maid who previously worked in this household," she explained. "We believe that Bernadette deciphered the coded letters and passed them on to her compatriots." She felt as if her heart was breaking, but she managed to keep her voice even.

"You would like me to pay a call on Lady Regina and somehow question her maid?"

Livie nodded. "She…Lady Regina would like to marry you, so she will admit you to the house. If Daisy or I tried to accost Bernadette in the street, the woman would never tell us the truth."

"I suppose that I am now eligible for marriage to such an exalted personage as Lady Regina," Joshua said, his voice flinty. "Given that the woman I adore has chosen righteousness over love, and assuming that my beloved brother will die without issue. I can't say that I look forward to the future."

He walked away with the brisk tread of a soldier.

"I'm sorry," Livie whispered—but she told it to an empty room.

Chapter 37

Kissing the Daughter of a Duke

Joshua walked into the library, noted that Frederick didn't appear to be sodden drunk, and told him, "Put on your coat. We're going to pay a call on Lady Regina."

Frederick's eyes rounded. "Not I!"

"Yes, you," Joshua said, hauling him from his seat. "I'll entertain the lady while you search the maid's room."

"The maid? Not the infamous Bernadette!"

"The same."

"What if Bernadette is *in* her room when I get there?" Frederick asked.

"What maid is allowed to rest before nightfall? If you encounter the woman, pretend that you're inebriated, and you've lost your way," Joshua advised.

"Even when sozzled, I don't invade the servants' quarters, but I suppose I can overcome my scruples in pursuit of a traitor. You aren't looking very cheerful, by the way," Frederick said, shrugging into his coat. "Oates-Plagitt informed me at breakfast that you had sallied forth to lay your heart at the feet of your lady."

Joshua uttered a silent curse.

"Don't ask me how he knows everything," his brother said blithely, following Joshua to the door. "As I see it, the good news is that since our butler determines the outcome of Father's cases, he'll ensure that your future father-in-law returns to the high seas— whether or not we find evidence for the man's innocence."

Joshua threw himself into the carriage, having informed the coachman that they would pay a call on Lady Regina. "You believe Oates-Plagitt has that much influence over our father?"

"Not to disparage our *pater familias*, but he and Oates-Plagitt discuss each case at length. Obviously, our butler uses his Machiavellian wiles to determine the outcome, allowing our father to conclude that he has reached an impartial, evidentiary-based conclusion." Frederick's snort made his opinion clear.

So much for Joshua's conviction that his father was unimpeachably just. He trusted Oates-Plagitt never to sway a case for personal gain, but obviously, his father's claim to impartiality was…complicated. "What will Father think when he discovers that Cassio was arrested under false premises?"

Frederick raised an eyebrow. "Didn't Oates-Plagitt inform you?"

"Inform me?"

"The captain's seal actually *was* attached to that sextant. I presume that Tyron gifted the instrument as a symbol of his intent to bestow Livie's hand in marriage. Likely he had intended Cassio to take his name along with his estate."

Joshua instinctively curled his lip. While gentlemen did occasionally adopt the name of their benefactor upon inheriting a fortune, he had never heard of a man changing his name to that of his wife.

"Didn't you learn anything from your moralistic attitude toward your would-be wife?" Frederick said irritably. "Try to be human rather than judgmental. Our father promptly changed his name on being given a title. Why shouldn't Cassio do the same? Am I to judge from your glower that the lady refused your proposal?"

Joshua ground his teeth. "She did."

His brother's hooded eyes narrowed. "Just how apologetic were you?"

"Very."

"I expect imminent parental execution casts a dark shadow over one's choices. You can try again once Livie's father is freed from the Tower."

"She assures me the case did not influence her decision," Joshua told him.

"Then you'll have to try harder, won't you?" Frederick remarked. "After all, given that I have no intention of marrying now or in the future, you are in charge of producing the future heir to the earldom. Speaking of which, Lady Regina seems willing to exchange her current fiancé for you, so be very careful while 'entertaining' her. I wouldn't put it past her to arrange a compromising situation."

"I shall not marry that woman, compromised or not," Joshua said, his voice just as firm.

"I thought the military required its young officers to be scandal-free? If you shrug off the daughter of a duke's claim to marriage, you'll be the talk of the ton."

"I'm useful," Joshua said flatly. "The army won't give a damn about scandal if I'm available to lead a battalion."

Frederick raised an eyebrow.

"Most second sons are shunted into the military," Joshua continued, "but that doesn't mean they can lead in battle, does it? Their fathers buy them a commission at the officer level, but they remain on the rear lines, playing chess in officers' tents while enlisted men risk their lives."

"I don't suppose I could convince you to stay in a tent? Being as you are responsible for our family's future?"

Joshua planned to leave London on the next available boat. "No," he said flatly.

They sat in silence until the carriage drew up at the Duke of Lennox's townhouse. When one of their grooms opened the carriage door, Frederick leaned forward and flipped him a card.

Two minutes later they were ushered into the ducal drawing room. Lady Regina was seated before a bow window, her head bent studiously over her lap, sunlight shining on her golden hair.

"Please forgive me," she said, rising gracefully as they approached. "I had no intention of accepting callers this morning, as

I am nearly finished with a set of embroidered chairbacks for our country estate." She scanned Joshua, head to foot, from beneath feathery eyelashes. "But I was happy to make an exception for you," she cooed.

Her expression cooled as she turned to Frederick. "And of course, you, Lord FitzRoy-Paget."

"Good morning, Lady Regina," Joshua said, adding, "Your needlework is exquisite."

Her smile showed a great many pearly white teeth. "My sister-in-law would be cross with me for entertaining two gentlemen without a chaperone, but how could I not trust the hero who rescued me from the ballroom floor?" She drew Joshua down to the sofa beside her.

Frederick picked up her needlework. "Interesting," he drawled. "You seem to be stitching a peach with white thread."

Regina snatched it from his hand. "I pride myself on the creativity of my renderings."

"If you'll excuse me, Lady Regina, your brother offered to lend me a copy of Volume Seven of *Plutarch's Lives*," Frederick said.

"The duke is not in residence," she replied. "I suppose you might go to the library and find the volume yourself."

Frederick bowed and headed for the door.

"Your brother is so amusingly brusque," Regina murmured. Joshua had edged away; now she leaned in until her breast rubbed against his arm. "Please tell me more about your military service. I am *fascinated* to hear of your adventures. Have you beheaded anyone in battle?"

"War is not adventuresome," Joshua said, rather taken aback by the mention of beheading. "One is generally too hot, cold, tired, or hungry to enjoy oneself."

Her eyelashes fluttered like the fly-swats their housekeeper used to eliminate pests. "Oh, but you're so brave, marching into battle as if your life wasn't at stake! I expect nothing terrifies you, does it?"

If anything, he was unnerved by Lady Regina. She was wearing a cloying perfume that hung thick in the air like London fog, choking his throat with every breath. "Like all men in His Majesty's Armed Forces, I understand that I may give my life in service to my country."

She swayed even closer, one of her hands closing around Joshua's left arm. "I wish there was something I could do to reward you for your sacrifice."

"Service is its own reward," he barked, thinking the lady would recoil. Instead, Regina fluttered her eyelashes even more; Joshua suddenly realized that she was on the edge of snatching a kiss. "We do miss the—the civilized comforts of home," he exclaimed, starting to his feet and pulling free of her grasp. "Music, for example!"

"Music?" she repeated blankly.

"May I beg you to grace me with a song?" Joshua asked, gesturing toward the pianoforte.

Lady Regina didn't seem entirely pleased, but she did rise, take his hand, and draw him over to the instrument. "You must sit beside me and turn the pages," she murmured huskily.

Joshua would guess that most soldiers reminisced about lusty ballads bawled in a pub. Surely they didn't daydream about a lady stumbling through a Chopin Nocturne, seeming not to notice that she missed half the chords.

By the time they reached the final page, Lady Regina was plastered against his side, having taken every opportunity to press her bony hip against him. He was seated on the very edge of the bench; he would fall to the floor if he moved any further.

When the instrument fell silent, he leapt to his feet and bowed. "What can I say, other than thank you?"

Regina rose and moved to stand just before him, her eyes glinting. "You can thank me properly, Major."

Without waiting for a reply, she threw herself at him, sticking her tongue in his mouth and moving it in a circle like a cook stirring a pot of soup.

Horrified, he froze; Regina promptly wound her arms around his neck and closed her eyes. Just as he put his hands to her shoulders to push her away, the door opened behind her back.

Since Joshua's eyes were wide open, he saw his brother Frederick's satisfied expression turn to horror. Behind him, stepping forward into the room, was a man whose hair rose above his forehead like a wave.

The Earl of Winchester.

Regina's fiancé.

Chapter 38

In Which Livie Learns of Lady Regina's Triumph

Meeting of the Special Commission

House of Lords,

Palace of Westminster

Heart thumping in her ears, Livie followed Lady Wharton into the Pugin Room, where the Special Commission meeting would take place. No matter how often she reminded herself that her "father" was not a blood relative, she couldn't bring herself to accept the fact that Captain Sir Tyron might face execution.

The heaviness in her chest was partly due to terror, and partly due to crying all night over Joshua. The moment he left, she longed for him to come back and try to change her mind. All he would have had to do was kiss her, and her silly argument would have crumpled.

Yet aside from a message affirming that he had paid a visit to Lady Regina, she had heard nothing from him. Her letter asking whether he had spoken to Bernadette had gone unanswered.

The Pugin Room was empty; Lady Wharton and Livie were the first to arrive. "Are you absolutely certain that I am allowed to attend this meeting?" Livie whispered, glancing around. The walls were hung with crimson flock paper and the ceiling decorated with patterns of roses. Huge portraits of august men hung on the wall, one of whom was presumably Joshua's father.

"I was assured that family is welcome. Moreover, you are here as a witness to the coded letters," her aunt replied.

"Yes, but Frederick—"

"I would advise you not to refer to a future earl so informally," her aunt said with a frown. "Lord FitzRoy-Paget will presumably attend, but since he is often inebriated and thus unreliable, your father's solicitor judged that you may be asked to provide a coherent account of the discovery. Moreover, given that his lordship is the Lord High Steward's son, we wish to avoid any suspicion of favoritism."

Lady Wharton removed her cloak and handed it to their groom, gesturing for him to wait in the corridor. "We have a half hour before the company is bid to assemble," she said to Livie. "I felt the need to gather my thoughts. When I visited the captain yesterday, I became concerned that my brother will not aid his own defense."

"I don't think Captain Sir Tyron realizes the gravity of his danger," Livie said. "When I visited him, he became so angry that…" Her voice trailed off. She had been agonizing about whether to tell Lady Wharton what her father had revealed about her parentage, but so far she had held her tongue. Her aunt had embraced her with such affection when she returned from the country that it seemed indelicate to raise the question of her mother's virtue or lack thereof.

"Come, Livie," Lady Wharton announced, leading the way to the end of a row of chairs lined up before a niche created by a bay window. The chair positioned in the niche wasn't precisely a throne, but it certainly evoked one: the back was enormously tall, and it was adorned with a crimson cushion. Two standing candelabras, easily twice Livie's height, were positioned on either side of the chair.

Once they were seated, Lady Wharton reached over and grasped Livie's hand. "Whatever happens, your uncle and I will never forsake you." She paused. "My brother's behavior has been remarkably foolish. In my opinion, he has rarely shown good judgment, but more recently he has been extraordinarily irrational, even for him. Still, idiocy is not synonymous with treachery."

Livie's eyes rounded. She had never heard her aunt say a disparaging word about her brother.

"You are old enough to judge the evidence yourself," her aunt continued. "Take into account the unkind letters he has consistently sent you, his cruelty toward his estranged wife, his devotion to a man who is as unprepossessing as dislikable. The captain had the effrontery to inform me that he planned to give your hand in marriage to this Cassio."

Lady Wharton's bosom swelled with indignation. "I consider you my own daughter. You will *never* marry below the gentry. Moreover, my brother informed me that he has shared with you his foolish surmise regarding your birth."

Livie felt herself turning pale. She bowed her head. "Yes, he told me of my—my shame."

"Nonsense!" Lady Wharton snarled. "You were born within the holy bounds of matrimony. I informed your father that if he told a soul about that wretched idea, I would never speak to him again, and I would withdraw Lord Wharton's support as well. We have great influence in His Majesty's Navy, given that my husband is close friends with Captain Sir Parker, the Chief of Naval Staff. The captain dares not disobey me."

Livie's mind whirled. Was her aunt saying that Livie *wasn't* illegitimate? "So you think I might marry a gentleman?" she whispered. She felt a bitter-sweet twinge of hope. Perhaps…just perhaps…she could write to Joshua, one last time.

Lady Wharton glanced at her. "Please tell me that you have not taken an interest in Lord Devin."

Livie shook her head. "Certainly not!"

"For all his power, his past is distinctly checkered," her aunt remarked. "You may marry as high as you wish, my dear. I should like to see the person who would *dare* to question your birth. Your father has no knowledge of female anatomy, and moreover, he could never count, even in the nursery, and so I reminded him. Trust me, he will never raise that subject again!" She frowned. "If not Lord Devin, have you a fondness for Lord Frederick FitzRoy-Paget? I know he was instrumental in solving the puzzle of my brother's letters."

"No, I have not."

"Thank goodness," her aunt said, taking a fan out of her reticule. She dropped her voice. "The man's an inebriate. The only eligible bachelor in that family is the younger brother."

Livie couldn't stop a smile. "Major FitzRoy?"

"Major FitzRoy-*Paget*," Lady Wharton corrected. "So you've met him? I understand he's quite handsome, and he certainly has a sterling reputation. He would be an excellent match, considering he has an estate of his own and may inherit the earldom, but I heard last night that Lady Regina has snatched him up."

If Livie had paled earlier, now she felt herself turn fully white with shock. "No!"

People were beginning to filter into the room, so her aunt lowered her voice. "Lady Regina is taking a risk, in my opinion. She had an earl in hand—Winchester—and she's thrown him over for someone who may or may not reach the same rank." She glanced over her shoulder and then hissed, "Some people are saying that she contrived to compromise him, but I trust that is a salacious rumor."

Livie felt as if she'd been plunged into icy water. Grief lanced through her, and her breath caught in a sob that she suppressed. She had *known* that Regina wanted Joshua, and yet she had sent him into the lion's den.

She felt utterly wretched. She had freed him, and then handed him to Regina on a platter. Remembering the avarice in Regina's eyes when she talked of him… Undoubtedly, the woman had compromised him.

Even worse, Joshua's "honor" would demand he marry her.

Chapter 39

The Plot Thickens

"There's my brother," Lady Wharton hissed, elbowing Livie. "The two men with him are our solicitors."

Livie couldn't summon a response. She sat, stricken, as the chamber filled with people. The captain glowed in his superb new coat and seemed to be in the best of spirits, though his mouth tightened when he caught glimpse of Livie.

Mr. Cassio was brought in a few minutes later. *He* was wearing handcuffs and didn't reply to her father's greeting. Frederick walked into the room accompanied by Lord Devin, his bloodshot eyes suggesting he was feeling the effects of drink, but was perhaps not wholly drunk. There was no sign of Bernadette, so Joshua's inquiries must have been ineffectual.

There was no reason for Joshua to attend, of course.

In fact, she may never see him again. Or perhaps she would, but only with Lady Regina on his arm. Pain stabbed through Livie's heart. Joshua would loathe being married to Regina. In fact, it wouldn't surprise her if he went to war, and…and sacrificed himself. Her stomach squeezed into a sickening ball.

She couldn't stop picturing the anguished love in his eyes, replaced by smoldering anger. She might have sent him to his death. Not that he—

Livie broke off that miserable train of thought as the heavy doors to the room closed behind the final member of the committee: Earl Paget, the Lord High Steward, had arrived. He seated himself before the group, twitching his velvet robes, and said without preamble, "This meeting has been called to allow Lord Devin to present evidence that implicates another defendant in the deplorable case of the attempt on His Majesty's life. This hearing will not determine Captain Sir Tyron's innocence, though he is present. His innocence or guilt will be addressed before a full meeting of the House of Lords; on that occasion, His Majesty's prosecutor will present his witnesses."

With a wrench, Livie pulled herself out of a black caldron of despair and tried to pay attention.

She glanced toward the other side of the chamber and found the captain smiling broadly. He assumed his innocence was a given—that's why he felt confident that he could save Cassio as well. Livie suspected that her father simply couldn't imagine a situation in which he was found guilty. He—or anyone else of his birth and rank.

Their eyes met, and the captain promptly looked away. Livie swallowed hard, her eyes smarting with stinging tears. She had to stop thinking of him as her father, given his contemptuous rejection.

Lord Devin described the discovery of coded letters, and the likelihood that Cassio had first transcribed and thereafter added coded ink blots as well as an incriminating sentence, reading it aloud: *"The dark shore of the heart may engender fornications, murders and thefts."*

The Crown's prosecutor, a Mr. Metrie, raised his eyebrows, taking possession of the letters and scanning them.

"That sentence sounds just like my brother," Lady Wharton admitted in an undertone.

After some discussion between Lord Devin and Mr. Metrie, Captain Sir Tyron was directly asked if he'd coded the letters, to which he answered a resounding "No." When asked whether Cassio had done so, her father said with raw conviction that he would trust his first mate unto death.

At that point, Cassio was brought forward and questioned. As expected, he denied all knowledge of coded language: "The captain reviews every letter after I transcribe it. He signs them and gives them to the quartermaster. I could add neither ink blots nor an extra sentence without his express knowledge."

Livie had to admit that it was a convincing point.

"What of the seal?" Lord Paget asked, leaning forward. "My understanding is that the witnesses for the prosecution maintain that instructions sent to French conspirators were affixed with Captain Sir Tyron's seal—his personal coat of arms—a seal that has been found in your possession."

"That particular seal was attached to a navigational device given to me by the captain, but since it was hidden in the index arm of the sextant, I had no idea of its existence. Another seal with the same coat of arms was stolen from the captain some months prior," Cassio replied. He paused. "It has since occurred to me that he may have gifted the sextant in order to cast suspicion on me if treasonous letters surfaced."

The captain turned his head to give his first mate an incredulous stare, but Cassio kept his eyes fixed on Lord Devin.

Called upon by the prosecutor, Frederick rose and stated that his butler had discovered the Tyron seal slotted into the index arm of a sextant on Cassio's table.

Yet Cassio again insisted that he knew nothing of the seal attached to the sextant. Moreover, he had been gifted the sextant after the captain's seal disappeared from his desk on board the *Royal Oak*.

"I did not inform Mr. Cassio of the seal attached to the sextant," Captain Sir Tyron stated, confirming his account. "I thought to show him the trick of it after he changed his name to Tyron and married my…Miss Tyron."

Cassio's lip curled. "I didn't bother to look closely at the sextant. I had no wish to marry Miss Tyron, and I shall *never* change my name."

"Yet you allowed Captain Sir Tyron to believe that you were interested in this marriage?" Lord Devin asked.

"He was the captain of the *Royal Oak*, and I, along with the rest of the sailors, did our best to keep him in a cheerful mood."

Livie watched as ruddy color faded from her father's cheeks.

"What do you mean?" the prosecutor asked.

"On more than one occasion, the captain threw men overboard for minor infractions, telling them to swim behind the ship." The chamber was utterly silent. "In at least one case, we could not rescue the sailor before sharks attacked."

"That's a damn lie!" the captain barked.

"His name was Jeremy Tulip," Cassio said, still not looking at his master. "You'll find his death listed as 'misadventure.' The captain left the deck directly after ordering the poor lad overboard and may not be aware of the outcome. He never paid much attention to the fate of his underlings."

The prosecutor shot a look at Livie's father that suggested he would soon be facing a charge of murder. "Are you saying that Captain Sir Tyron never queried whether Mr. Tulip had been safely rescued?"

"Never." Cassio's consciously sober expression struck Livie as deceptive, but on the other hand, she could easily imagine her father tossing a man overboard and dismissing the occasion from his mind. "Tulip was not the first to go overboard, but the only one I know of who did not return."

"I am the master of my vessel!" the captain thundered. "I assure you that if this Tulip was lost to the deep—which I doubt—he was a miscreant who thoroughly deserved it! I consider myself stern but just, and any number of seamen who have served under me will assure you of that."

"No one on board ever questioned the captain's decisions," Mr. Cassio said, entirely ignoring the captain's bluster. "He was feared by all. Certainly I would never have angered him by admitting that I have no wish to marry his daughter. My life was at stake."

Livie glanced around the room, horror surging in her chest.

"He's very clever," Lady Wharton said quietly.

"I had no idea that the captain had plans to bring enemy agents to England, but I was aware that his opinions of the Crown were…unflattering," Cassio added.

"I have the utmost respect for His Majesty," the captain growled. "I will admit that I did not always review letters I dictated as closely as I might have. The sentence in question may not have been written by me."

"Yet you did review each letter before signing it," Mr. Metrie prompted.

The captain's head bobbed. Livie had the sense that he was suddenly—finally—aware of his danger. "I merely glanced," he admitted. "They were unimportant missives, meant solely for Miss Tyron's eyes."

"Would you describe this language—'*The dark shore of the heart may engender fornications, murders and thefts*'—as characteristic of letters sent to your daughter?" The prosecutor's tone made it clear that he found the sentiment worthy of a pastor, not a father.

"I have always tried to direct Miss Tyron to the paths of righteousness," the captain stated.

"This subject will be further discussed during Captain Sir Tyron's trial before the House of Lords," the Lord High Steward said. "This meeting is solely to determine Mr. Cassio's involvement. The theft for which Mr. Cassio has been imprisoned has been shown to have no bearing on the case before us. He may be freed."

"If you'll forgive me, Your Lordship, we would like to summon one more witness," Lord Devin announced.

Lord Paget frowned at him. "This is most irregular."

"It was important that we first establish the fact that Mr. Cassio had no intention of marrying Miss Tyron."

"I fail to see the relevance," the judge complained.

But Livie was watching Cassio, and she saw his body still. In her imagination, he suddenly looked less like a put-upon subordinate and more like a predator.

Lord Devin left the room. When he pushed the door open again, Bernadette entered, her arm firmly held by Joshua. An unquenchable longing surged in Livie's blood at a mere glimpse of his face.

She forced herself to look at her former maid instead. Bernadette's head was high—and her ringlets in perfect order—but her eyes were darting from face to face. Her bosom was rising and falling rapidly; she was clearly close to panic.

"I recognize Major FitzRoy-Paget," Lord Paget said dryly, his eyes resting on his son's face. "Introduce your new witness."

"Bernadette Fournier was employed in the Wharton household for a number of years," Joshua stated. "As everyone surely knows, the Crown's investigation of the incident on French soil took two years. She left her post only after Captain Sir Tyron's arrest was made public."

"I fail to see the significance of such household trivia," Lord Paget said.

"Miss Tyron can confirm that during Miss Fournier's tenure as a personal maid, she had ready access to all letters sent by Captain Sir Tyron, including the coded letters."

"It is our contention that Miss Fournier was responsible for recovering those letters, deciphering the code, and passing on messages to her co-conspirators, affixing those letters with Captain Sir Tyron's stolen seal."

"What is the evidence for your accusation?" Lord Paget inquired.

"This seal was found in her trunk," Joshua said, pulling a seal from his pocket.

Bernadette gasped, the air rattling in her throat.

Lord Devin stepped forward. "You shall hang for this conspiracy," he informed Bernadette, "unless you tell us who is the mastermind of this plot."

"Captain Sir Tyron," she gasped.

"Mr. Cassio is about to be released," Lord Devin said, his voice dry. "Like you, he is in possession of a seal and has thrown blame on Captain Sir Tyron. Unlike you, he has successfully argued that he had no knowledge of the seal's existence. You cannot argue the same. Your innocence is not in question."

Bernadette's gaze flew to Cassio's face; Lord Devin allowed himself a smile. "May I ask how you know which man I am referring to, Miss Fournier? I was careful not to look at Mr. Cassio when I mentioned his name."

"I must have seen him while I served in the Wharton household," Bernadette said.

"Cassio has never entered my house," Lady Wharton said, rising and then seating herself immediately.

Lord Devin nodded at her. "I wish to make certain that you understand the outlines of the plot as we have uncovered it, Miss Fournier," he said. "The captain or another man sent coded letters to the Wharton household, where you were serving as maid. You marshaled these letters and arranged for a number of Frenchmen to be waiting on shore one particular evening, when a boat was sent to shore from the *Royal Oak*. The prosecutor for the Crown suggests that the men were meant to infiltrate the boat, return to the ship, and then make their way to London in order to assassinate His Majesty."

Bernadette made a small noise, like a cough.

"Perhaps you find this plot as unlikely as I do," Lord Devin said peaceably. "Miss Fournier, it is my contention that this plot had nothing to do with the king, and was never an assassination attempt. Do you agree with my surmise?"

Bernadette gulped again.

"Because if you do," he said, "the charges against you would cease to be high treason, and you would face imprisonment rather than execution. I'll remind you again, Miss Fournier, that the seal was found in *your* possession."

"They meant to take the ship," she blurted out.

Livie gaped. Bernadette's French accent had vanished, replaced by a Liverpool twang.

Mr. Cassio made a sharp movement.

"What did the conspirators plan to do with the *Royal Oak*?" Lord Devin asked. He held every person in the chamber in the palm of his hand; his polished, urbane tones were at once intimate, as if he were speaking only to Bernadette, and yet loud enough to be heard by all.

"Pirates!" Bernadette cried. "They were to be pirates. With the Frenchmen and others on the ship already."

"Mutiny?" Lord Devin asked.

Bernadette nodded, though her chin was trembling so hard that her assent was difficult to confirm. "He…the captain isn't a decent man. They meant to take the ship from him. 'Twas nothing to do with His Majesty," she said in a burst. "He is a good king, and sick in the bargain!"

"I see you are a patriot," Lord Devin said soothingly. "Is that why you stayed on in employment at the Wharton household after the plan failed?"

She nodded. "In case of another opportunity."

"Is your name truly Bernadette?" Lord Devin asked.

Bernadette paused. "It isn't," she said reluctantly. "My name's Dora."

"I must have your last name as well," his lordship said.

"Cassio." She raised her chin. "Dora Cassio."

Chapter 40

We all Need a Daisy in our Lives

"I cannot believe it!" Daisy squealed. "What did Cassio say when Bernadette told everyone she was his wife—not to mention, *not* French, and *not* Bernadette?"

Livie had scarcely removed her pelisse after returning from the Special Commission meeting before Daisy dragged her upstairs, demanding a full account.

"Then Cassio told Dora to 'Shut her giff,'" Livie replied, reaching the most exciting point in her story.

Daisy was sitting opposite her on the bed, hugging her knees. "Very unpleasant."

"Dora tossed her head so hard that her ringlets rose in the air and fell back around her face just like that statue of Medusa we saw in the museum. She wouldn't have hesitated to turn Cassio to stone right in front of us all."

"I see her point," Daisy observed. "*She* was about to be convicted of treason, whereas *he* was about to be set free. I presume the plan was his?"

Livie nodded. "Cassio was the ringleader of a mutinous group on the *Royal Oak*. He needed a few co-conspirators that would obey him without question, so he recruited Frenchmen with talk of regicide. Once the ship was his, he meant to turn pirate. They would never be able to rebel against his command, if you see what I mean."

"No, I don't see. Why didn't he just hire some criminal Englishmen?"

"Lord Devin says Englishmen would be far more likely to stab him in the back and take over the ship themselves," Livie answered. "Or turn him in."

Daisy rolled her eyes. "Oh, well, if *Lord Devin* says so, then it must be the case."

"Frenchmen who had joined a conspiracy to kill the King of England wouldn't be able to argue with Cassio because he had evidence of their regicidal plans to hold over them." Livie flopped down on her back on the bed. "The captain's face was so sad. He had no idea that his crew loathed him so."

Daisy laid down on her side, propping her head on her hand. "Not only that, but presumably Cassio would have made my uncle walk the plank." She grimaced. "That's a terrible thought."

"I couldn't even look at his face," Livie said, squinting at her cousin through a blur of tears. "He loved Cassio so much, but the man showed utter contempt for him. I couldn't offer comfort because…because the captain is so contemptuous of me. Even after the meeting, when he was being taken back to the Tower, he wouldn't speak to me. I shouldn't care, but I couldn't stop myself."

Her voice wobbled—she felt as if her entire world had crumbled. The family had always believed that her father was one of the best captains in the navy, but that was before they'd known that that poor boy, Jeremy Tulip, had been eaten by a *shark*.

"I am trying very hard not to be rude about my uncle," Daisy said grimly. She hesitated. "Did my mother share the news about Joshua?"

A sob broke from Livie's chest. "He's marrying Regina. Because I sent him to her house."

"You have to take him back," Daisy ordered. "He's yours, Livie. You may have temporarily tossed him out, but he was always supposed to return."

Livie swallowed hard. "You *know* what the circumstances of my birth will do for his career."

"Your birth?" Daisy snorted. "My mother says her brother can't count to nine months."

"The captain told me he was on board ship for over a year." She kept hearing his ringing denunciation in her ears.

"My mother won't let him tell anyone. More to the point, you're acting as if there are a hundred men out there just like Joshua."

"No, I am acting as if I *care* about him and his future!" Livie snapped.

"That would be the future in which he marries Regina and becomes an earl? He'll surely inherit the title, because if poor Frederick doesn't die soon, Regina will probably throw her brother-in-law under the wheels of a carriage to ensure she becomes a countess."

"Daisy!"

"So it's absolutely fine with you if the major marries Regina, as long as his career and title are preserved?"

"Joshua wouldn't be engaged to her unless he wanted to," Live said, her voice rough with tears.

"You know better than that," Daisy retorted. "My mother said that they were caught kissing, so as a gentleman, he has to marry her. Unless *you* save him, because you are *not* a lady, Livie, no matter how hard you've tried to be one. And no matter how desperately your father has tried to force you into the mold!"

"I *am* a lady!" Livie retorted, but her voice was hollow. No lady lay back in a cupboard and allowed a man to pleasure her.

"You are a *woman*," Daisy said, her voice gentling. "Don't you see how much better that is, Livie? Whatever anyone says about Regina, she is decisive. She wanted Joshua, so she took him, wielding the same rules of propriety to take him that you used to reject him."

That hadn't escaped Livie's notice. She put a hand on her chest, wondering if the searing pain she felt was permanent.

"Why should Regina get what she wants, and you shouldn't?" Daisy demanded. "That's not even taking into account what Joshua wants." She rolled onto her back and looked up at the ceiling. "I want a man to look at me the way he looks at you."

"He didn't even glance at me during the meeting."

"He's in Regina's grasp now, caught in the…in the toils of his honor," Daisy said, waving one hand in the air. "He saved your father by nabbing Bernadette. I'll say it again—it's your turn to save *him*."

"I'm not actually certain that my father is 'saved,'" Livie said, taking a shuddering breath. "They didn't release him from the Tower."

"Because of that business about dropping a sailor overboard? I'm sure it's untrue, made up by the horrid Cassio, who would do and say *anything*, obviously. Pirates throw men overboard—never Englishmen!"

"He threatened to throw me overboard once," Livie whispered, her voice rasping.

After a moment of leaden silence, Daisy sat up. "Do you know what I think of your father, Livie? Do you?"

Livie shook her head.

Her cousin reached out, caught up the water glass on her bedside table, and threw it into the fireplace, where it shattered.

"Oh," Livie whispered.

"He is not your father," Daisy stated. "He's nothing to you. He's as broken as that glass, every bit as nasty and as sharp—and a murderer, to boot! What is the obvious solution, Livie?" Her voice sounded exactly like her mother's: as imperious and fierce as a queen's.

"Marry Joshua?"

"Precisely. Put the captain's fate out of your mind. My mother will ensure that her brother isn't tried for murder."

"Is that fair?" Livie asked.

"Fair? When is the world fair? If he truly ordered a man overboard, my mother will force the captain to give the family of the dead sailor a large sum of money. It won't bring the man back, but neither will a murder trial, especially in front of the House of Lords. The captain will be acquitted, Livie, because the world isn't *fair*." With that, Daisy swung her legs off the bed and got up. "We'd best summon your maid."

"Why?" Livie made her way off the bed slowly, feeling old and tired.

"Because I wrote to Joshua and requested that he pay us a call—signing your name, naturally. I sent a separate letter to

Frederick, who will throw Joshua into a carriage and deliver him to you."

Livie frowned. "Why did you do that?"

"Because I love you," Daisy said, kissing her cheek, "and Frederick loves Joshua. We both know that the best way to keep Joshua alive on a battlefield is if he has you to come home to, Livie."

It was a simple fact.

Livie felt the truth of it in the deepest part of her bones. Still... "To marry me, he'd have to jilt Lady Regina, the daughter of a duke."

Daisy nodded. "Do you need me to shatter another glass to illustrate what I think of Regina?"

Forty minutes later, Livie was bathed, her hair had been brushed into silky ringlets, and she was dressed in her favorite yellow gown.

Daisy looked at her from head to toe, and then darted toward her, a tin of lip color in hand. "You are exquisite. Smile at him, and he'll fall at your feet."

Livie didn't agree. Did honor and reputation matter more to Joshua than she did? He had gotten over the first affront—when he thought she was asking him to interfere with his father's judgment—because he'd been mistaken. He hadn't risked his honor by finding Bernadette.

If he didn't marry Regina, he would be branded a dishonorable scoundrel throughout polite society.

Worry spun through Livie's mind. Her father wasn't her father, and he was likely a murderer. She was either the daughter of a criminal or illegitimate or both. She kept trying to weigh her certainty that she and Joshua belonged together against an equal certainty that marrying her would result in his being shunned by his superiors in the British Army.

What could she—what *should* she say to him when he came?

In the end, it didn't matter

He didn't come.

She, Daisy, and her aunt sat through four courses, Lady Wharton too angry at her brother to do more than growl; even Daisy's chatter couldn't distract her mother. Livie tried unsuccessfully to stop watching the door, hoping that Joshua would come in five minutes… In another half hour… In an hour.

After their tea grew cold and bitter, Lady Wharton led the way upstairs, still grumbling. Heart leaden, Livie removed her pretty gown, washed the paint from her face, brushed out her curls, and let her maid braid her hair.

Joshua had honor deep in his bones. An honorable, betrothed man does not engage in clandestine correspondence with another woman. He doesn't answer that woman's summons. She blew out the candle and stared into the moonlit room, wryly amused to discover that her father—or was it Cassio?—had been right.

The dark shore of the heart may engender fornications, murders and thefts.

She wanted to steal Joshua.

She could cheerfully murder Regina.

She wanted…

She wanted what no lady wanted.

Fornication.

Chapter 41

Who Deserves Honor?

Livie was still staring bleakly into the moonlit room, brushing away the odd tear, when she heard a carriage draw up before the house. The night soil man, she thought numbly. But that vehicle usually trundled through the alley to the servants' entrance in the rear. Perhaps the milkman on an early round? But again, why—

She sat bolt upright as Daisy's footsteps pattered down the corridor to the staircase. Frowning, Livie swung her legs out of bed, caught up her bedside candle, and lit it from the embers in the fireplace. Her heart started thumping so hard that it felt as if her ribs might crack. Thank goodness her aunt slept in the back of the house.

When footsteps came up the stairs, she opened her door—and stopped short. Daisy put her finger to her lip and pulled someone very large from the shadows behind her.

Someone male.

Livie grabbed his hand, drawing him into the room. Daisy closed the door quietly from the corridor, and though Livie didn't hear a giggle, her imagination supplied it.

They moved without thought or words: Joshua's arms wrapped around her, his cheek against the top of her head, both of them murmuring inarticulately. Livie clung to him, breathing his earthy, clean scent, unwilling to raise her face. She couldn't kiss him.

Because—

"You're betrothed to another woman," she said, pulling away.

"No." Joshua stepped toward her, cupped her face in his hands, his broad fingers reaching all the way to the back of her head. "How could I marry another woman? I love *you*."

Even in the dim light, she could read his expression, and part of her melted with pure happiness. Yet she had to say it: "You compromised Lady Regina, and my aunt says that you are betrothed."

He bent his head and brushed his lips over hers. "Lady Wharton is mistaken."

Despite Livie's shiver at his kiss, her aunt was so rarely wrong that she shook her head. "Were you seen kissing her?"

"No. She was seen kissing me."

"Isn't that a matter of semantics?"

At his expression, a seedling of hope sprang to life in her heart.

"I explained the difference to her and to her fiancé as well, since he was present," Joshua said. "The earl appreciated the clarification. She did not."

"But I thought—" She broke off.

"Lady Regina appears to believe that telling people her version of the truth will make it a fact," Joshua said. "I immediately informed her that I would not marry her. I left the room when she and her fiancé began arguing."

Livie was at once stunned and unsurprised by Regina's presumption. "Yet she informed people that you *are* engaged?"

"That seems to be the case," Joshua said, his tone unbothered. "Fair warning, Livie, my reputation will be destroyed once it becomes known that I refuse to marry a duke's daughter. Frederick told me that I'll never again be admitted to Almack's— though of course, he was drunk and seemed to consider that a badge of honor."

Livie swallowed. "I don't care about Almack's. I don't want to go there again." Thinking of Regina's face, she added: "*Ever.*"

"I will marry you, Livie. Or, if you won't have me, I won't marry." Joshua's brows drew together. "That sounded as if I meant to blackmail you, but I don't mean it like that."

"I refused you," Livie repeated, knowing that her words had no force.

Only one candle and moonlight—but she saw laughter in his eyes. And tenderness, along with hunger.

"You did say no." He pulled her closer, tilted her head back, and kissed her again. "I made myself wait until after the meeting to ask you again. I was hoping that finding Bernadette would work in my favor. But then your father—"

"No," she choked. "I don't want to talk about him."

Joshua's mouth came to hers again, tasting spicy and male. Heat burned down Livie's body, and she swayed into the hard slab of his chest. Those callused fingers slid into her hair, and their kiss deepened until he made a hungry noise in the back of his throat. His fingers slid down her neck and then shoulders.

Livie suddenly remembered she was wearing only her nightgown. It was too late to gasp—besides, his touch was tender, his hands slipping down her arms until their fingers entwined.

"I do think we have to talk about the captain, love."

"All right," she said with a gulp.

He looked around the chamber, at the bed, sheets rumpled and thrown back, glowing white in the moonlight.

Livie's heart thumped. "We could go downstairs."

Joshua shook his head, drew her over to the bed, curled his hands around her waist, and put her at the head. "I'll sit at the other end." His voice seemed to rumble from his chest.

Livie watched as he pulled off his boots and sat opposite her, knees up, his hands dangling between them. Light from the window behind him caught his face, moonlight edging the strong lines of his jaw.

"I feel as if we're on a raft," she said.

"Floating on a dark ocean? Just the two of us?"

She followed Joshua's gaze to the pale curve of her breast, just visible through the lace edging of her bodice.

"If it were a raft, I would be next to you, making certain you didn't unbalance," he said, hunger threaded through his words.

Livie took a deep breath and then pulled her bodice up.

He made a fierce sound, like a groan, and she couldn't help smiling. Her biggest, most joyful smile. The one her father never saw, and wouldn't welcome. The one that Daisy said was a "naughty" smile.

Joshua froze and then said in a deep growl, "How was I lucky enough to find you?"

The smile fell away. "I lied when I refused your marriage proposal," Livie said, blurting out the words she had rehearsed in her head.

"I thought perhaps that was the case," Joshua replied without censure in his voice. "The only reason I could imagine you lying, love, was if you were trying to protect me."

"Oh...well, yes." Then she remembered her script. "I was born after my father had been at sea for a year."

He frowned.

"The captain had been gone more than nine months," she said, wondering if men knew anything about pregnancies.

"Are you saddened to know he's not your father?" Joshua asked, clearly picking his words with care.

"I'm illegitimate!"

"No, you're not. You were born within the bounds of matrimony. You are *entirely* legitimate."

"You know what I mean."

He rolled his eyes, looking just like Daisy for a moment. "Who cares?"

"The captain—" She cleared her throat. "He has threatened to inform any man who asked to marry me."

Joshua's crack of laughter was too loud.

Livie sat up. "Hush!"

"As if his opinion matters? He's not your father, Livie, thank God. He's not…a good man. Ironic, given the content of all those letters he sent you."

Livie was still having trouble working it out in her head. Her father had murdered a boy, thrown him away like a piece of rubbish. He had harangued her for years about her virtue—then thrown her away like another piece of rubbish. She was lucky to have been on land, because she had a strong suspicion that he might have chucked her overboard.

"Love," Joshua said softly. "Come here." He held out his arms. "I can't come to you because it wouldn't be proper."

Livie's laugh was a squeak in the back of her throat as she tipped forward and crawled toward him. "Proper! None of this is proper. My aunt would…"

"She wouldn't be pleased," Joshua supplied, scooping Livie into his lap. "I have to remind you of a newly discovered fact, Livie. I am no gentleman. As such, I'll soon be infamous for jilting Lady Regina. I might as well be hanged for a sheep, as a lamb. Consider yourself compromised."

"Even if no one learns of my true parentage, my 'father' is in the Tower for treason," Livie offered.

"He'll soon be there on a charge of murder," Joshua said cheerfully. "Luckily, he's not really my father-in-law."

"But your career!"

Joshua shrugged, his arms tightening around her. "I inherited money and can support us. I'm a good soldier, Livie. If that doesn't work out, I'll be good at other things."

"It sounds so simple," Livie whispered longingly.

"It *is* simple. Your father disregarded the lives of the men under his command. True, I am jilting the daughter of a duke, but I treasure the men I lead, the men of my battalion. That's where true honor lies, Livie, and the captain doesn't have it. Honor has nothing to do with rank or convention or tradition—it lies in devotion, in kindness, in respect for one another."

Joshua's words were deep and heartfelt, emerging from his core. "It lies in love, Livie."

Livie nestled against him, thinking. "You're a gentleman with honor because you behave with honor."

"And you are a lady because you behave like one. You are kind-hearted, loyal, intelligent, brave, delightful, and in love with your husband-to-be. Moreover, you are *delicious*." The last few words were muffled because his lips were sliding, warm and firm, along her neck.

"Daisy says that it's better to be a woman than a lady." Livie took a deep breath, eased off Joshua's lap, and lay back on the bed.

"Have I told you how much I appreciate your cousin's wisdom?" Joshua breathed, moving forward so he was on his hands and knees, looking down at her.

Livie smiled. Her naughty smile.

Chapter 42

Whither Thou Goest

Joshua looked down at his wife-to-be, her untidy braid standing out against the white sheet, lips curved in a mischievous smile, cheeks flushed with desire. His entire body longed to make her his, but his conscience was nagging at him.

He may have thrown aside the rules of gentlemanly behavior in refusing to marry Regina, but he didn't want to take advantage of the woman he loved, either. "Are you quite certain, darling?"

Livie answered with a smile, but he waited until she wound her arms around his neck and whispered, "You're mine, Joshua. So yes, make love to me now, and when we're married, and when we're eighty."

"Before we say our vows?" he said, wanting her to be absolutely certain.

"I will never regret making love to you, be it outside the bounds of matrimony or even in a wardrobe," Livie told him. "You and I, Joshua, are not bound by the rules society dictates for men and women,"

Joshua winced. "To be honest, I'm traditional at the heart, Livie. I want you to be mine. My wife."

Livie brushed her lips over his. "I feel the same."

Joshua eased down on his side next to her, one hand freeing the last twists of her braid and sinking into her unruly curls. "Will you accompany me when I am dispatched abroad?" he asked, his voice uncertain even to his own ears, his heart thumping in his chest. "You wouldn't be the first woman to join the campaign. I have a friend whose wife travels with him—not into danger, of course," he added quickly.

Livie came up on one elbow and leaned toward him. "*Whither thou goest*," she whispered, echoing the age-old vow, "*I will go. And where thou lodgest, I will lodge. Thy people shall be my—*" She spoke the last word into his mouth, because Joshua rolled forward and sank into a kiss so loving and profound that he would remember it for the rest of his life.

One of his hands clasped her rounded hip, and for long minutes they merely kissed. She tasted like honey and love—like the most intoxicating liqueur he'd ever sipped—yet he reined himself in, kissing her over and over until she pulled back.

"What's next?" Livie breathed, her eyes sparkling in the moonlight, cheeks flushed.

Joshua choked back a laugh. "May I touch you?"

"As you did in our wardrobe?"

"Is it *our* wardrobe?"

She nodded. "No one else has shared such pleasure in that wardrobe. I'm certain of it."

Joshua swallowed Livie's giggle, letting her joy fill him as his hand slid from her waist to her breast, turning the silken fabric of her nightgown into a caress. She gasped when his hand ran over her nipple, so he rubbed his palm in circles over that little nub until a throaty plea broke from her lips.

Thus far she had kept her arms around his neck, but now her hands began flying across his chest as if she were measuring him for a new suit of clothing. She nipped his lip and kissed his chin, raining kisses down his neck.

Joshua relaxed into her gentle push, rolling to his back, giving his body up to her exploration, allowing her to tug off his coat and unbutton his waistcoat. Between them, they pulled the clothing from his upper body, until his unfashionably burly chest was bared to her view. She didn't seem to mind his muscles. In fact, she sprawled over him, kissing and licking until his heart was pumping ferociously, and air sawed in his lungs. Finally, he swung his legs over the bed, stood up, and stripped off his remaining garments, baring the scars hidden beneath his waistband.

Livie didn't notice them at first. Her eyes widened as she looked from the arrow of hair on his chest, past his rigid tool, down his thick legs. He was built for a battlefield, not for a ballroom, his battered body no match to the silken, slender elegance of her limbs.

When her eyes returned to his waist, she instantly came to her knees and put her arms around his hips, tenderly kissing the proof of his injuries, with no sign of the repulsion he had imagined fine ladies exhibiting.

"Does it still hurt?" she asked, brushing her fingers over his scars in a caress.

Joshua shook his head. He couldn't stop looking at her curves, so much more lush than they appeared in docile white muslin. Her hair fell almost to her nipped-in waist, curling in wild abandon over her bare breasts. His blood raged like wildfire in his veins, desire burning in his every fiber, passion racketing down his legs.

Everything he knew of virgins—precious little—suggested that they would be fearful of intimacy. Yet Joshua abruptly decided that very little would frighten his wife-to-be—not uncouth muscles, not scars, and certainly not intimacy. Perhaps Livie had developed fortitude to weather Captain Sir Tyron's constant reproaches. Year after year, she had faced the worst—daily condemnation from the man who should value her most—and survived, nay, thrived.

A lesser girl would have cowered at the captain's hectoring letters, not to mention the venomous lectures that he likely delivered in person. That lady would have been forced into a pale imitation of a woman, trembling at the mere idea of breaking social rules, terrified to do more than lisp in the presence of a man.

But Livie had survived years of parental loathing with courage, so much so that she went to a disreputable party—where she told Clod Tyrwhitt to jump, tripped him up, and shouted at him. Livie *would* sail away to a foreign country at Joshua's side. When he went into battle, she would wait for his return with fear in her heart, but her back would be straight and her eyes brave.

"Joshua," she said now, lifting her arms. "Come to me." Her smile was the sensual smile of a woman who knows the man before her is hers, body and soul.

He came, because he would always come to her. It was his turn to rain kisses down her neck, although he didn't stop there. He unbuttoned her nightgown, lips following fingers as he unfastened each in sequence, leaving a trail of kisses like footprints in fresh snow. He drew his tongue over the slope of her pale breast and finally closed his lips around her nipple, making her squeak and then sigh with delight.

Soon after, her nightgown was tossed to the floor, and their hands ran over each other's bodies like water. They kissed wildly, tumbling over one another, taking turns on top or sinking back, weak with longing.

Joshua felt his caresses shifting from tender to rough; with a choked sound he pulled away from Livie just enough to run his hands to her knees and ease her legs apart.

"Oh, *that*," she said, eyes lighting up. "I thought perhaps that was a matter reserved for masquerades and wardrobes."

"No, for every day," he managed, but he scarcely tasted her before she bowed upward, a shudder rocking her body and a hoarse sound breaking from her lips. He stayed with her through every quiver, until she took a shuddering breath and calmed.

Then he moved up and asked, "Livie?" A question, because she might have changed her mind—had the right to change her mind.

She opened eyes, slung her arms around her neck, and asked again, "What next?" Her voice was dazed with pleasure, yet eager for more.

Starting with another long kiss, he taught her what came next, beginning with cautious, slow thrusts, then deep and long, until she caught the rhythm and began arching to meet him. By then he was burning with impatience, sweating and panting; he pulled back and tilted her hips, plunging home again.

Her ripe mouth opened in a wanton cry that he only just caught with his lips. His large hand closed on her bottom and pulled Livie snugly against him, drinking in her feverish delight until they exploded together in a shuddering, uncivilized burst of pleasure.

Afterwards, they lay entangled, damp and overheated, grinning at each other like fools because they had discovered something astonishing: a pleasure so fierce that it could be experienced only with the right person. Only when life gives you the greatest gift of all.

"I would happily throw away my career for you," Joshua said, sliding one finger down her damp cleavage, admiring the curves of her breasts, even though lust had been temporarily burned out of him. "I would throw away the world for you, Livie. I don't care if you're a footman's or a traitor's daughter. The only thing that matters in my life is *you*."

Her smile was lazy, replete…tender. "And I don't care that I've stolen you from a duke's daughter. You'll never dance in Almack's again—and you'll never become an earl, for I intend to make Frederick give up his brandy."

Joshua would have said there was no room for any more joy in his heart, but it turned out that there was. A few minutes later, when she flipped onto her stomach and laughed at him over her shoulder, it turned out that lust wasn't burned out of him, either.

He pulled on his clothing at dawn, leaving a blissful lady sprawled on the bed. Her last kiss sustained him through a long day of difficult conversations, beginning with a meeting with Lady

Wharton, who was outraged when informed that their marriage must occur immediately; she sharply told him that she expected wanton behavior from her daughter, not her niece. From there, he went to the Tower to meet with Captain Sir Tyron, who had finally realized he was in serious danger. The man not only expressed disinterest in Livie's future, but informed Joshua that he needed her dowry for his legal defense, and thus Joshua should expect to receive "nothing but a shameless libertine" from this betrothal. Next, Joshua met with his own father, who proved incredulous at the idea that his son would refuse to marry the daughter of a duke, let alone that he'd propose to the daughter of a murderer.

And finally, long day over, he found Frederick in the library. His brother toasted his escape from Regina's clutches with a swig of the very best brandy. "Livie is the best sort," Frederick said, putting down his bottle. "She looks civilized, but she's not, is she? She'll go with you to war."

Joshua nodded. "Fair warning, she plans to take away your brandy and marry you off so that I never inherit the title."

His brother snorted, but if Joshua had to bet, he would back Livie every time.

Joshua did not sneak back into Wharton house that night nor did he climb a convenient tree outside Livie's window… Instead, he bought a special license and married his lady two days later.

Much to the scandal and fury of polite society.

Especially Lady Regina.

Epilogue

Ten Years Later

Livie hopped over a puddle, fell short, and swore under her breath—an unladylike habit she'd picked up during their years in Spain, where the sun shone daily, and no one paid attention when one of the "Lady Grenadiers" cursed.

"What's the matter, Mama?" Sara called, as she jumped the same puddle. "Are you feeling the cold in your bones?"

"I find the mud tiresome," Livie offered, smiling at her seven-year-old daughter. In truth, though, it was the city she found tiresome. While abroad, she had ignored the tenets of propriety that had mattered so much to Captain Sir Tyron.

She'd been free to try new things and seek new experiences without fear of reproach, whether from society or her father. Not that his opinion mattered at this point; the captain had died of an apoplectic fit on learning that he was almost certainly going to be convicted of manslaughter.

"You'll be used to the rain in a few days, Mama," Sara proclaimed, not without justification. "See, it's stopped sprinkling.

Now Nanny will take me to Hyde Park to play with Thomas, and you and Papa can nap, the way grownups do." On her third birthday, Sara had proudly consigned naps to adults and babies.

"*Mi preciosa*," Livie said, tweaking one of her daughter's curls.

"Thomas will be waiting for us!" Sara cried, trotting down the sidewalk, her red leather boots sending rainwater splashing. She loved her cousin Thomas, Daisy's son, as much as she loved her little brother—perhaps more, because Freddy was too young to do more than give his sister a gummy smile.

"Slow down, Sara," Livie called. "I can't run while holding the baby." Freddy was tucked in a sling that polite society would find outrageous—almost as outrageous as a lady swearing under her breath, or speaking in Spanish, for that matter.

In the last decade, as she and Sara had followed Joshua wherever the military sent him, Livie had readily adopted practices that English ladies abhorred, such as nursing her own babies and making dear friends amongst women of all ranks. With Joshua absent for days or weeks at a time, she and the other Lady

Grenadiers had befriended Spanish women who taught Livie the language and inspired a love of coffee and dyed leather.

In fact, now that Joshua had resigned his command and the family had relocated to England, Livie meant to begin importing red leather boots and perfumed leather gloves for ladies—and perhaps for gentlemen brave enough to start a fashion rather than follow it. In the last decade, Daisy had become a successful entrepreneur, much to the shock of her mother, and she had promised to teach Livie everything she knew.

They rounded the corner onto Green Street, where Joshua had purchased a large townhouse only a few blocks from his father's house. Lord Paget still attended the House of Lords daily, but he loved having his grandchildren close by.

Sara danced up the steps, smiling at their butler as he opened the door. "Mr. Augustus, we met such a strange lady in the bookstore!"

Livie smiled ruefully. "Thank you, Augustus. Sara, please remember to be polite and kind in your description."

Sara handed her pelisse to a footman. "Her name was Lady Regina, and she had her nose so high in the air, like *this*!" Sara squared her shoulders and pointed her little nose toward the heavens. "When Mama greeted her, the lady looked as if she had swallowed a flea—the same expression Papa had when that *pulga* flew into his mouth—but I was very polite and did not laugh even a little bit."

"Lady Regina was merely surprised to see me," Livie said. "Nanny will be waiting for you in the nursery, Sara. Augustus, will you please ask a nursemaid to take Freddy?"

"I shall be happy to escort Master Frederick to the nursery," their butler replied, holding out his arms.

"Thank you," Livie said, handing over the baby. "Is my husband in his study?"

Freddy opened his eyes, nuzzled against Augustus's chest, and went promptly back to sleep. After three years serving under Joshua's command, Lance-Corporal John Augustus had sold out, donned a different uniform, and spent the last five years running their household, including the country estate Joshua inherited and the house in Madrid where they planned to spend several months a year.

"Major-General FitzRoy is upstairs with your cousin, overseeing another furniture delivery," Augustus said, tucking

Freddy carefully in the crook of his arm. "Also, Lord Frederick FitzRoy-Paget is in the library."

Thanks to Daisy's exquisite taste, their house had been furnished with great elegance before they arrived in London, but chairs and smaller pieces were still arriving every week.

Livie handed a footman her wet pelisse and paused for a moment before a mirror to tweak the chignon currently fashionable in London. She wrinkled her nose, thinking of Regina's horrified expression on seeing her again. True, Livie's skin had been tanned to golden hue and she carried a baby in a sling, but surely that wasn't enough to cause Regina to slap her hand to her bosom and appear likely to faint from shock?

Or perhaps it was.

After all, Regina's skin had clearly been whitened with arsenic powder, which Livie strongly suspected to be poisonous. She followed a commonsense rule: if you couldn't swallow it, you shouldn't put it on your skin.

She poked her head into the library. "Hello, Frederick."

Her brother-in-law glanced up from his book, a snifter of golden liquid at his side. "Darling Livie, good morning. Oates-

Plagitt sent me forth to take exercise, so I walked all the way here, where I am now hiding from the rain."

"That was a five-minute walk," Livie pointed out.

"More than enough," Frederick stated. "I am weak from lack of my normal sustenance. You'll be happy to learn that I am eschewing brandy, after Joshua informed me that my spirituous breath might stifle my young namesake. Also, I mean to play spillikins with my niece when she returns from the park, and I need my wits about me."

"Bravo!" Livie said, eyeing his glass.

"What you see here is a snifter of the very best...*tea*. Oates-Plagitt suggested that I drink tea in snifters since I'm used to sipping. I must say, it seems to help."

"Double bravo!" Livie cried, running across the room to give Frederick a kiss on the cheek. "I'll happily join the game of spillikins."

Upstairs, she followed the sound of voices to the bedchamber she shared with Joshua, paused in the doorway, and burst into laughter.

Two footmen had just moved a large armoire into an alcove designed for a writing desk. Daisy was supervising the process; she twirled about and clapped her hands. "There you are! What do you think, dear? Joshua's idea, obviously." She gave the armoire an affectionate pat. "Now I must rush. I'm already late to the palace!"

She darted over to kiss Livie's cheek. Half of her curls were confined in her chignon; the rest tumbled past her shoulders. "Your hair," Livie prompted, giving her a squeeze.

"I'll fix it in the carriage. I mustn't keep the queen waiting. Goodbye, darlings," Daisy cried, trotting out the door and down the stairs.

Joshua dismissed the footmen and moved to stand behind Livie, wrapping his arms loosely around her waist. "Good morning again," he said, kissing her neck. "Please tell me it's naptime."

"That armoire looks very familiar," Livie said, tilting her head back and smiling widely up at her husband. The blue armoire was unmistakably that in which Joshua had seduced her, all those years ago at the masquerade ball. "How on earth did you talk the duke into selling it to you?"

"I offered him twice its worth. He laughed and gave it to us as a belated wedding present."

Livie leaned back against her husband's strength, happiness saturating her being. They were home, and Joshua was safe. As much as she loved traveling and living in new countries, she had begun to find the anxiety of watching Joshua march off to battle at the front of a battalion wearing.

"I'm so grateful that you left the army," she said, not for the first time. "Even though you would have been a general in a few years."

Joshua kissed her neck again. "My ambition waned when I considered the possibility of leaving you, Sara, and Freddy in the world without me."

Livie turned around in his arms, draping her arms around his neck. "I love you, husband of mine."

He kissed her until she was aching with desire. "Nap time?" Joshua's voice had a deep throb that was a promise in itself.

Livie nodded. "Augustus took Freddy off to the nursery, and Sara is going to the park to play with Thomas."

"In that case, I'd like to show you the intricacies of the armoire that has been so kindly bestowed on us."

Livie blinked, rather surprised, since she would have expected to find herself on the bed, her husband hovering over her with a wicked grin. "Oh?"

"I had it refurbished," Joshua said. He strode over to the armoire and turned the knob, opening the right side. "You do remember the interior?"

"Well, I remember a velvet curtain—" Livie broke off because Joshua had thrown open both doors. Rather than shelves or hooks, a bed had been built inside. It was made up with snowy white linens and a crimson velvet blanket was draped at the foot. "Oh, Joshua!"

Her husband grinned at her with all the naughty joy she'd come to expect in their bedchamber. Expect *and* adore. He held out his hand. "My lady?"

Livie undid the simple bow at her neck before she pulled her light morning gown over her head, throwing it on the bed. She wore no corset, and her light chemise strained over her breasts.

Breastfeeding Sara had changed her figure for good, which Joshua definitely appreciated.

"Come here," he said hoarsely, kicking off his boots. "Please."

He already had his coat off by the time she sauntered over, her chemise dangling from one finger. "Joshua?"

"Yes, love?"

"Jump."

He kissed her before he complied, jumping high enough so that she could deftly topple him onto the armoire-bed before throwing herself onto his chest, swallowing his bellow of laughter with her kiss.

Two Lies and a Lord
The Seduction, Book 4

A gown that falls off on the dancefloor. A baby left on a doorstep.
A charming young lady and a grumpy lord.
And (of course) a forced marriage.

~ CURRENTLY SERIALIZING ON AMAZON VELLA ~

Chapter 1

April 18, 2016

Lord Rothingale's Masquerade

The Right Honorable Lord Devin—who thought of himself as Miles, though only his sisters addressed him as such—strolled into Lord Rothingale's masquerade planning to stay for ten minutes. At most, fifteen.

Earlier in the day, at their club, Rothingale had announced that the most beautiful ladies in London would attend, although his wink promised lady*birds*. Sure enough, courtesans were swarming the ballroom, eagerly looking for their next protector.

Miles didn't have a mistress.

He didn't want one.

He felt like that absurd Shakespeare character who moaned about losing his mirth. The lines had been drilled into him at Eton, so they jumped into his head, willy-nilly: *I have of late, (but wherefore I know not) lost all my mirth.*

Oh Christ, he was quoting the ultimate dreary prince, Hamlet. That had to be a sign of mental deterioration.

Hamlet's malaise had dramatic origins—father murdered, mother remarried, etc.—but Miles's complaints were mundane. Mirth had gone out the window a couple of years ago, after his best friend Jonah fell in love and moved to Suffolk with his wife.

In short, he was lonely.

Not that Miles begrudged Jonah the lovely Bea, but he missed his friendship. And damn it, he was jealous. Jonah and Bea

didn't coo at each other like doves; they squabbled and laughed.
They were happier together than apart.

These days he spent his days in the House of Lords, serving
as the head investigator for charges of murder and treason amongst
the aristocracy, but filling the hours didn't help, perhaps because the
cases were so beastly—and the criminals so infrequently punished.
He found it hard to shake off the stench after talking to a lady who'd
been egregiously abused, knowing that her husband would walk free.

Miles skirted an over-rouged ladybird whose mask didn't
conceal her avaricious eyes.

Years ago, he would have relished the seductive impropriety
of this masquerade, but no longer. Glancing at a couple leaning
against the wall, the man's hips pumping rhythmically, he felt only
distaste for such vulgarity.

So far he had resisted his family's insistence that he find a
wife, but it seemed the time had finally arrived. He was almost thirty.
Given that his sister Clementine was betrothed, he would have
nothing else to do while roaming around society events this Season.
His two younger sisters wouldn't debut until next year.

Obviously Lord Rothingale's house was no place to find a respectable woman to marry. Hell, the man had tried to entice Clementine to elope, so if Miles hadn't known Rothingale all his life, he wouldn't even have darkened his door. But the man was a nobleman, if a degenerate one.

He was turning to leave when his eye was caught by tumble of white-blonde hair, almost silver under candlelight. The woman in question wore a masquerade hat ringed in violets, her face concealed by a veil that ended just above her plump lips.

She was peering about as if she had lost someone, presumably not the young lout standing beside her, trying to get her attention.

Acting from pure instinct, Miles strode directly to her and smiled. "Good evening."

She tilted her head and blinked at him from behind her mask.

Miles's whole being stilled.

He knew those lips. He had met this lady at her debut ball. He had danced with her, talked to her, eaten with her—before she was temporarily exiled from polite society due to her uncle's trial for treason.

Anger surged in his veins. What in the hell was Miss Daisy Wharton doing at one of the most disreputable parties in all London? He had judged her something of a nitwit with a penchant for mischief—albeit a strikingly beautiful one.

But this was more than mischief.

If anyone recognized her in this den of iniquity, she would be exiled from polite society forever, rather than for a mere Season.

Moreover, the last thing Captain Sir Tyron needed was for his niece's disgraceful behavior to cause another scandal in the family. The captain was currently imprisoned in the Tower of London; the Lord High Steward had accepted the case for adjudication in the House of Lords, which meant it would soon be handed to Miles to investigate.

The man standing on Daisy's other side said aggressively, "You'll have to wait your turn. I already asked this lady to dance, so I claim her. She's mine for the evening."

Miles threw him a glance that made the man pale and fall back a step. "She's dancing with me." He caught Daisy by the arm and drew her deep onto the dancefloor until a crowd of inebriated dancers blocked her admirer's view.

"Sir!" she protested, pulling back.

"Don't you mean 'my lord'?" Miles asked grimly, snatching her right hand as the strains of a waltz began. Naturally, Rothingale's orchestra was playing the newest scandalous dance, one that required a man to hold a woman in his embrace. "You know perfectly well who I am, Miss Wharton." He placed his left hand on her back and moved into the waltz, hoping that no one would notice them in the mass of dancers.

She gracefully matched his steps, for all she was scowling at him from behind her mask. "Anyone could recognize you, Lord Devin. You are not wearing a mask, and you're taller than most."

"More to the point, what if someone recognizes you? No proper young lady would darken the door of Rothingale's house: the man is a well-known degenerate."

"I was just starting to realize... But how could I have known? My mother received an invitation!"

"Lady Wharton was invited to this event? Impossible." He said it flatly because Rothingale would never make a mistake of that nature.

Her brow pleated. "I suppose my father's name may have been on the invitation. I didn't notice."

"I suggest that you do not open your father's mail."

"'Twas one of a pile of invitations!" she protested. "Why would my father receive an invitation to such a ramshackle event? He spends most of his time in the country."

Miles had no intention of answering any questions about her father. "Given that you are here without a chaperone, you would be courting scandal even if this were a respectable event. I surmise that you stole out of the house like a schoolboy avoiding chapel."

She didn't answer; she was looking about with bright curiosity, not looking in the least repentant.

"Surely you don't need me to tell you that your reputation will be ruined if you were recognized here," Miles added in his most autocratic tones, ones that cowed everyone except his sisters.

Rather than bursting into tears, she curled her lip. "You are here as well, Lord Devin, unmasked and known to all."

"Irrelevant."

"I think not."

"You are an unmarried young lady, and—"

"So no one will want to marry me based on this evening? What of you? You're an unmarried man!"

"The comparison is irrelevant."

"Granted, you're not precisely an unmarried young man!" she said furiously. "My presence here is due to a simple mistake. Your presence indicates that you welcome distasteful attachments that have nothing to do with marriage."

Miles prided himself on having an even temperament. When other men raged and stormed, he maintained equanimity. Yet now he found himself so angry that his heart was thumping in his chest. "I'm not yet thirty," he retorted, avoiding her second point.

"As I said: old!" She tossed her head and more silver hair spilled down her back. "I suppose you came here hoping to make a...connection, shall we say?" She turned her head from left to right, her plump lower lip curling as she surveyed the crowd. "I am loathe to offend you by questioning your judgement—or your taste."

"I was just leaving."

She raised an eyebrow, so he growled unwillingly, "No, I do not have a mistress, nor was I looking for one. You are remarkably blunt. I should be greatly offended if my younger sisters brought up this topic."

"You can be comforted by the thought that they probably haven't the knowledge to do so. Ignorance makes it easier for gentlemen to indulge in extramarital activities."

Daisy said it evenly, without bitterness or sarcasm, but Miles winced inwardly. She was right, of course. He whirled her out of the way just in time to avoid the drunken lurch of a giggling couple.

"You waltz very well," he said.

"You also dance well," Daisy said with the air of someone forced into civility. "Unfortunately, the scandal surrounding my uncle means that I shan't have a chance to waltz again until next Season, when I'm approved by Almack's patronesses."

"If anyone recognizes you here, Almack's will be the least of your problems," Miles stated. "As soon as this dance concludes, we will slip away, hopefully without notice."

"I shouldn't have made such a personal remark about your reasons for attending this masquerade," Daisy said suddenly. "I apologize. We genuinely thought it would be akin to that given annually by the Duchess of—"

Miles interrupted her. "We?"

She looked surprised. "My cousin Livie and I."

Of course, Daisy wouldn't have snuck out alone. He should have known that Olive Tyron would have accompanied her; they had grown up together. He took a breath and controlled his temper. "Where is Miss Tyron?"

"Livie is here somewhere," Daisy said, glancing about. "She was just behind me, but a press of people entered with us, and I lost her in the crowd. I was looking for her when you pulled me into this waltz. I think she must have gone right when I went left, so likely she's in that room." She nodded toward an archway.

Miles's temper slipped its leash entirely. "You are a pair of idiots," he said scathingly. "Don't you know that a group in the House of Lords is investigating your uncle's supposed treason—an investigation that I will be running? Believe me when I say that the last thing Tyron needs is for his daughter to create another scandal to burden the family name. He must keep the sympathy and loyalty of his fellow aristocrats in order to beat this charge."

Daisy missed a step, her mouth rounding with horror. "I had no idea."

"Not to mention the fact that your cousin might have been accosted by a lecher like the one back there who 'claimed' you for the evening."

She raised her chin. "Livie would never allow herself to be taken advantage of."

"You have no idea what you're talking about. A man could jerk you into his arms and kiss you—or worse—and no one here would bat an eyelash. We must find her immediately."

"Livie can defend herself," Daisy snapped.

Thankfully the music was ending so Miles wrapped his arm around her waist and drew her to the side of the room. She fit perfectly into the circle of his arm.

"You are holding me improperly. I am contemplating whether to kick you sharply in the shins or stick you with a hatpin," Daisy informed him.

She was an extraordinary mixture of sophisticated and naïve, old and young. "The next time a man embraces you, I suggest that you act rather than air your options."

She rolled her eyes at him. "It's just you."

Miles wasn't sure how to take that. "What is Miss Tyron wearing?" he asked, as they walked through the archway into the other chamber.

Daisy cleared her throat. He glanced down at her.

"My cousin…" Her voice faltered.

"What?"

"She's there…over there on that settee."

Miles looked.

A woman in a scarlet domino wearing a masquerade hat trimmed slightly differently than Daisy's was sitting in a young army officer's lap, her arms wound around his neck, kissing him enthusiastically.

"Bloody hell," he growled.

Daisy looked up at him, eyes wide. "Of the two of us, I'm the naughty one."

What he said next was unrepeatable.

Chapter 2

Seven Months Later

November 1, 1817

"We must behave as if we are in half-mourning until Christmas at the earliest," Lady Wharton instructed. "No bouncing around the dancefloor or loud giggling, Daisy. If we display the slightest hint of pleasure, we shall be accused of being unfeeling."

"Yes, Mother," Daisy replied, nodding.

"Tomorrow night, at the Duchess of Trent's opening ball, I will conduct myself soberly, as if garbed in sackcloth and ashes."

Daisy knew perfectly well that her mother planned to wear a magnificent gown of periwinkle-blue satin adorned by a circlet of diamonds; a costume farther from sackcloth could hardly be imagined. She nodded again. "Of course."

Her mother looked at her sharply. "My gown is *dark* blue. Very close to grey. I believe sackcloth is brown, but the color is ruinous for my complexion." Dismissing that sartorial question, she began leafing through a thick stack of invitations that had arrived in the previous week.

Before her uncle's trial for treason, followed by a second for murder, Daisy would have relished a lively debate on the suitability of diamonds and sackcloth, but these days she tried not to upset her mother's equilibrium.

"Everyone but the highest sticklers will welcome my daughter back to society," Lady Wharton muttered to herself. "Daisy's dowry and breeding are excellent, and her beauty is incomparable."

Last Season, the thoroughly dislikable Lady Regina had mocked Daisy for being "short, fat, and unkempt," which stung at the time—but based on male glances, Daisy had concluded that her bosom was an asset in husband-hunting. Lord Argyle had not labeled her hair unkempt, but compared it to a moon's nimbus.

Which he then kindly defined as a "luminous cloud of moonbeams."

So who cared what Lady Regina thought?

"Livie and I had plenty of suitors before my uncle's circumstances forced us to withdraw last Season," she reminded her mother.

"Your cousin's marriage does clear the field," her mother said, taking a practical view of the matter. "Unfortunately, Mr. Robert de Lacy Evans is now betrothed, and Lord Argyle married over the summer. It's a pity he didn't wait for you." She brightened. "Of course, Livie's brother-in-law, Lord Frederick FitzRoy-Paget, is a future earl."

"Fond though I am of Frederick, he's an inebriate," Daisy noted.

"The Earl of Winchester is looking for a wife after his betrothal to Lady Regina broke down," Lady Wharton added, with a touch of uncertainty.

The man she and Livie had compared to a scallion? Never. "Any man foolish enough to betroth himself to Regina is not someone I'd care to marry."

Lady Wharton snatched a missive out of the pile and broke the seal, her fingers trembling slightly. A ticket fell out. "Thank goodness," she cried. "Lady Castlereigh has reissued your Almack's voucher."

Daisy scowled. "What about Livie's?" Back when Captain Sir Tyron was first accused of treason, Almack's had promptly withdrawn both girls' vouchers.

"Livie no longer needs a voucher," her mother said, looking up. "She is happily married to Major Fitz-Roy and living abroad, as we shall inform anyone impertinent enough to inquire."

"Yes, but Captain Sir—"

"Do not mention his name!" Lady Wharton's voice rose to a pitch. "My brother, my own brother—" She choked, dropping Lady Castlereigh's note back on the table before she rose and walked across the room to the window, wrapping her arms around her waist.

Daisy hopped up and went to her side, giving her a consoling hug and a handkerchief.

Her mother blotted her eyes. "It was bad enough when Tyron was accused of treason! But *murder*. How shall I ever live it down? I dread the thought of walking into a ballroom."

"We must remember that Capt—that *he*—was acquitted," Daisy offered.

"Pshaw! That poor boy," her mother continued unsteadily. "That poor, poor boy."

Captain Sir Tyron—Daisy's uncle—had ordered a young sailor named Jeremy Tulip overboard for a minor infraction, and the lad had either been eaten by sharks or drowned. The captain was exonerated because…that's the way the world turns. He was a powerful aristocrat, and the Tulips were poor and illiterate.

Yet everyone who knew of the case recognized the truth.

"Naturally, my brother has no concern about the damage he's done to our family! He has put the whole unpleasantness out of his mind. That's what he called it: an 'unpleasantness.' Sometimes I just hate men." Lady Wharton's voice crackled with grief. "Do you think for a moment that if I were the captain of a sea-going vessel I would tolerate that sort of behavior?"

"Of course not!" Daisy said, handing over another handkerchief; she had begun carrying three or four.

"I never contemplated such shame from within my own family. My brother may have left for the new world, but that's not far enough. I would be pleased never to hear his name again. *Ever.*"

Daisy had never liked her uncle, so she entirely agreed. "The former captain will never return to England, Mother."

"The moment I walk into the Trent ballroom, he is all anyone will speak about. They'll be asking me with feigned sincerity how he fares."

"Not for long," Daisy promised. "The world will quickly move to the next scandal."

Her mother swallowed hard and mopped her eyes again. "Your father and I have spent years establishing ourselves as ethical, upstanding members of polite society."

"Livie cannot be blamed for her father's transgressions—and neither can you, for your brother's," Daisy said, for approximately the thousandth time.

Lady Wharton drew in an unsteady breath. "At least the Tulip family will live in comfort from now on."

Daisy nodded. Her mother had forced her unrepentant brother to give the Tulips a large sum of money. "Every family has a black sheep, Mother, and my uncle is ours. After a few months, no one will consider the murder again, any more than they talk of Lord Byron's *affaire* with his half-sister."

Her mother gasped, and her mouth fell open.

Oops.

Daisy had a tendency to speak—and act—before thinking.

"*Daisy!*" Lady Wharton dropped her handkerchief to the floor and clutched her bosom like an actress at Drury Lane. "I cannot believe my ears! That my own daughter should allow such odious words to cross her lips! I am shocked...scandalized...*disgusted*!"

"I apologize," Daisy said, ordering her features to look as penitent as she could. It wasn't one of her skills; she should probably practice that expression before the mirror. She could employ it when people asked about her uncle.

"How do you even know of that blackguard, let alone his brazen-faced sister? Who would tell an innocent young lady about a disgusting personage as Lord Byron?"

Daisy sighed. "Everyone knows. Augusta Leigh bore him a daughter, after all."

"But you are a young, untouched, innocent—"

"My point is that scandals come and go," Daisy said, before her mother could start thinking too hard about her supposed innocence.

She wasn't dissolute, though she knew more about the world than Lady Wharton would imagine. Most young ladies hadn't read a useful book called *City of Eros*, for example.

Daisy had read it twice.

"If you are tarred with the brush of hedony," her mother gasped, getting up a new head of steam, "if society decides that you are a debauched coquette, that will be the end of this family. *The end!* I shall live out my final days in sackcloth in a darkened room! *Brown* sackcloth!"

"I don't think 'hedony' is a word," Daisy observed.

"Stop smirking and mark my words. This family's reputation will recover far faster from my brother's inequities than it would from a scandal along the lines of Lord Byron's!"

"That's so unfair. Murder is far more indicative of a corrupt soul than wanton behavior."

"Not in the civilized world," Lady Wharton declared. "If a woman is not chaste, she is *nothing*. If the subject ever rises again, you must pretend that you have no idea how babies are made." She narrowed her eyes. "Which I gather you do. Somehow. I certainly have never mentioned the subject."

"It's absurd that women have to pretend to be ignorant of basic facts," Daisy said, beginning to feel heated. "Everyone knows that gentlemen have fancies outside marriage. Of course, it would have been far better of Bryon to seduce someone other than his half-sister—"

"*Daisy!*"

"It was terrible, most improper," Daisy added hastily. "He is a dissolute rake—"

"Never let his name pass your lips again!" her mother cried wildly.

"But a good poet," Daisy finished.

"The verse of an incestuous devil!" Lady Wharton gasped. "Surely you have not read that inexecrable nonsense."

Daisy wouldn't say that she had a penchant for fibbing. But quite often one had to find one's way *around* the truth. For example, Captain Sir Tyron wouldn't allow his daughter to read anything but the most deserving texts, so Daisy had read aloud many books to her cousin Livie.

City of Eros, for example.

And Byron's *Fugitive Pieces*, which had been remarkably instructive, as when Byron vowed to enter his lady's chamber and "love for hours together."

Obviously, she and Livie had needed to understand what "love" meant when used as a verb—in the context of a bedroom. Their maid at the time had been most enlightening.

"I don't believe most of Byron's works are in print," she said tactfully.

"You must never read them," her mother demanded, her eyes bulging slightly. "This family stands on the very edge, the precipice of ruin, and your behavior must be impeccable. Tomorrow, you will look like a subdued angel, your eyes cast to the floor, modesty and remorse on full display."

Daisy couldn't stop herself. "To be honest, Mother, I'll look more like an Egyptian mummy than an angel."

"Nonsense!"

"Remember all those panels of white satin? I had my final fitting yesterday."

Her gown was constructed of panels of satin falling from a high waist, designed to lightly float around the wearer's body. But

Lady Wharton had ordered the *modiste* to add three times as many panels as in the original design.

If Lady Regina thought Daisy was fat before, wait til the lady caught sight of her in this gown.

"Nonsense!" Lady Wharton snapped. "The dress is fashionable and appropriate. Your hair will stay in a chignon, or I'll fire your maid. No lip color, of course. A *jeune fille*, but without French sauciness."

Daisy nodded. She could do it.

And she *would* have done it too…

If the entire back of her gown hadn't ripped clear off her body.

On the dancefloor.